A RED NOTE SERIES NOVEL

the REBOUND

BESTSELLING AUTHOR OF KISS ME LIKE YOU MEAN IT

J. R. ROGUE

THE REBOUND

RED NOTE SERIES
BOOK 1

J. R. ROGUE

CONTENTS

Content Warning	ix
Author's Note	xiii

PART ONE

Chapter 1	3
Chapter 2	6
Chapter 3	7
Chapter 4	11
Chapter 5	15
Chapter 6	16
Chapter 7	21
Chapter 8	25
Chapter 9	26
Chapter 10	30
Chapter 11	34
Chapter 12	35
Chapter 13	37
Chapter 14	42
Chapter 15	43
Chapter 16	47
Chapter 17	53
Chapter 18	54
Chapter 19	60
Chapter 20	64
Chapter 21	65
Chapter 22	71
Chapter 23	74
Chapter 24	77
Chapter 25	78
Chapter 26	81
Chapter 27	85
Chapter 28	86
Chapter 29	89
Chapter 30	93
Chapter 31	94
Chapter 32	97
Chapter 33	102

Chapter 34	103
Chapter 35	107
Chapter 36	110
Chapter 37	111
Chapter 38	116
Chapter 39	121
Chapter 40	122
Chapter 41	124
Chapter 42	127
Chapter 43	128
Chapter 44	133
Chapter 45	138
Chapter 46	143
Chapter 47	144
Chapter 48	148
Chapter 49	152
Chapter 50	153
Chapter 51	157
Chapter 52	161
Chapter 53	162
Chapter 54	166
Chapter 55	169
Chapter 56	170
Chapter 57	176
Chapter 58	182
Chapter 59	185
Chapter 60	189
Chapter 61	195
Chapter 62	200
Chapter 63	203
Chapter 64	207
Chapter 65	208
Chapter 66	212
Chapter 67	216
Chapter 68	217
Chapter 69	220
Chapter 70	223
Chapter 71	224
Chapter 72	229
Chapter 73	233
Chapter 74	234
Chapter 75	237

Chapter 76	240
Chapter 77	243
Chapter 78	245
Chapter 79	247
Chapter 80	248
Chapter 81	250
Chapter 82	252
Chapter 83	253
Chapter 84	256
Chapter 85	262
Chapter 86	263
Chapter 87	267
Chapter 88	269
Chapter 89	273
Chapter 90	276
Chapter 91	277
Chapter 92	279
Chapter 93	281
Chapter 94	287
Chapter 95	289

PART TWO

Chapter 96	295
Chapter 97	299
Chapter 98	301
Chapter 99	305
Chapter 100	308
Chapter 101	312
Chapter 102	314
Chapter 103	317
Chapter 104	320
Chapter 105	325
Epilogue	330
Acknowledgments	339
About the Author	341
Also by J. R. Rogue	343

Copyright © 2019 by J. R. Rogue
All rights reserved.

All rights reserved. No part of this publication may be reproduced, distributed or transmitted in any form or by any means, including photocopying, recording, or other electronic or mechanical methods, without the prior written permission of the publisher, except in the case of brief quotations embodied in critical reviews and certain other noncommercial uses permitted by copyright law.

This is a work of fiction. Names, characters, places, and incidents are a product of the author's imagination. Locales and public names are sometimes used for atmospheric purposes. Any resemblance to actual people, living or dead, or to businesses, companies, events, institutions, or locales
is completely coincidental.

Cover art by Murphy Rae
Print and E-Book interior design by J.R. Rogue

J.R. Rogue
PO Box 984
Lebanon, MO 65536
www.jrrogue.com
contact@jrrogue.com

CONTENT WARNING:

Spousal abuse, anxiety, depression, rape

For Shawn Mendes.

You were a beautiful and pure muse when life was dark.

Writing this book has helped pull me out of the abyss.

AUTHOR'S NOTE

Although this novel was inspired in part by my love for Shawn Mendes, you don't have to listen to his music to enjoy the story. I do, however, recommend that you listen to his cover of the Kings of Leon song "Use Somebody" when it is mentioned in the book.

PART ONE

ONE

SEAN

**PRESENT
TORONTO**

"THIS IS ABOUT REVENGE. He's leaving so he can fuck his uncle's wife! Some rebound bullshit!"

Those are the words I hear floating over my shoulder as I board my jet, phone clutched in my hand, vision blurry.

I'm used to the language from my manager, Jesse, so I don't respond. Instead, I just put one leg in front of the other, higher and higher, step after step, until I'm surrounded by clean white and silence, save for the rapid beating of my heart.

The jet door shuts, and I'm alone with myself. With my thoughts. With the images. The muffled moans I heard just hours earlier.

My first anxiety attack happened right before a show. I could hear the thunder of the crowd, my name being chanted. I felt it, the rhythmic prayer. The demand for my voice. I felt it, but it could not drown out the sounds inside. The erratic beat in my chest. Moment after moment, faster. My throat was dry, and I could hear the voice in my head. The one that made no sound but was so loud I couldn't breathe when it started chattering and cawing.

I locked myself in my dressing room and grabbed my phone, texting Jo, but she didn't answer.

She was sick at home—at *our* home. She was the queen of the world we built together. I would let her rule and rest, and I never regretted letting her have anything she asked for.

The first Toronto show of the weekend would be the end of my tour. My team and I planned it this way. Three nights: Friday, Saturday, and Sunday. Then we would finally be able to rest. To take a moment for ourselves before I looked forward, to the next album.

I could finally shut out the voices of every single human that demanded my attention, my voice, my input, my energy.

I needed Jo in that moment of panic, as I started to sweat, to go blurry at the edges. I needed her delicate wrist and her full lips. I needed her to touch me in some way so I could feel the quiet. Her phone went to voicemail thirteen times before I shoved it in my pocket and screamed.

I didn't tell anyone I was leaving. It was unlike me, but I couldn't settle the buzzing inside.

I felt off.

Then, I felt like something was wrong with Jo. I needed to be near her.

She didn't hear me when I unlocked the door to our apartment. She didn't hear me call out her name. She didn't hear the flick of each light switch I turned on.

But I heard her.

The tragic sound of the air leaving her mouth. The distinct whimpers she made when a mouth touched sensitive peaks. I knew her sounds, her warmth.

I was not pulling these sounds from her.

I stopped in my tracks when I realized what I was walking in on, but I was too far in. My hand was on our bedroom door, and I could see the way the light of our bedside lamp illuminated her. The shadows carved out her shoulders, the cherry tattoo on her hip as it bobbed up and down. Two legs covered in dark hair spread out toward me. The arms that snaked around her were tan, hard. Long fingers pressed into her ass cheeks. The man's head was back, lost in her.

So was Jo's, lost in him.

Her pink, bubble gum hair cascaded down her back, and I felt like an intruder in my own home.

It was a flick of the wrist that stopped them. I pushed the door open hard enough to hear the doorknob ruin the sheetrock of the wall it collided with.

They sprung to action immediately. Jo twisted, her face scrunched up in terror. My uncle reached for a black pair of boxer briefs on the floor next to the chair they were fucking on. His eyes met mine, and my vision blurred at the edges. I felt that familiar pain I got when I was holding back tears. A red hot throat and a thundering chest, the sound overtook everything.

It was a nightmare, and I thought I was through with nightmares. I was forced to turn away from them. I left right that moment.

I left to get to Calliope. His wife.

TWO

CALLIOPE

APOLLO
This is what you wanted. You had someone who loved you. And you wanted this. You wanted us apart. You did this. If you don't tell him that, I fucking will.

THREE

SEAN

**PRESENT
THE LAKE**

I DIDN'T ORDER an Uber for my arrival. I kept my phone off the entire flight, eyes clenched, brow drenched in sweat, knee bouncing in an unsteady rhythm.

When the wheels of my jet hit the runway, I open my eyes, finally.

My hand feels heavy, where it grips my cell phone. I don't want to turn it on, but I know I must. So I stand once we've settled, then run my moist left palm down my black jeans twice.

A strangled noise leaves my throat as I toss the phone in *her* seat and run my hands through my hair, resisting the urge to pull it all out.

It's getting longer on the top. Jo loved it that way. She loved to grip it when she was on top of me. She said I looked more like a man each day, and I smiled, head back, lost in her. Lost in the same way *they* were.

I see it now, the warning. The way she always held her age over me like a weapon. Calliope was right, and I wonder what she'll say when I arrive on her doorstep. I know she's there, in the woods of the Ozarks, in the large house they visit in the summer months. The first house that felt like a home to me.

Burning up from the weight of everything, I give up, grab my phone, and power it on.

My eyes are tearing, and I want to tell the captain to take off again. To take me somewhere remote where no one knows me.

The device vibrates in my hand. One alert after another. I scroll quickly. Texts from my best friend, manager, Jo, even my fucking uncle—Apollo.

> APOLLO
> Don't you fucking tell her.

I feel a shiver move through me. Then I delete the text and block his number.

The walk to the estate is too short. I need the sounds of the country around me, but I see the lights of the driveway too quickly. The words I'm practicing over and over in my head feel heavy in my mouth, not ready for her ears, not ready to be spoken at all.

I didn't turn my phone back off after the onslaught of messages coming in, but I did turn it on silent.

It sits in my pocket like a heavy weight, a dark carrier of false words and manipulation.

When I reach the property, it looks like every light in the house is on.

I can see Calliope in the living room.

She looks nothing like I remember her.

Her once short brown hair is long, far past her shoulders. My crush is reignited, conflicted, as little hints, small offerings from the Calliope of the past, flash in my mind. A kaleidoscope of clues I'd pushed away.

In front of me, the Calliope of the present spins in the dining room to a song I cannot hear. Her eyes are closed, but maybe she senses me. She opens her eyes, and her steps falter. She grabs the dining room chair next to her and clutches her chest. I see her lips say my name. *Sean.*

I smile, but I know it isn't reaching my eyes. My hands dig into my pockets as I watch her go through the house. Too many large windows, too many secrets seen. Fifteen-year-old me loved that about this house. Twenty-year-old me, constantly chased down by paparazzi, wonders how I'll hide here. I have to hope no one will leak my location.

I hear Calliope before I see her again, and dam the tears I can feel streaming down my face. I turn when I hear the name I saw her mouth earlier.

"Sean, what are you doing here?" She looks around, her small arms wrapping around her chest.

It's late April, and a chill clings to the air. I saw through the glass what her modesty now protects.

"How did you get here?" She glances over my shoulder. "I don't see a car."

I turn, run my hand through my messy hair. "I walked from the runway." I was once a runaway showing up on her doorstep. I'm running again, and this is where the compass pointed.

"What's wrong?" She grabs my hands from my hair; the left was joined with the right, and I was tugging before I could stop myself. She is so damn close to me.

I look at our connection, two pairs of pale hands. I feel it—*us*—in the pit of my chest. "Have you talked to Apollo tonight?" I ask her.

She blinks at my words, dropping my hands.

My uncle, Uncle, Unc. I never called him by his name. The way a child never calls his father by his birth name. My uncle was the title, the authority, the one who took me in and changed my life.

"No," she says. "Why?"

Her cheeks are pink, like I've struck her, and I wonder where their relationship has taken them since I last saw them together at Christmas.

"I caught him..." I can't finish. The words lodge in my throat, and I suck in a breath when I feel Calliope's thumb on my cheek, just over the scar that lingers there.

"Your tears always pooled there," she says, pulling her hand away.

Touching me like that isn't something she has allowed herself to do in years.

"I'm sorry," she says. "What did you catch him doing?"

She looks resigned. As if she knows why I'm here. As if it cannot wound her.

I look at her hands. There is no wedding ring.

"Fuck!" I scream. The woods swallow the sound of my grief, and Calliope startles. "You know?"

"I don't know why you're here. Tell me why you're here, Sean."

I look over her shoulder to the guest house Jo and I spent the summer in before our lives changed. Inside is the bed I lost my virginity in. The bed Jo told me she loved me in.

I pull my eyes away and stare into Calliope's. The opposite of Jo's. Deep dark to her clear blue. Calliope's eyes look even darker against the pallor of her skin.

"He fucked her," I say. "He fucked Jo."

Calliope nods and grabs my hand, leading me inside.

FOUR

CALLIOPE

PAST
THE LAKE

WE ALL HAVE weapons we can use against others for survival, to cause chaos. My mother made it clear she would use hers, and I should use mine for escapes, for amusement. For pleasure and whatever else I saw fit. It was my right as a woman after everything men took.

I always watched my mother for clues, for practice. The incessant chatter she spilled and the lack of boundaries she erected left me with little else to do. And I knew my mother was right, in the end. I wanted out of the life I was born into.

Shady Croc's was on the water. Rich and tan, loud and smelling of sweet liquor—those were the men who frequented the bar. I watched and waited for the perfect meal ticket. The opportunity on two legs to take me away.

My two-bedroom trailer was closing in on me every day, and I relished the thought of suiting up for work every night, craving the noise of the crowd, the demand for what I could offer. I served drinks—an easy job—and the flesh that reached for the escapes I offered served, in return, as my reward.

I saw him as soon as he walked in. Tall and dark, with the darkest brown eyes I'd ever seen.

His friends smelled like money, and he was the leader. There was always one. They stand taller, talk lower, and the others lean into every syllable they speak.

I was on shot girl duty that night, free to roam, but I didn't go to him right away. Instead, I circled, played the game, and felt each and every time his eyes landed on me.

My weapons were loaded and ready. Short shorts, a tank top knotted in the front, and the Missouri heat was wet and relentless. Even with the sun fading, I was sweating.

His friends had accents, and I smiled as I handed out sugary shots, ears trained on them. They were from Chicago. I was familiar with the accent, but I couldn't place the alpha, and when I turned to them, his eyes were on me, waiting. So I smiled, pretending the thundering in my heart wasn't getting to me. "Shot?"

"Hello, future wife," he replied.

I'd heard similar lines night after night, felt hands on my ass, and hot breath on my neck. Many times from men old enough to be my father, but I'd learned to choke it down, to play the role. This man—his vibrato, his heat—made me feel weightless.

I winked in reply, then turned to his friends. "Shots, boys?" They weren't boys. They were older than my twenty-one years, and I'd been waiting years to be old enough for a job like this. Everything the lake offered, everything my mother taught me—*use what you have, use it on them*—had been lost on me until now, until this opportunity. Now that I was alone and in desperate need of a miracle, of a reprieve from the misery.

"We've only just gotten here. Shots already?" The blond one was slender, a crooked grin on his face. His eyes were green and messy.

They'd been to another bar already. Their noses were red, and I could feel the heat of their bodies. The sun lingered on them. Maybe they were on the boat all day.

"It's never too early for a shot," I said with a smile, waiting for the wanting. To see their faces painted in yeses or nos.

The alpha's boys nodded, held out their hands, so I supplied, before turning to the one I wanted, watched him fish out his wallet. As he paid, I stepped closer. His friends started talking behind me, recounting their day, and it became background music.

"Future wife, what's your name?" he asked.

I looked down at my name tag, then back up to his eyes, stepping closer.

"Calliope." He said it slowly, pronouncing it right, which was more than I could say for many intoxicated bar patrons.

"Yes, sir," I said, taking his money, giving him his shot.

He downed it, eyes on my own. "Tell me your story, muse."

I shook my head, smiling, tingling. "I'm impressed."

"With what?"

"You," I replied, taking one of the shots. "Not only do you know how to say my name, but you also know the origin. So what's your name?"

His smile was big, like the rest of him. He cropped his stance wide, lowering himself closer to her level. I'd left my heels at home that night.

"Apollo." He reached out, taking my hand.

I laughed in return, and it was real. Then, pulling the shot tray close as I let his hand go, I returned his endearment. "Hello, husband."

"I think you should stay with us for the night. Don't leave. I'll buy the shot tray." He reached for it, and I pulled it away.

"Twenty-two dollars. High roller. Good try, but I need to sell more than one tray tonight if I want to keep my job."

"Go get your boss."

"I'm not for sale."

"Your time is. Your boss bought it for the night. Now I want to buy it."

"There are plenty of women in this bar." I wanted him to work for it. Just a little.

"There are plenty of women on this lake. There are plenty of women in Chicago," he said, telling me that even though he didn't share an accent with his friends, he shared their home, "but I've yet to meet one with a name like yours."

We stared at each other then. Daring, electric. He smelled like the lake, the sun. Sweat and Jack.

"Let me get your waitress. Eva is pretty. You'd like her." I amused myself with the offering, knowing he wouldn't dare take it.

"Get your boss." He said it like a man who wasn't often denied.

There were so many like him there. Powerful men, taking. But I could stomach *his* plea because I wanted to give him what he wanted.

My boss sold me for the night. Everything—and everyone—has a price. And I stayed close to Apollo after that as he told me about his life in Chicago, his roots in Toronto, and I sold my past to him in return. Alterations and embellishments rolled from my tongue, and I was shiny and new. I wanted to stick.

He didn't leave with my number; he left with me, our hands linked. I slept on the boat he owned, woke with him between my legs, a repeat of the fucking I begged for only hours before.

I was taken, toying with his plans. Making sure I was in them.

FIVE

CALLIOPE

APOLLO
Remember when we met? What you were? You were nothing. I gave you everything you have.

SIX

SEAN

**PRESENT
THE LAKE**

MY PHONE IS BLOWING up on the countertop, and Calliope and I are both doing a shit job at pretending we can't hear it. The music she was listening to is now low, and I can't make out who it is.

I walk around the island in the kitchen as Calliope rifles through drawers. I don't want her to ask why I'm here, besides the obvious—the news I delivered—because I don't have an answer. Not one I can say out loud, anyway.

The woman in the room with me, pretending to look for a wine bottle opener when I can see it sitting next to the toaster, is a stranger to me. We have kept our distance, pretending we both don't know the reason and that my being here violates the agreement we silently made.

I can't help the wonder inside me, the wonder at her thoughts on revenge. "It's next to the toaster," I say, pretending I just now caught sight of what she was seeking.

"Oh," she says breathily. Her full voice is soft in this space. She grabs the wine bottle from the countertop and fastens the clamps around its mouth.

"Is this wise?" I muse, out loud, no humor.

"Is what wise?" She doesn't look at me, her hands working slowly.

I hear the cork pop, her wine glass sliding across the granite. "Drinking right now?"

"Are you still opposed to it?" she asks.

"I'm still not legal, you know."

She looks me over. It's intimate, intimidating.

Calliope has seen every change in me. From a scared boy in dirty clothes on her steps to the man I've grown into. We've eyed each other over dinner tables and across rooms during the holidays. There was never anywhere else for me to go when the world dispersed and forced merriment down my throat through their forced poses next to pictures of twinkling lights.

The world knows of my past, my parents, and my tragedy, but I've trained them to believe I left that all behind. That my surrogate family has filled the gaping hole in my chest. One half of that family stands in this room with me, and I'm making her nervous.

"Are you ever going to stop growing?" Her question is offered to the glass of wine in front of her, too full.

"I think I have." I'm six foot two, but not as tall as my uncle.

"It's funny, you know." She doesn't continue, and I know she wants me to pull her thoughts from her.

"What is?" I ask.

She takes a long drink. "All the things you used to worry over. Your height. Your eye. Your scars. Your anxiety. They love all of it. Everything about you. No one wants a perfect hero. It's dull."

I haven't heard her speak this candidly to me in years. It was in our agreement. We never laid out rules, but it was the survival we both needed.

I feel like I'm being interviewed, so I offer a manufactured answer. "I still let it get under my skin, though."

"Look at your life. Look at it." A switch is flipped. She seems agitated. Like my presence has disrupted her routine, her safe space.

I know how important those things are to her.

"I know."

"Three albums. Three world tours. A dozen songs in the Billboard top two-hundred. Do I need to continue?"

"I wish you wouldn't," I say, but it's a lie. It isn't vanity that wants her to continue listing my accomplishments over the past four years; it's the noise. Her voice is drowning out the sound of my phone. The sounds of Jo's moans as she fucked my uncle in our bed.

"Well, what do you wish I would do?" she challenges.

"Tell me why you didn't look surprised when I told you I caught them." I cross my arms and stare at the skylight above me.

"Your uncle and I have been separated for about six months now."

I look back at her, untangle my arms, and stand. "Christmas?"

"We've been pretending for a little while now. It was just too much to deal with. Family and all that." She waves her hand like it was nothing to pretend they were together still. She says *family* like there is anyone to impress.

She has no family. And my uncle has me and his older sister, my Aunt Bet, who I only met three years ago.

I look at Calliope hard, and she takes another drink of her wine. I find the barstool again, watching her as I sit.

"Work-family, and friend-family, not just blood," she says.

She has a leg to stand on here. Every other weekend they would host a lunch or dinner at the Chicago house.

"Are you getting a divorce?"

"He said he was going to file last week." Her cheeks are flushed. From the wine or the words, I don't know.

"Was it for Jo?"

"He didn't file, though. I think you're getting ahead of yourself, Sean. We don't even know what's going on between them or how long it's been going on." She sounds robotic, resigned.

"Do you care, though?" I ask.

"I care that you're hurting," she offers.

"Don't talk to me like that." I hate the way my voice sounds. Angry and cracking. *Don't be a fucking pussy*, Jo would say. I should have seen it then in the beginning.

"Talk to you like what?" She looks at me as if I've slapped her. Taken her concern and used it as a weapon.

"Like you're my mom. You don't look at me like that."

"And how do I look at you?" she asks.

It is with this question that I know why I'm here. Jesse, that fucking asshole. He isn't right, but he knows more than I wanted to admit, and it makes me wonder what my best friend—August—tells him when I'm not around.

"You look at me like I'm something you want, but you can't say it out loud."

We stare at each other then. Daring or begging, I don't know. I just know it's honest, the way our eyes speak when our voices will not.

"You're hurting." She doesn't go further with the statement. Instead, she downs the rest of her wine and brings the empty glass to the sink.

I watch the way the muscles in her back move, the way her hair sways over her shoulders. She looks delicate, and I would never have used that word for her as a teenager. She scared me then. I think I scare her now.

When she turns to me, her eyes are a little bloodshot. "I'll make up the bed in the guest house."

"You don't have to do that. I know where everything is. I'll see myself out. Thank you, Calliope."

I can feel her anger mixed with want as I walk away. But maybe it's just my imagination. Maybe it's just what I want to feel.

SEVEN

SEAN

**PAST
CHICAGO**

WE'D BEEN AWAY from home for two weeks when we arrived on their doorstep in Chicago. I could finally see out of my right eye—my good eye—when I knocked.

I expected my Uncle Apollo, but a woman answered the door. She was small, with large dark eyes and a shade of dark beneath them. "Well, hello," she said upon seeing us. "Can I help you? Fuck, are you all right?"

We did not look all right. We smelled like shit, and large backpacks were on the stoop, next to our feet. Every belonging Jo and I could not part with when we left Toronto.

Jo's hand clutched mine. I turned to her, kissing her dark roots quickly before turning back to the woman. "I'm sorry, does Apollo live here?"

The woman's face relaxed. She kept her eyes on us as she yelled over her shoulder. "Pol!"

She pronounced it like Paul, and I hated it. Why would you shorten a name like Apollo? It was so cool.

I could hear the heavy footsteps of my uncle approaching. The sounds of the busy Chicago street behind us threatened to amplify my growing anxiety. The woman in front of me lowered her hand on the door, and the diamond there caught the waning daylight, pulling my eyes to it.

I knew nothing of my uncle except his name and where he lived. An address I lifted from my dad's dated address book the night we left. It was our only hope, and Jo and I clung to it tightly on the nights we felt none.

When the woman moved and the towering presence of my uncle replaced her in the doorway, I couldn't help but shrink a little. His white shirt was crisp and clean, his sleeves rolled up, revealing large forearms. I caught a large arrow tattoo on the right one before my eyes met his.

He looked so much like my father, a massive beast of a man with a broken mind and hands that beat. However, the man before me was younger than him by more than ten years.

"Sean?" His brows were furrowed, and he pulled a pair of glasses from the neck of his shirt.

I wasn't expecting him to recognize me right away. The last time I saw him, I was seven, and the memories of that day came to me more from the photos my grandmother took than my mind.

"It's me." I attempted a smile but quickly abandoned those efforts. If I smiled, it moved the muscles around my eye, and my head felt like it was on fire. I hadn't smiled in weeks, though it felt like it could have been even longer than that.

I felt Jo move behind me, her hand gripping mine.

"Come in, come in, both of you." His eyes wandered to my skinny companion.

Jo was almost as tall as me, but my legs ached every night. I knew I still had inches to go before I reached my full height, which would surely match that of the man letting me into his home.

We both grabbed our bags and walked in. The foyer was white, every light in the living room, dining room, and kitchen was on. A record player was spinning on the wall behind the couch. I saw the woman who answered the door staring at us behind the bar. It was open and clean. I wanted to cry, but I knew that would hurt, too.

"Do you guys need something to drink?" Her voice was deeper than one would expect from someone so small.

I looked at Jo, her eyes level with mine. She nodded.

"Yes. Thank you, ma'am," I said.

She smiled at the respect I offered her. She didn't look like a ma'am, but she was an adult, and manners were something my mother taught me.

"Sean, son, what's going on? What happened to your eye?"

I flinched at my uncle's words. He was standing in his living room. The couch separated us. I let go of Jo's hand and cleared my throat. "Well, sir, um, I had to leave my house."

"Leave your house? What does that mean?" he asked.

"There was this field trip to the states for school. That was a couple of weeks ago. I snuck away. We planned it a long time ago, Jo and I. This is Jo, my girlfriend." I was rambling, my words could roll like a runaway train if I let them, but I was trying to be clear, concise. My father hated it when I mumbled.

"And you were on this school trip, too?"

"No, sir," she answered.

I knew it wouldn't be lost on him that Jo was older than me.

"And your father? Does he have any idea where you are?" he asked me.

"No," I said.

"No," he repeated, running a hand over his chin. "Okay, Sean, walk me through this."

I walked around the couch, made my way for an oversized loveseat. I could hear Jo following. When we were both seated, I grabbed her hand. I stared at my uncle's feet as I started. "I know what kind of father you and my dad had. He thinks he wasn't that kind of father either. But that's bullshit. He's just like him. A drunk. My mom is gone. She left one night six months ago, didn't even try to wake me up." I looked up after this admission, into my uncle's eyes. I felt Jo squeeze my hand. "He's been beating the shit out of me for years now. If I didn't leave, he was going to kill me. I guess my mom thought the same. Every man and woman for themselves, I guess." I forced a laugh, and it hurt.

But not as much as the knowledge that tears were forming. I pulled my hand from Jo's, and it joined my left one on my face, covering the evidence.

I heard my uncle's wife—fiancée? I didn't know what she was, but I heard her move into the room. The unmistakable sound of glasses hitting the coffee table in the center of the room was deafening.

"Fuck," my uncle muttered.

"They have to come with us," the woman said.

"Shit. I know, Cal. I know. Go make up the spare room."

And just like that, I had a family. And I thought, *I'll never be alone again.*

EIGHT

CALLIOPE

APOLLO

I just wanted a family. Why couldn't you give me that? You're so fucking selfish.

NINE

SEAN

**PRESENT
THE LAKE**

"NEW NUMBER. NON-NEGOTIABLE." I sigh into the phone.

Jesse is focusing on everything but what I'm asking him for. This has been a weakness of mine. Letting my manager treat me like a son, like he's in control of everything in my life.

In truth, I call the shots, but I forget it. All the time. Jo always made me feel like shit for it. But she was right about one thing: I can't keep looking for father figures in this life.

"But what about your next two shows? Are you really blowing them off? You flew out there quick enough, Sean. You can fly right back just as quick."

"No. The tour is done. Make an announcement. Tell them I've fallen ill."

"Even on Instagram? Because I seem to be locked out of that."

"I changed the password. I'll be the only one running it now." I'll stay up all night disabling comments on every photo if I have to. I don't know when the public will find out about Jo and me, but I can't look at the flood of comments.

My birthday is in two days. Twenty-one, finally. I pull my phone from my ear and delete the Twitter app as Jesse babbles on and on about responsibility and bad publicity. I hit the speakerphone button and turn the volume low just in case he expects a response to anything.

The guest house looks different. New decorations. The posters Jo and I hung up are long gone. There is a large trunk across the room. I shoved notebooks of poetry and songs into it that summer five years ago. Words about learning to drive, losing my virginity, falling in love. All the sweet things I could think of. All to fit the image Jo said I needed to perfect. The sweet Canadian singer. The perfect boy. I always tried to be the man my handlers wanted me to be.

I was a puppet, and I no longer want to be a puppet.

"Are you listening to me, Sean?"

"Yes, but you might as well be talking to a wall."

"You always listen when I give advice."

"You want me to power through when you know I can't get the image of my girlfriend and uncle fucking out of my head. So it sounds like nothing more than concern for the money I make you. Just focus on making sure none of this comes out. That's the bad publicity you should be worried about."

"You're right. But who would leak it? Have you told anyone? Jo wouldn't want that coming out. The public would skin her alive. And I would say your uncle wouldn't want his wife to find out, but I'm assuming you already told her."

"Yes. I told her."

"Don't do something you'll regret. Calliope *das Dores*, Sean. Think about that. She has the same last name as you."

"I have thought about that." I pause, and we let the silence surround us. "I gotta go. Let me know the new number when you get it." I hang up and throw the phone on the couch next to me.

I can feel the anxiety growing. A gnawing unseen presence living in my skull. It wants me to listen, but I can't. I start to count, eyes closed, so I don't react to the voices beginning to rise. They echo the chanting of a crowd as I walk out. Except there is no cheering, just jarring jeering and every insecurity I've ever owned, repeated from the phantom voices.

A knock on the door pulls me from my nightmare. I turn to see Calliope beyond the glass door.

I don't break eye contact as I walk to the door and hit the latch to unlock it. She opens it, and I shove my hands in the pockets of my black jeans.

"Have you eaten? You should eat, right?" she asks.

"I don't feel like I can."

"If anyone asks if you're here, what do I say?"

"I think you know the answer to that," I say, stepping back into the guest house.

"He won't come here. This is the one thing I wanted in the divorce. This house. I can't be in Chicago with him."

"You had a life there, too, right?" I sit on the couch. Her gaze grazes my knees as I spread them.

"That's how divorce works, I guess." She makes a motion with her hand. "You slice your life down the middle. Half and half." She shrugs, laughs to herself. "Or something like that."

"I haven't forgotten that you're an orphan like me." I was surrounded by them, and we made a makeshift family. They tore it apart.

"I didn't imagine you did." She crosses her arms and surveys the room. "Doesn't look like home anymore, does it?"

There are boxes along the far wall. Packing tape and markers sit on one that's low to the floor. "What is that stuff?"

"Your uncle's stuff. I've been packing it up. Fed Ex has been coming once a week, making pickups."

I stand at her words, make my way to the door. "I can't sleep in this room with those things here." I brush past her.

"Understandable."

I turn at her words. This is one of those moments. I make statements, and when Jo isn't around, I fill in the blanks. *Don't be so dramatic. It's just stuff.* That's what she would have said to me.

Though the main house is large, there aren't many bedrooms. I always found it strange. But for a vacation house that rarely housed guests, it made sense. My uncle and Calliope never entertained guests the summer we spent here. My uncle would leave some weeks, coming back on Friday nights. Calliope would go shopping. Decorate. Water the plants; there were at least a hundred of them. It looked like a jungle in there.

I decide I need to eat, so we walk to the house. When Calliope offers to make me something, I brush her off. I need to busy my hands because I know it'll distract my mind.

I pull cheese from the fridge and search for the bread while Calliope makes herself another drink. I catch her eyes on my forearm as I flip my grilled cheese.

I was right. I'm making her nervous.

And I like it.

TEN

SEAN

PAST
THE LAKE

MY LIFE WAS NEVER about wealth. My family got by, but my father didn't have the kind of success with his business my uncle had. My father was a real estate agent. Uncle Apollo was a real estate company owner.

After staying with Uncle Apollo and his wife—Calliope—for two weeks in their Chicago home, we left for their lake house in the Missouri Ozarks. It was where he met her. Where she grew up.

The home was on the water. Glass windows from floor to ceiling. They said you could see the runway of the small airport we flew into when it was wintertime, when the leaves on the trees gave up. Now, you could see spring green, and white blooms in the woods. *They're dogwood trees, my favorite,* my uncle's wife had said.

Calliope was welcoming. At first, she doted on Jo and me, but I heard her worries one night after dinner in the city. She told my uncle my relationship with Jo concerned her. That the age gap needed to be addressed, but he told her to leave it alone. To calm her crazy ass down. The tone of his voice made the hairs on my arms raise, but I brushed it away. He couldn't help sounding like my father.

When we walked into our new home, the detached guest house, I had a hard time believing Jo and Calliope couldn't hear my heart beating in my chest.

The center of the room was home to a huge bed. Bigger than anything I had ever slept on. I looked at Jo, then Calliope, over her shoulder.

"I told your uncle one of you should stay out here and one of you inside the main house, but he said if you hadn't come to us and had been living on the streets you would be sleeping together anyway."

I didn't know what she meant by "sleeping together". It could have been sex, or she could have been talking about us sharing the same bed; either way, she broke the connection between our eyes. There was no way I was bringing up that I was a virgin.

I pressed Jo for her reasonings in the beginning. Why she wanted me and why she wanted to uproot her life to follow me on the road.

She said that in the darkest moments of her life she heard a voice and when she heard mine for the first time in the stairwell of the town library she knew it was what she had been searching for. She believed in fate, the stars, and every myth her mother taught her. I wasn't sure about destiny, but when she told me she could guess my middle name with no clue, and did, I thought maybe I should just shut up and listen to everything I felt when she touched me.

Calliope left us to unpack. We showed up with one bag each, but now we carried more, thanks to their hospitality.

When Jo heard the click of the door, she let out a sigh. "Thank God. I've wanted to get you alone for weeks now."

She threw her bag on the bed, pressed her lips to mine, and wound her fingers into my hair. She tasted like the peppermint gum she had been chewing on the entire flight.

I pulled away and looked out the glass door.

Jo glared. "What? She already thinks we're fucking. I doubt she is watching." And then, after a moment, she continued. "She bugs me."

"Why?" I never knew when one girl disliked another back in school. They played it cool, wore faces I couldn't read, and then the truth came out.

"She acts like she's an adult and I'm a kid, but we're both adults." She liked to say that a lot, as if she was on trial.

"I'm not," I reminded her.

"You're an old soul."

I rolled my eyes at her words. I didn't care about our age difference. When I was older, it wouldn't be an issue at all. And now that we were starting over, no one would know about it unless someone else brought it up. And people, more often than not, didn't like bringing up awkward questions like that.

I scanned the room, walking away from Jo. My fingers slipped from her hand, and she sighed.

"I need to find a place to record," I said.

Her eyes lit up, and I winked at her.

I had plans, and Jo wanted to see those plans become a reality.

You're going to be a star.

She said that to my face the first day we met in that stairwell. I blushed, but she reached out and ran her thumb over the scar on my cheek. I was never going to be anything if I didn't get out of my house. If I didn't escape my father. I was going to end up in a casket.

Jo was living in a motel five miles from my house. We were inseparable from that moment on. She would hitch a ride with the woman who rented the room next to her down to my place, sneaking me out of my window, taking me downtown. Once there, I would sing, and she would dance, no matter who watched. Her pink hair and long legs drew them in.

You're going to be a star. A star.

I believed her some nights. When the tips filled her black hat, when the crowd was large.

I believed her when she said I should start posting videos online. I believed her when the followers filled the black hole in my chest. I believed her when the views reached thousands.

The only moment I didn't believe her was when my father found us recording in my bedroom. He was supposed to be showing a house, but he got stood up. So he came home early.

That was the night we left. He said no one would watch a skinny, pussy Canadian sing songs and play the guitar.

He said a dead eye was better than a lazy eye, so he put his fist into it. As Jo screamed, as he kicked my ribs with his shiny dress shoes, I heard him say a dead son was better than a lazy son who wanted a get-famous-quick scheme to determine his future.

I brought my hand to my face, sick at the memory. It was no longer tender there, but I still winced.

"Here. Right here," Jo said, behind me.

I looked across the room to where Jo was standing. A large window with a seat. The forest opened up beyond the glass, and the sun blinded me as it reflected off the water of the lake.

ELEVEN

CALLIOPE

APOLLO
He's soft. We both know that. And you don't want soft.

TWELVE

SEAN

**PRESENT
THE LAKE**

I SEND THE TEXT, not to be dramatic, but to get her near me as soon as possible.

She finds me in the guest house on the bathroom floor. My bare chest is covered in sweat.

I've suffered through anxiety attacks before. But never back to back like this.

I feel like I'm dying. I'm dizzy, crawling in my skin.

Calliope falls to her knees when she sees me. "Jesus, Sean. What's wrong? Are you okay?"

Her hands are all over me. My neck, my chest, my wrists. I wish I could feel it. I just feel numb.

"I couldn't breathe for a minute there. I think I'm okay." My voice sounds muffled in my ears. I close my eyes because all I see are stars and what looks like the sun, but I know it's just the bathroom light.

My adrenaline brought me here, to her home. I had a purpose, a truth to tell. A scar to create. One in her to match my own pulsing pain.

It hits me then that I'm in my boxer briefs. I see my jeans hanging over the side of the tub, and I groan. I try to sit, and Calliope's hands wrap around my forearm. I'm embarrassed, but the nausea is clinging tightly to me.

"What happened?" she asks, running her hand across my face, feeling my forehead.

It feels like something a mother would do, a comfort I barely remember, so I reach up and grab her hand. "I think, I think it just all hit me. It hit me at once. And the walls caved in on me."

She stands then, grabbing a glass by the sink, filling it. She kneels down when it's full, pressing it into my chest. "Just have a drink, and you'll feel better."

I can't taste it, but I drink anyway.

Her hand is on my thigh. Skin to skin. It's all I can focus on.

I give the glass back, crawl to the toilet, and gag.

Hot spit and acid. It's all I have.

THIRTEEN

CALLIOPE

**PAST
THE LAKE**

THE GIRLFRIEND LIKED to leave him alone. Often. Too often, for my liking. And I found the age difference unfair—a mismatch. But my concerns fell on deaf ears when I voiced them to Apollo.

The car that picked Jo up had left a half-hour ago. Sean was sitting by the pool, his guitar laying by his side, his feet in the water as he scribbled furiously in a notebook. The only light was the moon and the lingering rays of amber from the candles I lit earlier to ward off mosquitos.

I should have stayed inside, watching him from there. But he would have seen me eventually. There were too many windows in the house. Too much glass, too eager to give away secrets to anyone willing to look.

I couldn't help but notice that he reminded me of my brother when he scribbled like that. I pushed the thought away as I reached him. His eyes met mine only at the last moment. "Holy shit, you scared me," he said, clutching his chest.

"Sorry. I don't know how you didn't hear me."

"I get in this zone, ya know?" He spun his finger in a circle near his ear. "It's like nothing else in the world exists when I need to write something down."

"How long have you been writing?"

"I think I came out writing." He smiled. It was a beautiful smile. All teeth and youth. The light played tricks, and I could see the scar on his cheek, even in the dimness.

"I started with poetry, and Jo said I could turn my poems into songs. That I'm a better sell if I write my own lyrics."

A better sell. That sounded like something Jo would say. The boy was talented. It was clear to all of them. And it was going to be clear to the world if their planning and plotting worked. Jo saw a meal ticket and took a chance.

I can't hate the little shit. The face of my mother flashed in my mind as I dipped into the past. "I had a boyfriend in high school who used to write poetry about me." He treated me like a doll, like something delicate and breakable. I missed that.

"With a name like yours, why wouldn't he? Was he aware of the meaning?" Sean asked, strumming his guitar.

"You're aware of the meaning?" I was taken aback, surprised by him. And, truthfully, it'd been a long time since I'd been surprised, genuinely, with no trace of horror intermingled.

"Yes. I've always been into mythology."

"Your uncle pronounced it right the first time I met him, but now he loves to say it wrong. On purpose." When he joked, I could almost remember why I fell in love with him. "I think you should say it the right way. Show him he's an ass."

"Deal." He set the guitar down, stared at his feet in the water. The moonlight reflected onto his pale skin.

"Where's Jo?" I asked though I knew where she was. My friends in the area still texted me sometimes, and you can't miss a pink-haired girl throwing her smile, her charm, all over, like confetti.

"We met some people at the mall a few weeks ago. A couple. So we've been hanging out a little bit. But they're all Jo's age."

"And they like to drink," I said as I looked at him.

"And they like to drink," he confirmed, reaching for his guitar again, and I wondered if it was a shield for him. A way to hide from the conversations he didn't want to have.

I saw him do it sometimes when Apollo asked him about his plans. His uncle was obsessed with goals, with charts and figures for the future. Maybe he saw a meal ticket, too.

"I'm sorry," I said, and then, "would you like a drink?" I looked down at the sweating glass in my hand.

"No. Jo, that's her thing. Not mine. It'll never be mine."

Red covered my cheeks as his response, and I was glad for the dim light around them. *I offered a drink to a teenage boy who had an alcoholic father. Jesus fucking Christ.* "I can't believe I just said that. Fuck. I guess I was just trying to be the cool aunt."

He blushed this time. "You don't feel like an aunt to me. How old are you?"

"Twenty-six."

"You look Jo's age."

"Not too long ago, I was Jo's age. And I was out partying at the lake. Every night."

"Where did you live here?" Sean asked.

"Trailer park about ten minutes east."

"How did you meet my uncle?"

I cleared my throat. "I was a shot girl. He was down here with some work friends for the weekend. The table, about seven dudes, ordered shots. I brought them over, and I never left the table. I got fired that night. Or I quit. I don't even know anymore. You can paint it any way you like."

"Why would you quit?"

The boy liked to collect stories, I knew that, but I gave him our story anyway. I trusted him. "Your uncle said he wanted to marry me. I knew he was drunk, but I think I wanted to believe him so badly I didn't care. I don't do reckless shit like that." A lie, but it sounded romantic. "How did you meet Jo?"

He blushed and couldn't help but smile. If he made it, women would go crazy for that face; the shy smile, the soft voice. He wasn't trying, and he may never need to. It was all there. *Genetics.*

"I don't want to say."

"You know, if you make it big one day, it's going to come out how you met. You're going to be asked. Better start practicing your truths and lies."

"She was my babysitter."

I choked on my drink, and Sean flew up, grabbing me under the arms. When I caught my breath, his fingers were wrapped around my elbows. I could feel spit on my lip, so I pulled my hand to the spot and wiped it away. "Holy shit."

"Are you okay?" Sean asked, releasing his grip on me.

"Yes. Now, wait. What?"

He stepped back, ran his hands through his hair. It was long on the top, floppy when he didn't fix it. "You told me to practice my truths and lies. It seemed like a good story. When you said that, it just flew into my head."

"You're already too young for her, Sean. Maybe don't make it worse."

"I'll be sixteen when the summer begins, and I've experienced more than most people have by that age. I've experienced more than Jo has in twenty-one years." His voice lost the laugh, the beauty.

There's a lot that can age you when you're young. I knew how he felt, so I couldn't argue about his maturity—it was apparent when he walked in our door with his dirty backpack. Jo's carefree vibe was evident then, too.

I caught Apollo chatting with Jo sometimes. They shared their own language. They talked about sports. It was coded, and I didn't understand it. I didn't want to understand it.

"Do you miss Toronto?" I threw out, wanting to change the subject.

"Yes. No."

"What do you miss?" I asked, looking at him.

"My mother. All my memories of her are tied to Toronto."

It was another tug at my heart. I was home, where every memory was tied up with my own mother.

And my brother.

FOURTEEN

CALLIOPE

APOLLO
He's heavy. You can't carry that shit. You're the heavy one. You're the one who needs to be carried. Don't think I don't know what he will be up to. I saw it then. I saw you two.

FIFTEEN

SEAN

**PRESENT
THE LAKE**

I OFTEN CATCH myself when I know I'm being a little manic, and when I couldn't catch myself, Jo always did. Or someone else in charge of my life and the carefully crafted image we all created—together—would catch me.

I look into the mirror, run my hand through my hair one more time.

I want it gone. I want it all gone.

I remember the way Jo's hands felt in it, the way she would pull on it when she was on top of me, making me see stars, making me wonder at the ways the world damned lust. It was too deeply intertwined with my love for her.

I search the entire bathroom and cannot find anything to stop the ache in me, so I walk outside, cross the yard. I don't know if Calliope is up yet, but the door is unlocked when I reach it, so I assume she must be.

I call her name and hear nothing.

It's just me and the silence I'm trying to escape until she finds me in her bathroom. Her hair is up, tiny tendrils of brown fall down in her face. She has a white mug in her hand, and her red fingernails stand out against the colorless porcelain. There is a dog at her feet—white fur, fluffy, and a little wet.

"What are you doing?" She doesn't sound mad, just curious.

"I'm sorry. I called for you, but you didn't answer." I stare at the dog, wondering if I see a ghost.

"I was down by the water. I like to go down there in the mornings." She has denim shorts on and an oversized sweater. Her pale legs look a little pink on the tops of her thighs, as if the sun has kissed her recently.

I want to kiss her.

"Oh." I look away, pull my hand from the drawer I was searching.

"Am I being robbed by Sean das Dores?" She offers me a small laugh, and I appreciate it.

"I was looking for hair clippers. So I searched the guest house and didn't find any."

"Well, the only ones I have are in there. In those boxes. I don't really have any use for them myself, but your uncle did." She pauses, her eyes following the dog as he walks to the toilet and sticks his head in. She clicks her tongue, and he runs out, knowing the sound. "What do you need them for?" she asks, her eyes finding me again.

"I want to cut my hair."

"You know some people might be concerned with that move."

"I know, but none of those people are here, right?"

"No. They're not."

Twenty minutes later, after a trip to the guest house, where Calliope dug through carefully labeled boxes—boxes she promised me would be gone by the end of the day, we find ourselves staring at them back in her bathroom. She pulls out her vanity seat and tells me to sit, so I do. I wanted to do this on my own, but she isn't leaving, and I don't ask her to.

"Take off your shirt," she says, running the fingers of her right hand through my hair. An act so loathed in my memory by one woman is giving me life now, at the hands of another.

"Why?" I ask, my eyes closed. I wonder if she can feel me shaking.

"So you don't get hair all over it."

I reach back, pull my white T-shirt over my head. She stares at me, at my body, in the mirror, her eyes avoiding mine as she examines, memorizes. My cheeks become ruddy, the way they always do when I'm nervous or turned on.

I look away from her reflection, my eyes caught by her phone lighting up by the sink.

"Do you leave your notifications on for Instagram?" I ask.

Calliope has a large following on the social media site. She dabbles in photography. When the public found out she was related to me, through our shared last name, her already large following quadrupled. Her account is verified now.

"Sometimes," she says, "but not always. It can drain the battery." She reaches for her phone, scrolls for a moment, then sets it back down. Face down.

I watch her busy herself. She plugs the clippers in, turns them on.

Jo used to say we are all bodies struggling to find peace in another body. She was pink and open and yet, red. A glaring red flag, right in front of my face.

My eyes are closed when Calliope presses the clippers to the nape of my neck. I keep them closed as she works to remove this part of myself I reclaimed.

My father had a head of hair like this. I got it from him. His dark hair and his dark eyes, matching my Portuguese last name. My mother gave me my pale skin, my cutting jaw. My softness.

I try to stop the tears at the edges of my eyes from falling, but it is useless. I am shedding, being culled of a hard-won part of my identity. My uncle has this thick hair on his head. It's another tie I wish to sever.

When she's done, when the humming is over, and I've successfully stayed still, her fingertips work over my neck and shoulders to remove strays. I keep my eyes closed. I let my face fall into my hands, letting the salt come.

I can hear her moving around me, letting me have this moment.

It isn't the first time I've cried in front of her, and it probably won't be the last.

When I feel her hands on my shoulders, firmly pressing, I still.

"Are you going to be all right?" Her husky voice pulls me. So different than Jo's mousy pitch.

My best friend—August—said it was annoying once, in another room, not to my face. But I heard it. And after that, it was all I heard when she spoke, though her souring words were the real cause in my shift of perspective.

"Yes," I say, pulling myself together.

Calliope lets go of me and walks to the bathroom door, so I reach for my T-shirt on the floor, shaking it clean when I sit up.

"I think we need to have a talk," she says.

Her arms are crossed, and I'm lost in my reflection. I don't know if I look older or younger now. I feel older.

"Okay." I don't ask what about.

We both know there is too much unspoken, too much that could ruin us.

SIXTEEN

SEAN

**PAST
THE LAKE**

MY UNCLE WAS out of town, and Jo would be out late. Without her, the guest house was quiet, and I couldn't stand the sounds in my head anymore.

They told me lies, or, at least what I *thought* were lies.

The plans Jo and I made seemed fragile, breakable every night she spent away from me, every night she came home smelling of malt liquor and sweet cigarillos.

She was gone a lot. Weeks of long hours working and breathless promises that she just wanted to save up for a car for us. She said *us*, and that's the only thing that kept me calm.

Deep in my chest, I couldn't shake this overwhelming fear that she would fly away across the lake someday like a butterfly or some kite I couldn't grab hold of.

I walked out onto the dock with one earbud in, watching the edges. I didn't want to fall in, but the sound of someone swimming pulled me.

I knew it was Calliope. This was private property. The dock was private.

She was wearing a tiny black bikini. She looked like a mermaid under the dark, filthy water. I took a seat at the edge of the dock, my white Converse tucked under my legs. The earbud came out when she placed her palms on the dock next to me.

Water trickled off of her as she pulled herself up the metal ladder. It wasn't until she was standing next to me, dripping, that she noticed me.

"Damn, Sean. What are you doing out here?"

I gave her no words, just held my phone up so she could see the song I was listening to. She nodded then pointed to her temple. I smiled at her mental note.

She toweled off next to me, the waning sun casting shadows all over her, and my cheeks caught a blush in the dusk.

"Want to see something?" she asked. The towel was around her waist, and she was walking.

I followed the sway of her hips and shoved my phone in my pocket.

In the corner of the main room of the guest house was a large trunk. The fifty-inch flat-screen was sitting on it when we moved in, so rummaging through the contents of the makeshift TV stand was never something that crossed my mind.

Calliope kneeled in front of it, digging out old records, sipping from a glass of wine.

I had moved the TV for her earlier, and now I didn't know what to do with my hands.

"Do all these old records belong to your brother?" I asked.

She had told me a story on the short walk from the dock to here. Her stories were always half-stories. As if she planned them in advance, or had told them a million times before, and knew how to make them entertaining while giving away as little of the meat of it all as she could.

"Yes. They were originally my dad's. It was all we had left of him," she said.

"I wonder what that's like." I pulled a record from the stack. The faded face of a star stared back at me. Not easily placed, like Elvis or Johnny.

"What?" She turned to me, and her brow was in a V.

"To want to hold on to memories of your father."

"Apollo told me about his father the first night he met me," she said, speaking of the grandfather I never knew. "I think it was the vodka talking. He wanted to tell me every little thing about himself. His past and his present. It's why I fell for him." She ran her palm over the record, lost for a moment. "I'm sorry your father turned out like their father."

"At least my uncle didn't turn out like their father. Right?" His voice frightened me at times, but just because it so resembled the deep baritone of my own father's. My voice wasn't deep, booming. Not when I was singing or speaking.

"Is there anything good you got from him?" she asked.

"The scar on my cheek." I pointed to it. As if it wasn't obvious.

She frowned at my answer. "And how did he give you that?" She rocked off of her knees, pulling her ankles around, sitting cross-legged, facing me.

"I was five. I talked back. He backhanded me."

"Jesus." Her face flushed, and the vein in her neck throbbed.

Her knee-jerk reaction to the violence of my childhood made me want to tell her more. "You see this eye?"

"Yes."

"It was really lazy when I was a kid. And he said he wasn't spending the money to get it fixed. That I could just look like that and learn to deal with it. So I talked to this kid Oscar at school. He had a lazy eye, but his parents wanted to do something about it. I couldn't go to a doctor or anything. So I just did the exercises that he told me he did in my spare time. It's still there. A little. Can you see it?"

She looked hard into my eyes, and I felt the blush creeping back. I looked to the right then the left for her.

She nodded. "Just barely. I wouldn't have noticed if you didn't say anything."

"What were your parents like?" I asked, moving away from her just a bit.

"My father is dead." She began rifling through the records again, and I knew these keepsakes weren't just about her brother.

"What happened to him?"

"He rode a motorcycle. He was hit. These roads are dangerous. All the curves." She appeared to be making two piles on each side of her thighs. The towel was coming undone around her little bathing suit.

"Jesus," I said, mimicking her earlier shock. "Your mom?"

"She fell apart afterward. He left us nothing, and she had a hard time. So we moved to a trailer park, and she got a job at a bar. When I was old enough, so did I. She told me I needed to marry rich. Get the fuck out of here. And I guess I did that. I think she would be proud of me." She shrugged.

"Would be?"

"She's dead to me."

The finality of those words, I couldn't argue with them, question, pry. She was a brick wall when you got her alone.

"You're an orphan," I said, reaching for a record on the top of the pile to her right. It was a Keith Whitley album.

"Yes."

"I feel like one."

"We are just a house full of them then," she said.

"Not Jo." I reached for the phone in my pocket. The screen showed no texts from her when I pulled it out.

"What's the family she ran away from like then?"

"Well, she didn't run away. She's an adult," I said.

"Are you?"

"Okay, I know where you're going with this."

"I'm sorry. It isn't really my business. I'm not your aunt. I mean, I am, but not really. I just wasn't sure if this," she motioned to me, "was just her particular taste."

"You can't really say anything about dating older. Look at you and my uncle."

Suddenly she was standing, and I looked up at a small, angry little woman. The towel was falling, and her knuckles drew my eyes in. There was a wide scar on her right hand.

"We were both adults," she said, using her bare foot to push one of the stacks she created earlier closer to the trunk. She swayed a little, and I wondered if she was tipsy.

"She isn't taking advantage of me," I said, standing. I towered over her. "I love her. She's the love of my life." I hated that I didn't sound convincing. I sounded like a little boy.

"Your life has barely started. You might think differently later." Instead of looking me in the eyes, she bent at the waist, grabbing records, ruining whatever sorting she had managed earlier.

"She saved me from the life I had before. This is weird." I laughed. It was awkward, not angry. I didn't sound convincing when I tried for angry. "You barely know me. I don't think you should be offering advice on my life." There was a teal chair next to the trunk, pressed close to the glass window that gave us a view of the lake we had just left. I sat down, watching her work.

"I'm sorry. You're right. Sometimes I have a drink, and I just say stupid shit."

"Not everyone wants a meal ticket," I said, hating myself for it as soon as the words left my lips.

SEVENTEEN

CALLIOPE

APOLLO
How long are you going to ignore me? Do I need to fly down there?

EIGHTEEN

SEAN

**PRESENT
THE LAKE**

THE SPRING SUN is hot above us on the dock. The water around us is muddy brown, unpretty. Calliope has a red bikini on, her brown hair is up. We are both so pale, the sun reflects off of us. You could probably see us from space. I look around, into the woods, at the dogwood trees, and they make me smile.

"How long do you want to stay here?" she asks.

"As long as it takes."

"To get over her?" She reaches for a pair of aviators on the dock, uses them to push the tendrils of hair in her face out of the way, so I can see anything she may try to hide.

"I'm over her now."

She laughs at me. "No, you're not."

"I saw her with him. I'll never be able to scrub that image from my brain. I'll never forgive her."

Calliope's face is the most expressive face I've ever seen. I used to try to analyze every tic, every muscle moved when I was a teen. I'm watching her now, back to old habits.

"You'd be surprised at what you can forgive." She pushes the glasses down, over her eyes, pushing me out.

"Do you want forgiveness for what happened between us five years ago?" I thought I would leave it unspoken. But it's the reason. It's the lingering question, and I want to uncover the motivation behind that night.

We'd swept it under the rug for years, pretended no intimacy ever lived between us as we sat down for Christmas dinners, attended Sunday lunches when I was in the city.

"It depends on the day," she says, lying back. She props her hand under her head, and I wish I knew if her eyes were closed or not.

"I think I could give you that power."

"What power?" The sunglasses come off, and she props herself up on her elbows.

"The power to ruin my life."

"You're like a young god, Sean. No one could ruin you. She can't. I can't. Your father couldn't, and Apollo won't either. You have the whole world at your feet, so I'm not sure what you're looking for here."

"I'm going to write through this. And you can say you haven't dissected my songs, but I think maybe that would be a lie. Because I made it obvious. Or maybe it wasn't obvious, but I felt so guilty for wanting that kiss, that I feel like I didn't bury it deep enough."

"Did you bury it deep enough that Jo couldn't find it?" she asks.

I lie back, stare at the clear Missouri sky. Places have memories. They never die away. The dock down by the water holds many of mine. So many words spilled to pages as I sat alone, my feet hovering above the lake water. I wonder what places hold Jo's memories. If I could feel them. "Maybe she didn't point it out," I say, "because she knew she had her own secrets to hide."

"Is that a statement or a question?" she asks.

I shake my head, saying nothing. I don't know her intentions; this is a different Calliope.

She is no longer the wife. The authority figure. She looks so young in the morning light. The warm glow of the Tiki torches I lit to keep the mosquitos away by the water casts her in warm shades, contrasting with the blue.

She asks me another question, abandoning the one from before, abandoning the sunglasses, her armor. "Do you write down every red thought in your head?"

"Red?" I arch a brow, kick my legs that dangle over the side.

"My brother was always so anxious. He called those his red thoughts. His life flashed in red and blue. The lows and the angry highs. It was telling. Who knew he was his own fortune teller? These were admissions he gave me before he started to get arrested for bar fights and possession."

"A different kind of red and blue," I supply.

She nods. "Do you ever lie to people?"

I shake my head, run my hand over my head, still looking for the past. Jo said if I ever wanted anyone to look at me, to listen to the words in my mouth, I should do that. That I could have everyone eating from my fingers. She said it drew her in. So I noticed when she stopped looking, I just didn't let myself confront it. "What's the use in a lie?"

"It lets you control the narrative. I want you to be honest with me. Why are you here with me? Why did you fly here as soon as you saw them together?"

"I wanted to make sure you knew."

"And why did you want me to know?"

"Don't you think you should have known?" I ask.

"That's not what I asked," she replies. "I want to know why you wanted me to know."

I can't look at her. I can't let her see a face so few have seen. I don't act on my deepest desires, step outside my comfort zone, unless I have a team behind me offering reassurance. Every daring thing I have done in my life has been with the knowledge that I have someone to pick me up if I fall to pieces. Here, I have no one. My family doesn't exist anymore. My girlfriend doesn't exist anymore. Once again, my hands find my head, and it isn't to draw anyone to it; it's to hide. I groan and hear Calliope shift on the dock. I sense her getting closer.

"Say it," she says, her mouth close to my ear.

I can smell sugar and musk.

With my eyes closed, I reach out, find her tiny wrist on the dock. My thumb runs over her pulse, searching for something. Confirmation that any answer I give her won't humiliate me. She responds by twisting away, running her hand up my arm. My eyes open.

"You're too tense, too scared of everything. Can't you see what you are?" She moves her knee over my lap, and I reach out. She is too close to the water.

I lean back and snake my arm around her waist as she settles on my lap. Her knees on each side of my hips. I can't help but lean back so I can look at her. "What are you doing?" I ask.

"Straddling you," she says, nonchalantly. "Did you hear me?"

"Yes. You asked if I knew what I was." There is a lump in my throat. I swallow, and her eyes follow.

"Yes. I did." Her hands go to the hem of my shirt and slip under.

I lean back, close my eyes. Desire trumps the noise, chases it out.

"Damn, Sean. Just say it."

"I'm just a guy. That's all I am. Just some guy."

Her hands move higher. "The world is watching you, screaming your name, and you can't see how beautiful you are. You can't see what they see because one little punk girl pissed it away."

I fall back, away from her, and she presses. I know she feels my response.

"What are you doing to me?" I beg, but we both know it's what I came here for.

"What you want me to do." She doesn't come down to my level, and I wish she would.

I've never pursued, for fear of what I may find. I've always been chased.

Jo chased.

I've watched girls chase me down a street from the blacked-out windows of a speeding SUV in Spain. As a result, I've developed an intimate love affair with running.

"This isn't right," I say it because it needs to be said, but I want her to tell me to shut up.

"You can't make me play her role, you know?"

I open my eyes, go up on my elbows. I still hold back from touching her, from taking what I want. "What do you mean?"

"I can't imagine what it would be like to step into that mind of yours. I can only dissect those songs. And you're right. I did."

"I know," I say.

She presses down, my eyes flutter. "Sean?"

"Yes?"

"Did you bury it deep enough that Jo couldn't find it?"

I grip her hips, pull her against me. "Did you want me to?"

"I'm not telling you..."

I hear the hitch in her breathing as she trails off. After a moment, I open my eyes. Her fingers count my ribs, and her warmth is pressed too close.

"I'm not telling you, sober. Tonight we are going out. It's your birthday, after all," she says.

With that, she stands up, leaving me alone on the dock, unable to move.

NINETEEN

CALLIOPE

PAST
THE LAKE

I MISSED MY GYM—THE smell of sweat at five in the morning on a Tuesday. The music filling my headphones, drowning the world out.

I relished routines; they kept my mind clear when the world fell apart. They kept me healthy, kept the blurred vision and blinding pain away.

I ran down the path of the woods, the lake in view, dogwood trees—my favorite—in full bloom, surrounding me. It was a beautiful alternative, but it wasn't what I would choose, and that's why my heart wouldn't allow me to like it. At this hour I could hear birds chirping, could smell the morning fog on the water.

Apollo wouldn't let me go to the gym. Not here, and not in Chicago. He said it was a meat market no matter where I went. He didn't want men looking at me there and said *I* shouldn't want men looking at me either. When I left my old life for him, I was expected to give up every desire that made me who I was then. He didn't even allow me healthy vices.

When I made it back to the house, much earlier than intended, I saw them. My left breast ached from Apollo punching me two nights prior in his sleep.

It was warm already. The day would suffocate you if you didn't stay inside or retreat to the water. I made a mental note to see if Sean and Jo wanted to go for custard after lunch, but that thought was abandoned when Apollo's profile met my eyes.

He was in his car; his windows were down. He had a bad habit of leaving them down, and I always scolded him for it initially because I was always punished with having to roll them up for him. He said I had no idea what it was like to run a company, let alone work a full day's work anymore, so I might as well make myself useful.

His head was leaned back against the seat, his eyes closed. I felt stuck in the moment for too long, frozen, where I couldn't figure out what I was looking at, what I was seeing. My mind was still waking up, despite my beating heart, my sweating brow.

I saw her hair next, the slow bob of Jo's head in Apollo's lap. I saw his fingers wound in the strands then, the deep swallow of his throat in ecstasy as she moved, rhythmically. They were in sync, and I was going to throw up last night's dinner in the bushes.

I moved to them slowly, got down on my knees. My hand muffled the heaving. I didn't want to be caught, afraid of the repercussions.

I can't have the friends I want. I can't go to the gym. I can't have my phone out at dinner. I can't follow other men on Instagram. I can't, I can't, I can't. But I can wake up each day and desperately try to find beauty in the world with my camera. I can escape these stifling Ozark trees when the season is over.

I can't lose those things.

So I crawled. When I looked again, the windows were rolled up. My heart thundered in my chest, and I wretched into my hand again. Nothing came up but hot spit and my eyes stung.

I didn't know if they saw me, so I fell back into the grass and leaves.

I knew I couldn't return to the house. I needed to give them time to perfect the lie.

The loose hairs around my face stuck to my skin, and my hands went up, pushing everything gone astray back into place.

After a while, I sat up, checked my watch. It was six twenty-three in the morning. Did they both wake up at the same time? Did they plan this around my run? Where did Sean think she was? Was he even awake?

The boy could sleep like the dead. I'd been forced to wake him several times. It made me feel like a mother, and I didn't like that. I wanted to be more like his friend, not his elder.

It had been a long time since I had done something as thrilling as what I had just witnessed. Even in my horror, I recognized that it was exciting to them. Humans got off on that kind of thing. I knew my own past was littered with scattered moments of debauchery before my married life.

But thrills like that don't make for a life.

Again, I pressed my hand to my breast. *A lot of things don't make for a life.*

I stood slowly, my right knee popping the way it always did. My shoes carried me on autopilot back to the path I'd abandoned. My eyes were awake now, my heart a thundering nightmare. Reluctantly, I stared at the house, at the windows. The long floor-to-ceiling curtains in the pool house were drawn, but the curtains in the main house's kitchen were open. I could see Apollo over the sink, Jo at the bar behind him, a white mug in her hands.

I was wearing black, lost in the green. I doubted they could see me, and at that moment, I didn't care, but it was fleeting. After that, my bravery succumbed to cowardice.

I took the long way around, stopped at the pool, kicked off my running shoes, taking a seat on one of the plush lounge chairs by the fire pit.

The sun was painting everything in orange, in fire. I saw my dog—Kanuk—down by the water, staring at a cluster of ducks on the glass surface.

One false move and they would fly away.

At that moment, I felt like the dog down by the rocky shore. One false move and it would all fly away, this life.

So I stayed still, watched the world turn warmer, brighter.

When enough time passed, I circled around to the open garage, entering the house from the door inside, finding it loud and full without me. The morning news was on. Apollo was sitting in the dining area. He had his coffee mug to the right of him, his iPad in his large hands. He was listening to the news and reading the news. It was his routine; he rarely strayed from it.

Jo was on the couch, lying down, her phone in her face, her feet up on the armrest, an ankle moving back and forth to an unknown rhythm. I looked at the girl's messy pink hair piled on her head, saw headphones in her ears.

"Did you sleep well?" I asked my husband, making my decision.

TWENTY

CALLIOPE

APOLLO
She reminded me of you. Don't you see that's why I did this? You used to be happy. You used to be fun to be around.

TWENTY-ONE

SEAN

**PRESENT
THE LAKE**

I DON'T WANT to be seen. The thought of being photographed out in public makes my anxiety spike, so I close my eyes, listening to the low hum of the radio, the gravel crunching under Calliope's tires.

I tensed at the idea of celebrating my birthday with her when she suggested it—or rather, demanded it—earlier in the day. I'd been planning for this day for five years. That's all gone now.

Calliope can read the lines on my forehead. She smiles, and it's comforting. Maybe that's why I came here. Maybe that's how she convinced me to do this.

"I promise no one is going to know you here. My mother used to go here to look for older men if that tells you anything. The average age is sixty-seven. They're all retired rich white dudes with huge boats and even bigger bank accounts. Their granddaughters know who you are, but trust me, they won't be here."

I run my hands down my black jeans, wiping away any sweat. "If you say so." My knee bounces. "Is there an escape plan?"

"Escape plan?"

"Yeah. If I'm spotted."

She puts her car in park and stares at the bar's neon lights. "I didn't think about it. So this is something you need to think about, huh?"

"Always. Or I don't because I pay people to think about it for me."

She settles her hands in her lap and breathes out, heavily. "The owner knows me. I'm sure he would let us through the kitchen. But, Sean, look at that place. It's tiny. What are you worried about?"

"A photo of us together making it online."

"How long do you think it'll be before someone spots her alone? Without you? And you're already radio silent. People are talking now. There's a reason you disabled the comments on your Instagram."

"You noticed that?" My phone feels like a heavy weight in my hand.

"Yes."

"My biggest fear is I'll wake up someday, and all of it will be gone. No one will care about me. They only know me one way. With her by my side." It's the first time I've said it out loud, Jo's role in the image I've created. I feel like shit. Like I'm calling her a prop, but I know Calliope would never accuse me of it. She never much cared for Jo, anyway.

"They don't listen to your music and connect with your songs because you have some pink-haired older girlfriend," she replies, confirming my memories.

"It's part of the image I've been living. I'm not the star who goes out to the bars, taking girls home, driving drunk, ending up with his mugshot on the *Entertainment Weekly* Facebook page. I'm the one who's been with the same girl since he was a kid. Just kids in love. People relate to that."

"I'm not going to pretend I know anything about this life you have. But I know this, and I hope you know this. You can't control what people say about you. All you can control is what you do. Do you want to do this? Because I don't want to make you do anything you don't want to do."

"I want to. My mind just won't relax," I say, adjusting my seat, leaning back. I imagine her eyes on my throat.

"That's what a drink is for." She squeezes my hand and exits the car.

I watch her figure in the headlights in front of me until they turn off. She isn't waiting for me, and I wonder if she would let me sit in her car all night with my demons, with the voices telling me to stay in the cell I've created.

Finally, I follow her.

The bar is small, like Calliope said. Black and smokeless, thanks to laws that weren't in place years ago. I can still smell the smoke in Jo's hair when she came home from drinking all those years ago if the memory strikes.

Calliope is at the bar; she stands out in her blue dress. I come up behind her and brush my fingers across the skin of her back.

She turns, an angry glare fixed on her face that softens when she sees it's me. "I didn't think you would actually come in this fast."

"I'm trusting you here."

There is something about touch. The way it conveys messages we cannot say. We often ignore them, waiting for words we hope will never come. Jo was sending me messages for months, maybe years. Calliope reaches out and touches me again, her fingertips on my knuckles. I boarded a jet here with harsh words trailing me from the mouths of those closest to me, declaring my intentions. I wonder if they will be right, if she will draw the ache out.

My biggest teenage crush turned into love. There was no reason Jo should have looked my way, but she did. A skinny kid too young for her, fresh out of braces, with a bruised chin.

A band behind me starts to warm up, and I shiver, though the bar is hot. The front door is now propped open. There is another open door to the right of us, leading to a balcony overlooking the water. I see the lights of boats and houses beyond the railing. There is smoke in the night. That must be where they go now.

Calliope hands me a drink, and I squint at it. "What's this?"

"Jack and Coke."

"Why did you settle on that?"

"It was just a guess. I used to tend bar, remember? I was good at reading people. I could tell what they would order before they even made it to the bar." She circles and produces another glass. This one clear.

"Vodka for you?" I ask.

"No. Water for you. I know this isn't your thing."

I feel like I'm forever being led into the dark by these women.

We find a table next to the wall. I survey the space while Calliope messes around on her phone. When I shift, she shifts. I'm not trying to look at her phone, but the mannerisms spark a memory. The way Jo guarded her phone more and more. The constant texts from a girlfriend I never met. I'm sure it was just a fake name for my uncle.

Calliope's hairline is dotted in sweat. I wonder if she's nervous. If she knows the way this could ruin our lives.

She finally sets her phone down and promptly downs her drink. "Why are you staring at me?"

"Sorry," I mumble, pulling my drink to my mouth. I like the earthy taste. The fizz burns down my throat.

Calliope catches my face and laughs.

"What?" I ask her.

"You look so young sometimes. Like you're still that gangly kid who showed up at our door."

"I'm not, though."

"No. You're taller but softer," she says.

"I've always been soft."

"No. I don't believe that. At least not in the way you're using the word. You're putting yourself down. But when you showed up on our doorstep, with that black eye, that girl clutching your hand, dirty and hopeless looking, I saw someone lost. You'd found us, but you were lost. And the person sitting here with me right now, he isn't as lost."

"I don't know what you're seeing, but that's not how I feel right now."

"You'll feel better, eventually," she says.

"Do you feel better?"

She takes a moment, as if she doesn't know why I'm asking. When she recovers, I see the mask she always wears. More familiar than her real face. I still remember it from that night.

"No. Not yet," she says.

"But you'll get there?" I ask, forcing a smile.

"Okay, how about this?" she ignores my question. "I don't tell you things you don't want to hear tonight."

"Okay."

"And, I also don't tell you the things you want to hear either," she says, the hint of a smile forming.

"What's left?" I'm relaxing. I forgot how much she settled me when everything rose in my chest. My nerves can be seen from a mile away by her.

"I'll tell you whatever I want. I won't worry about whatever box you want it to fit into. Your jaw gives you away, you know?"

"It aches at night, sometimes." I grind my teeth. It's a reflex.

"It's one of the places you carry your tension."

The silence stretches between us. It feels like the loud sounds of the bar, conversations, and drinks hitting the tables in front of the patrons can't penetrate it. Then, finally, the band starts playing. Calliope's phone lights up on the table, but she doesn't look at it. Instead, she's scanning the room, her leg rocking back and forth under the table. Her foot hits me a couple of times, and I wonder if it's on purpose. My legs are spread, I'm invading her space under there, but I don't move.

"I don't know what it's like to be you, Sean," she says.

I turn to her, watch her grab her phone, and shove it in her purse, dangling off her chair.

She bumps my knee again, and she's looking me in the eye this time.

TWENTY-TWO

SEAN

PAST
THE LAKE

A HUNDRED THOUSAND views and counting. Jo and I refreshed the screens of our phones. It was a game, a thrilling chase. I saw the pride in her eyes, and it was addicting.

"This is the best one, Sean. The best one and they can see that."

YouTube wasn't getting us where we wanted me to be. The new app we were uploading videos to featured small clips, bites. I worried it meant I could only be taken in small doses. Jo argued it was our rapid-fire minds and short attention spans.

She often talked of people our age as if she wasn't our age. As if she was an outsider looking in. I would never have considered her an old soul, but if she claimed the title, I wouldn't argue. I would let her claim to be whoever she wanted to be.

"What do you want to tell the world? Because they are going to listen." She leaned back on the couch in the center of our little living room in the guest house. Her pink hair was orange on the ends now. Another color, another phase.

I never wanted to be one of her phases.

"I don't know."

"What do you want to write about more than anything?" she asked me.

"Being human," I said, staring at my shoes as I set my phone on the floor. "It's weird and beautiful and sad."

Jo crawled off the couch, found me on the floor, and climbed on top of me. "Don't get emotional on me. This is all part of the plan, and we got this."

I hated cracking around her. I felt like I was letting her down, like I was too much. Like she left her old life behind for a boy with no follow-through when she could have had any man back in Toronto.

"We got this," I said into her summer hair. She smelled like lemons and sugar. I watched tiny drops of sweat trickle down the side of her glass of lemonade on the coffee table behind her.

The sun was setting, and Calliope would call us for dinner soon, but I didn't want to leave our bubble. I wanted to pretend we lived—and loved—here alone.

I pressed my hands into her hips, pulled her close. God, I wanted her. But she kept me at bay.

"Sean. Not now. It's not our time yet."

"I'm just so happy," I said, leaning up, burying my face in her neck. "I love you. I love you so much, and this is all because you believed in me." I wanted her to know the nothing I would be if not for her. I didn't want to fuck her. I wanted to love her. To show her how much I loved her. To feel every bit of her. I didn't want her to think I was like the guys who hurt her before.

"Your aunt could come out here any moment to get us for dinner."

"Lock the door," I replied, tracing the vein on her neck with my tongue. I felt her reaction, the press of her hips, unprovoked by my hands. "You're my world," I admitted.

And she sighed.

And I tried to pretend it was from pleasure, not anything else.

TWENTY-THREE

JO

**PAST
THE LAKE**

SHE NEVER WANTED to be the world for anyone. Being the world meant your presence mattered, and if you took it away, the guilt came. And she was so tired of the guilt men rained down upon her when their worlds crumbled, no care for how they wrecked hers.

Jo watched Sean sleep. His jaw begged to be touched, his soft hair called to her fingertips, but she wouldn't wake him, wouldn't take him in her mouth. She didn't want to tease him the way she did other nights.

Instead, she slipped out of the covers. She tiptoed across the room, to the large window paned doors.

Sean didn't hear the click of the door when she closed it from the other side. She watched him for a minute, satisfied, when he did not stir.

Her phone felt heavy in her pocket. She wanted to make sure Apollo didn't text her in the middle of the night and wake Sean.

She changed his name in her phone to a girl's name, but still, she didn't want Sean to find her missing from bed.

Apollo was gone, back to the city, but she just needed to be away from the anchor. The hope Sean carried in his chest for her, and their future. She needed to get away from his need.

She found the main house locked, pulling a curse and Calliope's name from her lips. The garage was open, so she went there next, trying the door inside that led to the kitchen. It was locked as well.

She pulled her phone from her pocket. It was two in the morning, and she wanted to text Apollo. But she didn't know what she would say. *I miss you?* They didn't speak like that. Not at this point. She hadn't led him there—yet.

She walked to the fridge on the far side of the garage, found a beer. The cool amber liquid hit her throat and she sighed. The sound she heard next chilled her. It was her own voice. Her own laugh. Her legs carried her from the garage, around the side of the house, to the noise, despite the goosebumps on her arm.

She saw Calliope, her face lit by the glow of her phone. One hand held the device, the other, a glass of wine. She was walking toward the dock in a little black bikini and denim shorts.

Jo followed her, in the mood for a fight. In the mood to gloat.

Calliope heard her before she saw her. Jo wasn't tiptoeing anymore. Her bare feet hit the dock, didn't slow.

One more swig of beer traveled down her throat before she spoke, after taking a seat next to the older woman.

"You ever sleep?" Jo asked, looking at Calliope's bare feet in the water.

"Don't worry about my sleeping habits," she replied, no venom in her voice, only boredom.

"What were you listening to earlier? On the way down here?"

Calliope looked at the younger girl then, blinked slowly, then looked down at her phone. She pulled a video up, tapped her finger on the screen.

Across the water you could hear Jo laughing, then the strumming of Sean's guitar. They were sitting by the pool. He was playing and she held his notebooks in her lap. To watch the video was to believe in a lie. A lie to her, but not to Sean. They looked in love, and she felt sick to her stomach as the song played on, as his falsetto hit her ears. "Turn it off," she said.

Calliope let it play for a few seconds more, then obliged.

Jo hated the smile on the other woman's face. What it meant.

TWENTY-FOUR

CALLIOPE

APOLLO

You think I care that I can't access the cameras down there? I don't fucking care. I don't care if you fuck him. She says he's a shit fuck anyway. He can't do what I did to you. You better hope no one finds out if you're doing what I think you're doing.

TWENTY-FIVE

SEAN

**PRESENT
THE LAKE**

"WHO OWNS THIS BOAT?" I ask, my nerves shot, already. I trip on a rope and nearly go down trying to keep up with Calliope. I watch her sway and move faster. I don't want her pitching into the water.

"Belongs to a friend. We aren't trespassing. I wouldn't do that to you."

The thundering lessens, a little. When I catch Calliope, I grab her hand, so she turns, looking up at me. My eyes are hidden under my ball cap, but I can see hers clearly.

"How drunk are you?" I ask.

"I'm not drunk. I promise. I just feel free right now."

I think of her phone, the point she made to run back to the car and lock it in the glove box. It looked like a disco ball on that table, lighting up, buzzing. I wonder if my uncle will show up in Missouri. If the violence I left behind can catch up with me. If new fists carry the same intentions. Intentions to put me in the grave.

She doesn't let go of my hand as we walk to the boat. I don't worry about being seen. We're the only ones down here. The music is muffled; the voices of the bar reach us, but barely.

When she reaches the boat, she drops my hand, throws her shoes onto the deck. It's a large boat for the Missouri lake, though I'd been on much bigger since leaving this place, years ago. It wasn't impressive, but I knew that wasn't what she was trying to do. Money didn't matter to me. I had it now, and it represented something for me that was not power. It meant stability. It meant freedom, though the strings of my career told me that was a lie, in some ways.

I follow Calliope below deck as my thoughts race.

There's a TV, bar, and bunk beds at the bottom of the stairs. A guitar sits on the other side. I want to pick it up. Calliope goes behind the bar and searches. When she pops back up with two bottles of water, my anxiety lessens even more.

"You worry too much," she says, throwing one to me.

"I know. I know." I grab the guitar, hoping she will drop it. Hoping she won't echo Jo's annoyance.

"That's my brother's guitar," she says, just as I'm about to strum a chord.

Her words still me. "What?"

"My friend, the one who owns this boat, he was friends with my brother. When I needed to move and was forced to get rid of everything that wasn't necessary, he agreed to take it. To keep it safe."

"Your brother played?"

"Not seriously. He was never as good as you are. And he didn't sing. I mean, he did sing, but not with hopes of making anything of it. Just to put words to the music he wanted to play. It calmed him. I wish he found more that calmed him. More that was healthy."

"I'm sorry," I say, setting the guitar back where I found it. I cross the space and take a long drink of the water. The cool liquid rolls down my throat as she burns me up with her eyes. She's watching me, I feel the shift. We haven't been alone all night. The cabin is small, pressing. When I'm done, I replace the cap, look at her. "What?"

"You're the most beautiful person I've ever met. And I know it's wrong to think that. And I know it's wrong to be happy that you look nothing like him. I couldn't bear it if you did."

"Are we really going to do this?" I ask, finally.

"Do what?" She wants me to say it.

"Rebound with each other." I set the water bottle on the small table next to me, cross my arms. I don't want to be closed off, but I feel incredibly vulnerable. Like she can see right through me.

"They deserve it."

"They do," I agree.

"We deserve this." She sets her water bottle on the bar.

"We do," I answer.

"It's inappropriate."

"What they did is worse," I offer. Because I know it's wrong, what I want from her. What I couldn't admit out loud when it was yelled to me on that jet ramp just a few days ago.

"If anyone finds out, even if they know what they did, they'll still say this is wrong. You can survive the fallout. I can't." Her hand is on her throat, and I know then, despite the evenness of her tone, she feels vulnerable, too.

"Then no one will find out," I say, regretting it as soon as the words are out.

I would never want a woman to think I was ashamed to be with her, but there is no escaping the reality of this. The truth of this is what makes me want it. And I think she feels the same.

TWENTY-SIX

CALLIOPE

PAST
THE LAKE

I GOT Jo a job on the docks pumping gas. They didn't have a spot for Sean; they preferred women. Women brought in boats. As a teen, I once held that job and bought my first car with a summer's worth of tip money.

I knew it was the only way I would drive myself, no longer hitching a ride with my brother, so I made it happen.

Jo got into the car, and I wanted to turn the music up to drown out any words the younger girl may say before she said them, but I didn't.

Instead, I placed the mask on cleanly. My face was serene, though the vein in my neck was likely throbbing. Most days, Jo got a ride from one of her new friends. But some days, I was forced to drive her. I hated those days.

We drove for ten minutes in relative silence until I couldn't handle it anymore.

"Would you prefer a summer here or back in Toronto?"

"Here," Jo said flatly, picking at the cuticle on her nail.

I tried again. "Do you think Sean would agree?"

"I don't know. You'd have to ask him." This time she reached for the vent by the passenger window, tilting it toward her face. Pink hair moved like waves in the air.

"Maybe I will ask him then. When I'm done dropping you." I didn't say dropping you off. I was specific in my words. She doesn't know who she is tangling with. She doesn't know what I know.

I did know that Jo was aware I saw right through them. The video I played for her the other night was an arrow to the heart. I saw it in the younger girl's face. The act, I saw right through it. I saw right through *her*.

Today, I wanted to push more. "Have you always liked younger men?" I was curious about Jo's past, her taste. I was curious about what led her to him. Their history was still a mystery to both Apollo and me. Or maybe it wasn't a mystery to him, just me.

"No," Jo said, turning to me, blue eyes piercing. "Before him, I was always with older men."

I expected her to leave it at that, but she didn't. So I kept my eyes on the road as the pink-haired girl continued.

"I lost my virginity when I was thirteen to my older brother's best friend. He was five years older than me. Two weeks later, he dumped me, but I still had to see him at the house and pretend nothing happened. Because whatever we had was just between us, and no one else knew. So I had to pretend my heart wasn't fucking trash. After that, it was always older guys. Flings, casual shit. My next boyfriend was when I was seventeen. He was twenty-one. I went to all his university parties, he got me a fake ID, and he took me to clubs, too. Then I invited him to my brother's birthday party, and his best friend was there. Somehow my drunk mouth spilled too much. I told him who was there, what happened three years earlier.

He got so jealous. That night while I was sleeping, he cut all my hair off."

I turned at that, my face red, the blush crept from my neck to my face. It felt too close to home, so I looked away.

Jo had no idea what new home she was slipping into. What door she was knocking on.

"When I saw Sean for the first time, I knew he wouldn't hurt me. I knew he couldn't hurt anyone but himself. He's not the life of the party, but he is safe. I needed safe," Jo said.

The muffled radio droned on for a moment, and I could see Jo glancing at my profile. The wheels were turning, and I couldn't stop them. I wanted to stop the car. To let her out. "Do you feel like he saved you?" I asked her.

"We saved each other," Jo replied.

It sounded so final. Like she was so sure. Moments ago, I was sure the younger girl knew I was onto them, now I wasn't so sure.

We reached the road to the dock, and I saw Jo go for her purse even though it was too early to be holding it. I recognized the lifeline, the shield.

"Plus," Jo said, after a moment, pulling a bright pink lipstick to her lips. "He's so eager."

"Eager?"

"Yes. So eager. He wants to learn everything."

I knew she wasn't talking about school. The blush was back as I put the SUV in park, hoping Jo would get out. I didn't want to hear about my husband's nephew's...*eagerness*.

Jo didn't leave the vehicle; instead, she turned to me, showing me she was better at the game. "You have no idea what it's like to have someone try to please you like that. To take every little direction," she said.

"This is weird," I said, staring out the windshield.

"Why? We're both women around the same age. It's just sex. Or, not sex. Not yet."

"Not yet?" I finally turned to her.

"Yes." Jo smiled, but it was not in her eyes. "Sean's a virgin."

"So the first time you got dumped. And the second time, you had all your hair chopped off." *Was there a third? Was it my husband,* she wondered. "What do you think he's going to do? Are you scared?"

"No. I just know I'll never let anyone have that control until I know for sure I can hurt them more than they can hurt me."

"And you think he can't hurt you more than you can hurt him?" I wasn't sure a girl like this, too familiar, too like the old me, could be hurt.

"Look where we are. With his family. His rich family." Jo nodded her head at me. "I have nothing."

I looked Jo in the eye, thinking of the secret I knew of the young girl and my husband. "Women with nothing should be careful of the risks they take, of the secrets they think no one knows."

Jo smiled at that, then got out of the vehicle.

TWENTY-SEVEN

CALLIOPE

APOLLO

I'm giving. I've always been giving. Look what I did for you. I just wanted to give. I wanted to help the girl. She had nothing, back then. Am I the bad guy because I wanted to help? I'm always the fucking bad guy to you, aren't I?

TWENTY-EIGHT

SEAN

PRESENT
THE LAKE

I DON'T REACH for her. I need to know she wants everything the way I do. I'm standing in front of the floor-to-ceiling windows in her bedroom when her hands go under my shirt, wrapping around me.

They start at my waistline, move up. I can feel her breathing into my back, and I know she can hear me breathing, too. My chin is down on my chest. I lean forward, letting my forehead hit the glass.

When she presses into me I move, pulling my shirt off, turning to her. Her mouth tastes sweet, and I am begging for her, needing her closer. When her hands go up, and there is no hair for her to pull, my body quiets. She runs her hands over my shorn head, sending goosebumps all over me.

It's a new memory, a new sensation that will be reserved in my head for her. Our first kiss wasn't like this. It was wrong and rushed. I'll take my time with her here, in this place we shouldn't be.

I walk her backward toward the bed. In my manic head, I've played imaginary sounds for days now. The way I imagined she would sound if I unraveled her. They don't compare to this.

"Are you sure?" I ask. It's not sexy, or maybe what she's used to. But I'll question her until I am convinced she could want me without it being wrapped up in other sorrows, other motivations.

"Yes," she says, her teeth on my earlobe. "Don't ask me that again tonight, Sean."

My hand reaches for the bottom of her dress, pulling it up, finding lace, freckles on her collarbone, and a tattoo of a swallow on her hip—matching the one on my shoulder now—that she didn't have years ago.

I drop to my knees and press my lips there, rewarded by the press of her hips. Her needful response spurs me on.

"What?" I ask, more words stuck in my throat, as I look up at her.

"Don't," she replies, drowning my question. She reaches down, her hand wrapping around my throat, pulling me up. "Don't ask questions, don't question yourself. I want you, okay?"

I nod, but it's a lying move. I question everything I do. I question every word that comes from my mouth. There wasn't a single show this last tour that didn't begin with me taking medication for my anxiety. And my heart is beating faster now than it ever did before those shows.

I never told Jo, but those shows were better than sex. The rush I felt, nothing compared to it. I look at Calliope and I wonder if she sees a fool, someone worth this.

Her eyes are so big, so dark. She moves to the bed, never breaking contact, pulling her dress off completely. "I want this."

There is fear, here, in my heart, in my mind. I'm not scared of her, but I'm afraid of my racing pulse, my ability to hurt people just by being myself.

"Okay," I say, pushing my jeans down, watching her watch me. I've never felt anyone look at me that way. Jo looked at me with familiarity, even in the beginning. I told myself it was because we were meant to find each other. And I still believe that's true, though the reason isn't what I thought it was back then.

Calliope is looking at me like I'm art, and I want to break open.

"Do you know what you're doing?" she asks, watching a shiver move through me.

"I think we're going to find out," I reply, terrified of the places she could take me, the weight of this, and what these actions say about me. That I could enter my uncle's home and take something from him. We are in control of our own actions, no matter who pushes us to extremes. *What does it say about me, that I want this so badly? That I want her so badly?*

I crawl into the bed, over her, and decide I don't care.

Before I can kiss her again, she speaks, and it's the last words either one of us says for the rest of the night. "We can get over them together, even if it's in secret, for a summer, but don't fall in love with me, Sean. That's the only rule. Because if you do, I'll break that love."

TWENTY-NINE

CALLIOPE

PAST
THE LAKE

"I'M NOT TAKING her out drinking," I seethed, baring my teeth.

"She's of age, Cal," Apollo replied, rolling up the sleeves of his crisp white shirt, dismissive.

"That's not the point. Do you really want to go out and leave him here? That's fucking shitty." My voice was low. I knew Sean and Jo were in the main house.

"Why? He can't drink. He can't go." He would often debate points with himself, rarely leaving space to offer my rebuttal. Case closed.

"Then let's go somewhere else. There are plenty of places he can get into. Plenty of restaurants that serve alcohol if that's what you're in the mood for."

"I know. But my friend Kenneth is here, and that's where he wants to go. He's the guest. We go to him."

"He would understand if you explained." I wound my hair around the hot wand in my hand, eyeing my husband in the mirror.

"Listen, I'm sure Sean doesn't want to be around a bunch of drunk people anyway."

"Well, then maybe his girlfriend shouldn't want to either." The hair wand clanked on the glass surface of the vanity. My curls wrapped around my ears, and my husband walked forward, brushing them away from my face.

"What's your problem with her, anyway?" he asked my reflection, his hand snaking down to my neck.

"I don't like her."

"That's been clear since she showed up. Are you still on that age thing? I'm older than you, Cal. Get off it. I hate it when you act crazy like this." He stared into the mirror, away from my eyes, fussing with his hair, bored.

Crazy like this. Crazy, crazy, crazy. Did he make me this way, or is it hereditary? I flashed through every fight my mother performed with her myriad of boyfriends. She was green, jealous, and fragile. I didn't have her shrill voice. My voice took after my father's.

I used to be so self-conscious about its deepness, the fullness. The words slipping out now still sounded like my mother's, so I fixed my face, choked it down. "You're right. The age difference is the same."

I turned to our large walk-in closet, gripping the hem of one of my shirts. I wanted to rip it off the hanger, pull the whole pole down. It'd been a while since I caused a scene, and I craved it. I felt like I was coming out of a deep sleep.

I wanted to give him chaos, watch him flutter between concern and rage. Love was fickle and ugly. I hated the way my face looked. I couldn't see it, but I could feel it—the violent lines, the creases in my brow.

I reached up and smoothed them away with my fingertips.

I could smell Jo on the shirt sitting in the hamper. Men think they are so clever. That we don't know when their dick wants to find a new home.

Temporary or permanent, it didn't matter to me. I couldn't accuse without hard evidence. And they were so lazy, I knew I would get it soon. They'll leave crumbs for me tonight. It's in their nature to be this hasty.

I grabbed a blouse, threw it on the bed. When I got back to the vanity, my cheeks were red, my thoughts, dancing in pinks and violence, painted my face. I grabbed my foundation brush, prepared to paint the rage away as I mumbled under my breath about my intuition.

I heard Apollo's footsteps before he filled the doorframe.

"What did you say?"

I knew the tone. I didn't want to speak, to get pulled in, but I also knew being mute wouldn't work. He wouldn't let up until I told him what I said.

"I said I trust my intuition. I trust my instincts." It was half a truth. But, unfortunately, my instincts didn't warn me of this side of him.

"Your intuition? What a laugh." He crossed his arms over his broad chest. "Where was your intuition when your junkie brother was tearing your family apart? Where was it when you thought he was sober, but he was shooting up down in that trailer park? You don't know everything. I know that seems to be some truth you hold onto. But you don't know shit about anything."

"I'm not a child, Pol. I've seen shit in life, too. The shit you just brought up." *And what you put me through, what you let me take the blame for,* I wanted to say. But I didn't. I hated the rise he got out of me. The way my mask slipped. The mask I built as his wife.

"And you didn't learn shit, apparently. I learned from my childhood. I moved on and grew up. That's what Sean is doing. He wasn't going to let it drag him down either. That's a smart, talented kid out there," he said, pointing his finger in the direction of the guest house. "You think he has bad intuition?"

"He's thinking with his fifteen-year-old dick. He doesn't know what's up with girls like that."

"Girls like that, or girls like you? I seem to remember you being all over me like a bitch in heat the night we met."

I set my makeup brush down, bit down on my tongue. "You sure didn't seem to mind." I resumed my painting. The mask was mine to reapply. Pride was harder to cover than finger bruises, but I knew how to do it.

"Just the way he won't mind when she comes home hot and begging for it when we get back."

I cringed at the words, but kept quiet.

I wasn't going to lecture him on appropriateness and skin crawling. He knew what he was doing. He could work words better than anyone I knew, and I fell into the hole every time.

Apollo paused, waiting for more, but nothing came. Finally, he looked past me to the blouse on the bed. "That what you're gonna wear?"

"Yes," I said, finding the pink lipstick I intended to wear.

He didn't respond.

He made a face, and it was all he needed to do.

THIRTY

CALLIOPE

APOLLO
You'll regret it. And I won't forgive you. I won't.

THIRTY-ONE

SEAN

**PRESENT
THE LAKE**

I DON'T LAST. Before I can stop myself, my climax falls upon me like a heavy bucket of water. Then the heat comes. My shame and desire intermingled.

I reach for my face, my hand covering most of it. I know I'm red, damp, flushed with undeniable youth and inexperience.

I feel Calliope's hand on mine and let her tug it away.

"What are you doing?" she asks.

"That was, wow," I groan. "I'm sorry. I can't believe I did that."

She laughs, and the sound is not like Jo's. No condescension. No pity. "Stop it."

"Stop what?" I ask.

"Being so apologetic. All the time."

"I'm not." I'm lying. We both know it.

"What do you want to feel?" She presses her palms to my hips.

It tickles and I bury my jaw into the space between her ear and her shoulder. After a moment, I pull out of her, but not before she clenches around me one more time. "What do you mean?" I ask, wincing.

"What do you want to feel?"

"Everything," I say, pulling my hand to my head, trying to run it through hair that is no longer there. "I'd rather feel absolutely everything. To the extreme. I'd rather feel it all than feel nothing at all."

"Did you feel something just now?" She pushes up on her side, props her head on a hand.

When I say nothing, she motions between us, and I don't know if it's a trap. But I don't care. "Yes."

"Then let's make you feel it again." She reaches to her bedside table and pulls out another condom.

She is not virginal, her lipstick is smeared and thoughts of her red apron flood my mind, I picture her in it five years ago when she made me pancakes. I picture her in nothing else, just the way I did back then.

Here now, my arms cage her, and she presses her head into the pillow. I see her neck, her jaw, the freckles there.

"You can't do that," I say, hoping I can hold it together.

"What?" she asks with a laugh, knowing.

"I'm not going to last. Again," I admit. She feels like nothing I've ever known.

Maybe we are all looking for something that feels a little wrong. Maybe we all get off on that kind of thing.

Her hands, moments ago, gripping the sheets, find my skin. She presses her forehead to mine, and we move like we are lost at sea, rhythmic, buoyant. Her fingertips are on my neck then, and I can feel her squeezing. Fuck, I would give everything up to feel this every morning. The reputation. The jets. The illusion of family.

"You can come." Her teeth are on me, and that's all it takes.

After, when my hand clutches to my heart, she climbs on top of me, presses her palms to my rib cage.

"Do you regret it?" I ask. I can't help but question every move she makes, everything we might do.

"No. And we aren't going to do this," she says, tracing the bones under my hands.

"Do what?" It tickles a little, but I hold still.

"Debate, question, tear it apart. You offered, I'm taking."

"It sounds like a business transaction when you say it like that."

"Don't twist things." She leans down, traces her tongue around my nipple.

"But *this* is twisted."

"And you wanted it." She bites, just barely, and I'm hard again.

I flip her over, press to her. "I do again. Can I just stay here?"

"For as long as you want."

"And you'll be my muse?" *Again.* I want to say *again*, but we both pretend it isn't there. The truth.

THIRTY-TWO

CALLIOPE

**PAST
THE LAKE**

THE NIGHT WAS RED. Red lips, red dress, red in my eyes.

I watched them when they thought I wasn't looking. When Jo wanted to tell Apollo something, she touched his arm. When he wanted to tell her something, he brushed against her.

They both loved hockey. I didn't care for the sport, but they were both northerners. So they used the bond to their best advantage, and I let them.

I knew people at the bar, and I let my husband and the girl carry on. It made it easier for me to get away.

My friend Ethan was bartending. I downed another drink and left Jo and Apollo to talk, drinking in Ethan's smirk as I approached the bar, letting it warm me. "Hey, stranger," I cooed, leaning over the bar.

When he kissed me on the cheek, I felt the hair on the back of my neck stand up. The loud beehive drone of the patrons around them couldn't distract me from my other senses. Fear and excitement, ache and a pool of dread deep in my belly. I closed my eyes for a moment, then opened them to my friend, his head cocked.

"Like a bad penny, eh?" The bartender laughed.

"Every summer. You're never going to get rid of me." I twirled a coaster in front of me until the bar logo was readable, shoulders tense, waiting for Apollo to appear behind me.

"Why don't you convince that husband of yours to just move down here?" my old friend asked, knowing it would never happen.

"This place is a trap," I said, settling onto the barstool beneath me when I was convinced my husband was staying put. I tried to cross my legs and fumbled a bit. My thighs would be covered in sweat on the leather in no time. "He'd never make money here," I continued, "and I like his money." I swallowed the lump in my throat, busying my hands with a napkin in front of me. The truth isn't easy to say aloud, but we wear it on our faces, so why not?

I needed stability. I needed some sort of family. I needed my cage, and I also needed to run. And these days, when I needed to run, I ran back here.

"Who's the girl?" Ethan asked, nodding over my shoulder.

"His nephew's girlfriend."

"Where's the nephew?" The tone was knowing. He saw what everyone else did. He saw everything, as most bartenders did.

"He's not legal," I replied, pointing to a bottle of vodka on the top shelf, over Ethan's shoulder.

He nodded, always knowing what I wanted. Then he turned, throwing a small towel over his shoulder. "In that case, you guys picked an interesting place to come to for dinner."

"I said I wanted to see you," I lied. I never brought Ethan up. He was the past, and Apollo wanted to pretend every part of my history

I still wanted to hold onto didn't exist. Tonight, he was too distracted to care. So I took a chance.

"Then let's get you drunk," he said.

The drinks were sweet, full of sugar. My finger traced the rim as I talked to Ethan.

He reminisced with me about the low seasons, the tourists he loved already this summer, and the songs he'd been meaning to send me.

He hadn't lost my number, but I stopped texting him back years ago, so I knew why I'd never heard the songs. I hadn't *lost* his number, but I had been through so many phones there was no way to save it. It was memorized, even though I never used it. Couldn't use it.

Since Apollo, I didn't keep guy friends. It was hard to be treated like a dirty little secret. To only be talked to in Snapchat conversations that disappear when texts are ignored. I didn't want to be sneaky—shady. But I got tired of cold shoulders and my phone being hidden when Apollo saw a guy's name.

It didn't matter how long I knew them, even if I'd known them since kindergarten. They weren't allowed. I knew my guy friends were safer for me to be around than his; we both knew that. But the knife in my gut was twisted too deep, too tangled up in my gray memories of the night I couldn't shake.

And Apollo said he didn't keep girlfriends, so I should treat him with the same respect. No conversations he couldn't see. That was the only reason I was allowed this one in the loud bar.

And I knew he would never show his jealousy in public. He owned a reputation, dignified, and he guarded it above all else. Jekyll and Hyde were never seen in the same place.

I didn't want to break the seal but knew I would have to soon. I didn't want to leave Ethan—didn't want to break the spell. His easy smile made me feel like I never left, like I didn't have to leave again when the summer ended.

After a few more minutes, my friend went to serve a woman down at the end of the bar, so I spun on the stool, looking at the table I'd abandoned. Jo was on her phone, texting, and Apollo's was to his ear.

He was standing by the railing of the outdoor patio, his back to his wife.

I stared at Jo, willing her to look my way, knowing she would, eventually. She would feel me.

As soon as the thought passed through me, Jo looked up, locking eyes with me. I moved my head from side to side, slow and deliberate. The younger girl stared back, not backing down.

She had balls; I gave her that.

I hopped off my stool at the bar, headed to the ladies' room. From the corner of my eye, I saw Jo follow.

There were two girls by the mirror when I entered. I cleared my throat, then headed for a stall and listened for the door to open again. It did.

Jo joined me at the sink when we were both done. The other bar patrons were gone.

"Having fun?" I asked.

"About as much fun as you are."

"And how much fun am I having?"

"I'm surprised you haven't crawled over that bar. The bartender is fucking hot. That's for sure," Jo smarted. Her weakness was in her delivery. The smugness on her face was comical, so easy to dismantle in girls like her.

"He is. Sweet as hell, too."

"How sweet has he been to you?" Jo asked.

I dried my hands slowly, the smile on my face getting broader and wider. The silence enveloped us, and the smile on Jo's face trickled away slowly.

I left the younger girl in the bathroom, returning to my table, not the bar.

THIRTY-THREE

CALLIOPE

APOLLO
Are you showing him a good time for his birthday? Bringing him to all the bars? Showing him off to all the guys you've fucked down there?

THIRTY-FOUR

SEAN

**PRESENT
THE LAKE**

THE AIR IS cool in the morning.

I sit by the pool in my denim jacket, one I wore when I was here, years ago. It was still stuck in the coat closet, to my luck, because I didn't bring much with me.

When Calliope finds me, I can feel her hesitation.

"I wrote this song once, never recorded it or did anything, but it was about how I can feel people. I remember telling my mom that when I was a kid. I said, 'Mom, can you feel people?' And she asked me what I meant so I told her. I could feel it when she and my dad were about to blow up and have a huge fight. It's like the way you can smell a storm coming. The rain. But it's not a beautiful thing, it was this pain I felt before the pain even landed."

"Do you think a storm is coming now?"

"Maybe," I say.

She sits down next to me, puts her bare feet in the water, kicks slowly. "I can be a storm." Her phone buzzes in her pocket.

"I can feel your regret."

"I pushed for this," she replies.

"We both wanted it. Don't end this before it even begins."

"End what? We said we'd rebound with each other. Rebound into each other's bed? Into my bed? We did that." She traces circles on her knees, watches her own movements.

I watch her movements, too. I always have. "I want to do it again."

"How romantic. You want to fuck me again."

She sounds sad, and I want to erase it. I turn to her, fully, wrapping my fingers around her wrist, stilling her. Her eyes map me, landing there.

"You have beautiful hands, Sean. I liked the way they felt on me."

"I like the way you make me feel. And I'm not talking about fucking." I know the word sounds stupid coming out of my mouth. I don't gossip about fucking, I don't write about fucking, and I don't sing about fucking. Because that's not the kind of guy I am. We both know this, but she has me worried.

"They're not going to let us be together if that's what you're dreaming up in your head," she says, resting her hand on my thigh, pressing her forehead to my shoulder.

She shivers, and I move to take my coat off. "Who's *they*?"

"The world. It's already looking for you," she says.

"What do you mean?"

"My Instagram. I took a picture of the sun setting last night before we left and posted it. Some people posted comments on it."

"Saying?" I ask.

"Your name and a question mark. They want to know where you are. You don't cancel the end of a tour and expect the world not to ask questions."

My mind races. I want to pull her to me, I want to call my manager, I want to text my best friend.

I want to disappear. But that may never be possible.

"Fuck," I say, my eyes on the pool.

"Jo's social media is gone, too, which is another red flag for your fans. They know something is up. I wouldn't go on Twitter if I were you."

"What's on Twitter?" I reach for my phone, but it isn't there. It's back inside.

"Just a bunch of gossip. I only know because I was tagged in a few threads. They're looking, and when they look for your name, mine comes up, which is a whole other level of fucked up."

This is the moment where breaking would be natural. I can hear my heart beating in my chest. I can see the carefully constructed image that has been created for me falling apart. I almost reach for my face, imagining cracks there. I have no springboard here. I have no one to go to for advice.

But, I'm not a kid anymore, and I can't expect everyone else to fix my problems. Even though that's exactly the kind of life I've been living since the world started paying attention to me.

Maybe this is growing up.

"I don't care," I say, my voice steadier than I thought it would be.

"Why?" She sounds pleading; the confidence she held last night is gone.

"Because I want you more than I want the lie to continue."

"What lie?"

"That I'll always do what everyone expects of me. That I'll always try to fit into molds others create for me."

"Let's change that then," she says.

She falls into the water, and I stand, eyes searching.

"What the hell?" I shake my head at her when she surfaces, her black nightgown billowing around her in the water.

She pushes her hair back, eyeliner from the night before is smudged under her eyes. "Get in here," she beckons, her fingers moving in the water, her legs kicking the ink-black fabric in circular motions.

I don't take my clothes off. I don't think.

I just do what she asks. I just do what I want.

THIRTY-FIVE

CALLIOPE

PAST
THE LAKE

I COULD SEE them in the woods. I was sick all day, in and out of bed. In the bathroom, heaving up last night's dinner. In bed, sweating, sorry, and moaning.

Apollo said he was going to the store to get me some soup. Such a cliché. He didn't know how to take care of someone when they were sick.

He didn't know how to take care of someone when their world was taken.

He took. He soaked up my blood, tears, and any ounce of life I used to own.

I was looking in the bathroom mirror just moments before. My skin was pale, my brow was damp, and my eyes looked lifeless.

What struck me was that they didn't look much different than my eyes on any given day. So it wasn't just my stomach bug making me look like a corpse, a sad version of my former self.

Movement in the window pulled me from the sad inspection of my face.

Two figures in the woods. On the side of the guest house where there were no windows.

Her hair is what caught my eyes. *Her hair is what will ruin her*, I thought, running to the bedroom, to my nightstand, grabbing my phone.

On my hands and knees, I crawled past the window, determined not to be seen.

Though they were lost in each other, it was likely their eyes were peeled for anyone who might see them.

But it was a dare, the way they played; I could see that.

Perhaps Apollo told Jo I knew. On the other hand, maybe it was only Sean who was being guarded now.

My husband pressed the young girl against the house. She was wearing a bright blue bikini. His hand was working her, his fingers moving in and out. The ink of the arrow tattoo on his arm marked him, damned him.

There was no mistaking the fact that he was fucking her with his fingers. There would be no mistaking it when someone looked at the photos.

I snapped—manic—the phone making loud shutter sounds.

The toilet bowl called to me, begging me to give up another bit of myself. Instead, I clamped my hand over my mouth—waited for the moment to pass.

When I was steady, I turned my attention back to the phone. Uploading the images to the Dropbox account I created after Apollo ran over my last phone in the driveway, furious over the time I spent up at the bar, chatting with Ethan. The girl hadn't distracted him enough, and he was spending a fortune on phones to keep me in my place.

I deleted all the evidence from my phone when I was done, then returned to bed.

I didn't want to see any more; I was numb to it now.

He could fuck the girl all he wanted. With his hands, with his mouth, with his dick.

He could fuck her with abandon.

I stopped loving him years ago, anyway.

THIRTY-SIX

CALLIOPE

APOLLO

You're tied to me. And you will stay tied to me until I untie you. Not when you want to be free. Not when he wants you to be free. Because you don't give up on someone just because you fuck someone new. I didn't. Are you going to? It's just sex. And if I can forgive you for the past, why can't you forgive me?

THIRTY-SEVEN

SEAN

**PRESENT
THE LAKE**

WE CAN'T STAY HERE FOREVER, I know it. But I can't stop writing with her like this. It's been three weeks, and I haven't slowed down. It's been three weeks, and she hasn't stopped capturing me with her camera. But I know I need to go. I have to go back to my life.

I'm lying on the dock, and the sun is setting. Calliope says we need the light, she needs to capture me in a way that's been in her head for weeks.

I'm wearing a white T-shirt, my distressed light denim jacket, and black jeans. She has me look to the side, runs her hand through my hair. It's getting a little bit longer. I have a dogwood branch in my hand, the flowers are wilting.

Calliope has on a blue dress, and her bare feet are on each side of my hips, the camera trained on my face. I wonder what the shadows are showing her. I swallow, slowly.

I hear the click, her movement. She stops, thinks, takes another photo. I don't interrupt her until I think she's done, turning to her. The strap of the camera is cutting across her dress. Her hands are on her hips, her fingernails red against stark blue.

I wrap my hand around her ankles, earning her gaze.

"What?" she asks.

"Where are you?"

"Here," she says, laughing.

I push myself up, press my mouth to her, over her dress, over her panties. It's not good enough. My hand slides up her thighs, the fabric is forgiving. She says my name, but stops there, giving way, making room.

I push her panties aside, taste her, feel her press into me.

She grabs my hair, stopping me. I don't like the look there when I look up.

"What?" I ask, then, "I'm sorry," just as quickly. I will never take.

She falls down to me, wrapping her legs tightly around me. Her head is under my chin, her arms under my shirt. "Don't ask me to leave here," she says, softly.

I know nothing of a home. I'm rarely at mine. I've made my own in people, in songs, in stadiums. The rush of a crowd, nothing can beat it. Nothing, but maybe, maybe this. "I need you to. I need you." I can't leave without her. If she isn't over everything, over him, I'll convince her. But I have to do it in my world. Somewhere he has never been. Doing something he could never do.

"Maybe I'll meet you," she says, and it sounds as weak as we both know it is.

"You won't come. I need you on the plane leaving here, with me." I know it's lust infused with my abandonment issues and my fear of the alone, but everything stills when I'm inside her. I'm quiet. She's quiet, but I hear her. I hear her through her skin, and I know you can give your heart away after the first time. I know the first time is something we romanticize, but it will fade. It has already faded into a mute memory. I recognize the co-dependency and the paper-thin promises Jo and I made with our mouths.

I'm here trying to make promises to Calliope with my skin that she can never wash off because I fear she will outgrow this. There is something dark and unreachable in her eyes. I see her staring off, and I know there's no going to the place she goes to.

Now, with my lust and longing—and perhaps love—reflected in her eyes, I feel safety.

Safety is an illusion I've created in her, but I'll hold onto this, and her, for as long as she'll let me.

I can never let a perfect moment lie, so I speak. "What is this between us?" I regret it. I regret the words I promised myself I would never ask.

She kisses me. Long and languid. I know she's trying to distract me, but I let her.

She surprises me with an answer as she pulls away. "This is a man and his muse."

It's nice to hear her call me a man, not a boy. No sharp reminders of my age. Not anymore. We are past that. The moment is halted when I feel her phone buzz on her hip, in the pocket of her dress. She sees the change in my eyes, rolls off of me. The heavy sigh she offers pushes me.

"Is it him?" I ask.

Apollo had been reaching out to me periodically over the last few weeks. Instagram messages asking if we can talk. Messages to my email. Messages to my Twitter inbox.

"I've been operating on a dead battery," she says, flipping her phone over and over in her hand, not looking at it.

When she avoids my questions, I volley between fascination and frustration. "What do you mean?" I ask her.

Her voice has changed. It has gone monotone, as it does from time to time. She changes it when she really wants me to listen to her. And it's always something rehearsed. Some shit I don't want to hear.

"When I met Apollo I was dead inside. I felt nothing. I had no one to pour myself into. My mother was gone. My brother was dead, and the bills needed to be paid. I needed to get to work. There was no time for grief. He made me feel something, and I didn't care what it was I felt. I didn't care about the boundaries he pushed. I just cared that I felt something."

"I feel like I'm just standing in his shadow. Like I'll always be standing in the shadows of more powerful men."

"You think they're more powerful than you?" She rolls to her side, runs her finger over her black camera. Her dark eyelashes flutter, and I shiver. Her blue dress is fanned around her. She looks like a tear.

"Yes," I admit.

"Then you're still under their influence. You think the same things are as powerful as they do. Do you want to strike fear?" She looks over, then up into my eyes.

I see no salt there, just her disappointment.

"Fear? No."

"Then what?"

"I want to be the kind someone can never get over," I say.

"This isn't what you think it is." She pushes the camera behind her, takes her phone out of her pocket, throws it on the pile of towels behind me.

I don't feel better with it out of sight. "You're still in love with him. Right?" I ask, lying back, closing my eyes.

"No. But, I'm still under his thumb. I'm still bound to him."

"I see." I don't know what she means. Emotionally? Financially? They're still married, and I feel like a child. Knowing nothing of that world.

"Do you want someone under your thumb?"

"No." I shake my head. I've never wanted to control someone.

"That's the difference between you and them," she says, taking my chin in her hand and pulling me toward her. Her fingers are soft, like her eyes in the light. "You don't have it in you to hurt like them, like me."

THIRTY-EIGHT

CALLIOPE

**PAST
THE LAKE**

I SAW him on the dock, white fur rustled by the warm lake air.

My feet carried me slowly, carefully. "Don't you dare jump in," I joked, not wanting to have to wash the dirty lake water off my dog.

When I got close enough, I saw the leash leading to the water, saw the rings and ripples in the water, circling out, away from the dock.

There was *someone* in the water.

A flood of words—threats—seized me.

I walked slower and made a chirping sound, the one he loved when I wanted to bring him in for the night to eat dinner.

The sound of the lake rebounding off my husband's body made me see stars.

"What are you doing? Little early for a swim," I offered, my voice aiming for casual, landing on a trembling stutter.

"You rise early for your runs. I rise early for this sometimes. You would know that if you gave enough of a shit to notice." His voice was calm. His arms moved through the water, the right clutching the long red leash.

It moved through the water like a ribbon. A red, ominous ribbon.

"I give a shit," I said.

"You give a shit enough to *spy* on me," he said. His white teeth flashed, his dimple succumbed to early morning shadows.

Every beautiful thing about him that once drew me in now made me sick to my stomach.

"What do you mean?" I suspected he knew, but I was hopeful that his distraction was too strong a drug for him. He wasn't as careful with my schedule, my routine. His attention was elsewhere. I should have known the girl didn't have a strong enough hold after the night at the bar.

"I know you saw us, Cal. I just need to know if you were a tricky little bitch."

"What do you mean?" I was inching forward, but he held up a finger, stilling me.

"Every relationship is give and take. I want something from you; you want something from me. I give you shelter, money, and the gift of time since you don't have to work. Since you don't have to tend bar, pass out shots, and sell that body of yours to the unworthy garbage men of this place you insist on returning to every summer. In return, you give me your loyalty; you give me your fidelity. You give me your body as long as I hold up the bargain. I am holding up my part of the bargain, but you are not holding up yours. We said vows, did we not?"

"Yes." My eyes were stinging. I knew I couldn't use my voice or words to cut him down in return. He had me frozen.

"We are supposed to cherish each other. You no longer cherish me. You have broken that vow, so I have broken mine. She gives me what I need, what you won't give me anymore. And I am going to keep taking until you see fit to take her place."

"Okay," I said, giving him permission to continue.

"Where is your phone?" he asked, wrapping the end of the leash around his fist in the water.

I reached into the back of my shorts where my new phone was nestled, snug between the elastic and my skin.

I held it up for him.

"Did you take any photos of what you saw?"

"No," I lied.

"I need you to throw it in the lake."

"What?" I balked, not wanting to give up my lifeline, again. He always waited a day or two to replace it.

"We will go get another one for you. But that one has to go."

"There's nothing on it."

"And I would love to believe that. But we both know you can't resist a tempting photo opportunity. I admire it, Cal, your eye. But not with this. Throw it." He pulled on the leash, and the dog jerked.

I did not hesitate. I did not make a scene. I knew better by now.

I tossed the phone, pretending it meant nothing to me. And in that instance, it didn't. Once it hit the water, I felt myself breathe. My watery eyes returned to Apollo, and he was smiling, shaking his head just a little.

"I don't like it when you make me like this. I don't like myself like this. So why can't we just be happy together?" he said.

"We can," I said, trying not to look at the leash still in his hand.

"I just want to know that you appreciate me and everything I do for you. I hate coming back here, did you know that? I didn't even want to build this house here. I did it for you. That is how much I cherish you." He swam closer to the dock, and my heart rate sped up.

"I know," I said, confirming, for him, all his love.

He placed a hand on the dock. The dog walked to the edge and licked the water from his knuckles. "This is a messy business. I don't want anyone to get hurt."

I knew he assumed I would think he was referring to Sean or Jo. But I knew he just meant me.

"I don't either." I lowered myself slowly to my knees, to his eye level.

"Can you prove to me that you cherish me again?" His other hand came up, ruffled the fur behind my dog's ear.

"Yes. Yes, I can," I said steadily. *I cannot cry. I cannot let anything out. He wants to know I'm listening.*

"Would you crawl for me? Do you still love me that much?"

His voice was cracked, and this was how he got me. This was where I was weak. He wept, and I didn't know what to do with it. My hands felt numb.

"Yes, I would." *I will crawl for this love if it means no blood is shed but my own.*

"Do it then. Prove it to me."

"How?"

"Crawl to me right now. Show me," he said.

I lowered my palms to the dock. It was moist, dewy from the morning. The air was cool on my thighs, and I knew my shirt was riding up. I didn't wear a bra out of the house.

The humiliation was his desire, above all else.

I moved slowly, not wanting to alarm him, to make him think I was going for the dog. When I reached him, I stared into his eyes, asking.

I never knew what I was asking for; maybe it was his permission to exist.

He looked down at his wet knuckles, then back into my eyes.

I thought of his nightmare moments, when he would hit me while sleeping, the torment, the way I muffled the cries from the blows.

Moving closer, I placed my hands on his. My forehead met his knuckles because I couldn't look at him yet.

I was afraid I would cry.

THIRTY-NINE

CALLIOPE

APOLLO

Do we all need to just sit down? Have a chat? All four of us?

APOLLO

I'll bring her there. Let's have a little family reunion.

APOLLO

I'll let him know what a tricky little cunt you are. I'll let him know all the shit from the past.

APOLLO

I know he's there. In my home. I won't stand for it. I'll be seeing you both soon.

FORTY

SEAN

PRESENT
THE LAKE

KANUK WAKES ME IN BED.

I hear his whimper to go outside, and when I reach for Calliope, she isn't there. Her phone is gone from the nightstand, and her side of the bed is made. The sun rising beyond the large windows in her bedroom paints the white down comforter in shades of fire.

When I reach the kitchen I see the real fire, down by the water. I open the kitchen door quickly, and it bangs on the home's brick exterior. I leave it open, in my haste, running down to Calliope.

I'm sure the fire can be seen for miles. The early morning fog and the smoke. And I see her watching the ghost dance, clutching her chest.

She doesn't hear me approach, so I stand behind her for a moment, not knowing how to proceed, how to reach her.

The phone in her pocket vibrates but she doesn't reach for it at first. I'm frozen, listening to the flames eat my uncle's clothes and other personal belongings, barely recognizable in the white ash in front of us.

The phone buzzes again, and this time, she moves. Kanuk gives me away, pressing his wet nose to her bare ankle.

When she turns to me she doesn't look alive, she looks like a shell, and it scares me. I want to reach for her, pull her close, ask questions to her temple, but I just look into her eyes, searching for something, though I don't know what it is.

In response to my quiet, she holds her phone out to me. I've fallen into too many traps in my life, so obvious in hindsight, as most things are, so I hesitate.

I don't reach for the phone. Instead, I reach for my hair, hide my eyes in the dark strands.

Her hand is on my wrist like I knew it would be, her foot lands on one of mine, and I sigh at her closeness. Her bare skin, so tender, against mine.

"Look at it, Sean. You've been wanting to look at it."

I abandon my juvenile hiding, my knee jerk escape, and take her phone. My uncle's name is at the top of the screen. I see messages from him trailing to the top of the screen. Unanswered messages, countless. I scroll a little, not reading the words, just absorbing the quantity. My thumb scrolls back down to the bottom. The last message, sent just a few hours earlier.

I know he's there. In my home. I won't stand for it. I'll be seeing you both soon.

FORTY-ONE

CALLIOPE

PAST
THE LAKE

THERE WAS mud in the SUV, but the leather seats would wipe clean; I didn't care. I was numb.

I pushed the dog's head down and drove down the driveway at a reasonable speed. Robotic. I was good at it. Good at this.

Apollo would thank me for his breakfast when I got back. He would smile, and I would kiss him, and only later would I break down.

I would cause a scene. I would shed tears and act the part of the distraught, the grieving.

Ethan's house looked the same, maybe a little less white. What color would you call it? Eggshell? Ozark poverty? I thought it looked like home, like everything I wanted to escape. But nostalgia like that, giving in to it, was something that couldn't be afforded. I wouldn't allow myself to fall into that hole.

I grabbed my dog after putting the SUV in park, pulling him over the console, cursing myself for not catching his leash but then remembering the way Apollo cataloged everything. If the leash were missing, he would know.

I held onto my dog's collar when he hit the ground, and we scurried up to the porch, looking like wild creatures, bent over, hobbling. Dirt dusted over my toes, dirtying my red polish.

Ethan opened his front door just as I reached the top step, making the screen squeak, and I winced.

"Callie, what are you doing here?" He eyed the dog warily.

"I need a favor," I started, letting go of the collar.

The puppy ran to my friend and started sniffing his leg, his fluffy tail wagging back and forth. Back and forth. I stared at it, transfixed, until my friend spoke, stepping away from the dog.

"Anything. What's up?" The wrinkles around his eyes made me want to cry. He looked so concerned for the friend who left, barely speaking to him.

"I need you to take my dog."

He stepped back, scrunched his face into an unnatural one for his spirit, so carefree and open. I'd never seen him in the morning, before coffee and other vices.

"Take your dog? Why?" he asked.

"I just hate the thought of taking him back and forth. He'll hate the cold." The words were out too quickly. My mistake was foolish, but I couldn't take back those seconds. I shook my head, embarrassed.

"Callie, he's a husky. I'm sure he hates being here in this muggy Missouri weather."

"He's weird."

"What's going on?" He walked to one of the wooden chairs on his porch, motioned his hand to the other one.

I knew I couldn't get away with a lie, not with a man who had known me since we were both five years old. I needed to tell the truth because my act would have to go beyond the home. It would have to extend to the internet.

Resigned, I took the seat, my head in my hands. Every tear I'd stored up for weeks was falling. I was a flood.

But I didn't want to run away. There was no shore to break upon.

Ethan was on his knees then, in front of me. He grabbed my wrists gently. "Callie, Callie. What's wrong? Fuck."

I leaned up, pulled away, not wanting his scent on me, and I knew I didn't have much time. "A lot is wrong, but I can't talk about it. I'm not even supposed to be here, and this is something you can never talk about." It wasn't the first time he had kept a secret for me. He had kept plenty of secrets from his best friend, my brother, years ago when we couldn't stop finding each other in dark rooms. But, he was the rare guy who could handle rejection—fall into a friendship so easily with me when that was all I wanted for the future.

"What do you mean?" he asked. He had my hands in his, and it was so comforting to be touched by someone who didn't want to hurt me.

"I just need to know if you can take him. And if you do, you can't say you have him. You can't react to anything I say online or at the bar that has to do with this."

The puppy was curled up in a ball on a rug in the corner. Red and blue and tan.

"Yes," Ethan said, standing, crossing his arms.

When I kept secrets, he closed himself off, but he wouldn't abandon me. I knew that, and I didn't have time to diffuse this bomb.

This one was child's play compared to what was at home.

FORTY-TWO

CALLIOPE

APOLLO
You think I care about those things? They're just things. You can't hurt me. You can't erase me. You can't burn me.

FORTY-THREE

SEAN

**PRESENT
TORONTO**

WE ARRIVE at my apartment by nightfall.

When we make it inside, Calliope retreats to the hall bathroom. I think she's afraid of what she may see. What traces of the past may linger, like hers.

But I see clean white when I look around. Every picture from the past is off the wall, off the nightstand. No more fridge magnets, letters tucked into books, or perfume on the nightstand.

Every memory of Jo is gone. I have purged. No, my team has purged this place for me. They've been waiting for me to come back. Since we landed, my manager, Jesse, and my best friend, August, have been sending me frantic, excited messages.

I thanked them for the work they did. For the work I wouldn't have been able to do.

Jo's belongings have been sent away. *Where?* I don't know. I don't care.

My empathy has limits. The welling of my heart can only stretch so far.

I look at my bed. New clean white sheets that I will taste Calliope on. Behind closed doors, I don't let the doubts, the whispers of wrong and right, find us. I don't let her look at me with that questioning stare. Calliope asks permission with her teeth, it's the way she takes the breath from me.

It hits me then that everyone has left her somehow, and she refuses to see that I'm not the leaving kind.

I don't think you can call my breakup with Jo leaving. She left while we were still together.

I set my phone down on the kitchen counter and pull out the Polaroid photo I keep in my pocket. Calliope is on the dock, her blue dress around her. She let me capture her, but with rules. You can't see her eyes, just her mouth, neck, and pale arms. You can't see her eyes, but I can. I can read her lips and posture and just know how they look.

I turn to Calliope as she enters the room, setting the photo down.

When she steps into my space I feel as though I may cry. I grip the granite of my kitchen countertop and stare out the window, into the lights of the city, hoping her vision is locking on anything but my face.

Everything is white, crisp, and clear because I wanted it to look like their lake house. I felt home there that first summer, so I recreated it.

When she looks at me I've mastered my spilling emotions. I hope to be unreadable. Just as she is now, staring at me. Pink lips and dark hair.

"Yes?" I ask.

"I didn't ask anything."

"You look like you want to," I say, running my hands down her arms.

She reaches, pulls them to her hips and she is close to my face when I lift her. I set her on the countertop and her legs go around my waist.

"I won't have trouble sleeping here," she says into my hair.

I rest my forehead on her shoulder, dissect her admission. If I close my eyes for too long I can smell smoke. I can see her standing by the water, her face unreadable. I can see the white fur of her dog, no soot, no ash. I can see the puzzle pieces falling to the floor, but I won't move a thing.

I feel a buzzing on my hip so I pull away, and I reach for my pocket, but remember I don't have my phone. Calliope is already pulling her own up. I watch her face go dark, the deep V of her brow.

"It's your uncle. He knows we left."

I stare at her and she shakes her head.

I believe in erasing those who have wronged you from your life completely. Forgiveness and I are not acquainted, will never be close friends.

She throws the phone across the room, I hear it break something, but it can't pull me from her.

She is wearing white lace, leaning back, showing me where she wants my focus.

Her hair is falling. I am falling.

I catch her pulse with my tongue, slip my fingers up the sheer fabric.

I've only ever been with one other woman.

The one who taught me.

One image of seeing Jo with someone else and it hit me. She was holding back. Every instance of her calling me delicate flashed through my mind on the plane ride to Calliope. Every instance of me accepting it as a compliment, and not the insult she was using the word to wield flashed through my mind on the plane ride back here.

Calliope doesn't act like she's going to break me. Instead, she acts like I am a twenty-one-year-old god, but I worship this.

I'm on my knees then. She leans back, her thighs falling apart, her head falling back.

I should feel wrong, being where I am, knowing who was here before. But I don't.

And that makes me wonder at the purity projected onto me, that I've always owned.

Flesh seeks flesh. Flashes of the last time I made her come make me moan into her, and she returns in kind.

"What would they do if they knew you were like this?" she asks, breathing the words.

"Who?" I ask, pulling away for a moment. We are high on the escape. I wonder if he's at the lake house, screaming into the night air, finding her gone. I hope the ashes meant something to him. The way they meant something to her before we left.

She answers me, her breath shallow. "The world."

"Blame you," I reply, and the regret is so quick when I see her eyes fall down to me, see them change. I stand, pull her closer, but her hand presses against my chest.

"Don't," she says, a smile at the corner of her mouth.

"I'm sorry," I rush, but she shakes her head.

"No, don't stop. Get back down there."

I know her brush offs, her insecurities, her frantic worries. Because I share them. I wish I didn't let the echoes of the world drown out my own desires.

I give her her wish. I bring her to the brink, but only give her the release when she grabs my hair; it's longer now, and all hers.

FORTY-FOUR

CALLIOPE

**PAST
THE LAKE**

MY EYES WERE PUFFY—RED-RIMMED. They matched the nail polish I was applying to my toes as the video played next to my foot on my phone.

Apollo was down by the water when I caught him again with my phone. So was Jo. He pulled the string of her bikini, and it fell. I imagined the girl blushing, pink like her hair. I saw her look to the guest house, look for her boyfriend. I saw Apollo lean over and grab the girl's perky breast in his large hand. Watched him suck her nipple in his mouth. Jo shoved him away, but she smiled as she reached behind, tying the strings again.

This was not the way I expected the summer to go. A married woman collecting evidence against her husband she wasn't sure she would ever use. Only now, when I was alone, did I look at the videos in my private collection. Sometimes just to make sure they were still there, hidden away in the Dropbox account. Sometimes just to remind myself who they were.

Because when Sean was around, they were so good at pretending they were innocent.

Apollo left on an early morning flight two days ago, leaving me in charge of the lake house, leaving me with my false grief over the disappearance of Kanuk. The false reason for which I blamed my real tears.

Sean woke up late every day for two weeks. He was sulking, lost in the absence of Jo, who flew to Toronto for a funeral for a middle school friend. Apollo didn't hesitate to offer our credit card to fund the trip when Jo brought it up over dinner one night, as a warm summer storm played in the background.

I smiled at his offer, giving my support, wanting the younger girl gone from my sight. But, unfortunately, she was often in my company these days, lingering in the main house more than she dared to before.

I saw the boy out the kitchen window when I walked in, stepping lightly so I wouldn't ruin my polish. In one hand was his guitar, and in the other, his phone. He wore that look on his face like his whole world was a series of events he couldn't get a handle on.

I pulled my own phone from the counter where I'd laid it and took a photo of him against the morning sun as he settled by the pool.

He reminded me of my brother when he was sixteen. Tall and gangly, wiry muscles and a big grin. He smiled about as much as Talan did back then. It was hard to pull them out.

I imagined this boy trusted as much as my sibling did back then. When you had a father who beat the shit out of you, a runaway mother, and a snake for a girlfriend, little smiles seemed impossible, I imagined.

I doubted he saw his little girlfriend for what she was, though. Men can be so fucking clueless to our intentions. Or they don't give a shit, because it lines up with their own plans.

He wasn't Apollo. He was a kid, so there was no way he knew what Jo was up to, what they were up to.

But I saw her coming home late at night. I heard her laughter as she exited the Uber cars, dropping her off.

I could smell her. *I've been there.*

I pulled my coffee close, walked to the open dining room door.

The summer heat was not here yet, so I liked to let fresh air in early in the morning, and I rarely slept these days.

I rarely stopped picturing them together.

I rarely stopped planning my escape.

After a while, Sean stopped playing, stopped writing, and came inside, joining me in the living room.

He sat before me, his long legs under the coffee table, when I broke the silence between us. "If you could go anywhere, where would it be?" I asked.

Though he was ten years younger, I enjoyed this friendship we were creating and tried to remember being a teen when he voiced his concerns for the world that awaited him. It was hard to be around him sometimes. I could feel his emotions, and I was afraid he could feel mine.

I suspected the world that awaited him could be different than any world a typical teen and young adult would live in.

"I would want to get in a car and just drive," he offered, writing in his notepad.

I caught glimpses of it sometimes. It was filled with lyrics, poems, and scribbles. And music. Notes and chords. There were little sketches in the margins that I suspected sprang from his mind when the words wouldn't come.

"Where would you drive?" I asked, tilting my mug, looking in, and finding it empty. I grabbed my phone and found the screen the same. Empty.

When Apollo left, he was distant, likely frustrated that the dog was gone, a tool he could use, taken from him.

It was a gift he was giving me, his walls.

One I yearned for since that night, years ago, in Chicago.

I was waiting, for years, stuck, wanting what felt like a fruitless wish. Finally, I moved my legs in the silence the boy was giving me against the soft area rug under the coffee table and looked at him.

His eyes went from his notebook, to his laptop, to his phone.

I knew the loop, the manic wondering of where your lover was. Only these days I knew where he was. And I didn't care.

The clink of my mug hitting the glass table in front of me caught his attention.

"I'm sorry, what? I'm a little tired," he replied, though I knew he slept in late.

The white of his eyes always caught my attention. It stood out around his dark eyes, caged by his long black lashes.

"Where would you go if you got in a car and could drive anywhere?" I asked.

He closed his notebook, then stared at me. "I've been looking up North American road trips. There are so many I want to make."

I was happy to pull a smile from him. "Any in particular that stand out?"

"Route 66. Jo thinks it would be fun to be on a tour bus, watching the country go by, but I don't know. I think it would suck to be spending most of the driving hours asleep, wondering what city was next. What if each crowd was indistinguishable from the last? What if you stopped in cities and didn't get to explore them before being pulled to the next one?"

"I suppose," I said, pausing, trying to imagine what a life like that would be like, "maybe you would be in charge of it? If it was your tour bus, your tour, you could dictate when you leave?"

"I don't think it works that way."

To me, he seemed burdened by the fame he'd yet to achieve. He was an anxious young man, and if Jo brought him anything, I thought, it was a balance to this. The younger girl wore a mask of no fear, no worries, and perhaps he needed to cling to that.

"Well, maybe one day you can just get in that car with her. Make the drive on your own terms. A vacation. Have you ever been on a vacation?"

"We didn't have many family vacations. Once, we went to Niagara Falls. I just remember my mother and father arguing in the car the whole time." His smile was gone. "Did your family go on vacations?"

"Once," I said, saddened by the similarities of our lives. "We went to New Orleans. My mother has family down there. Hell, that may be where she is now, with her sister."

"Did you have fun?" he asked, his finger running along the spine of his notebook.

"No," I replied, taking a long drink, staring out the window, hiding my eyes from him, knowing he could feel me anyway.

FORTY-FIVE

JO

**PRESENT
CHICAGO**

THE THRILL OF THE CHASE. *God, how lost we can become in it,* Jo thinks as he eases in and out, moaning.

She knew this. She'd been chased before. Though her experience was limited in this regard to men, she'd been there before.

The last two men she wanted—one a boy, one the man above her—she chased.

Doe-eyed Sean was easy to capture.

Apollo was a harder one to claim.

It started sooner than the lake house. Sooner than she would ever admit to a soul. When confessing, she would fast track the events that led to their first kiss, make it seem like he chased her. And Apollo likely thought he did.

The only one who saw through her was Calliope. *Perhaps she saw a likeness,* Jo thought.

She knew the older woman wasn't as kind and ivory intentioned as she tried to pretend. She knew she wore a mask, could be cunning.

Above her, sweaty and heavy, Apollo finishes. Inside her.

She told him she was on birth control months ago, and he seemed disappointed.

She wasn't a womb to fill, but she wondered what he wanted. He's the kind of man to have a five-year and ten-year and fifteen-year plan mapped out in his head.

Jo didn't have next week mapped out, and being here with him now in his bed was never part of her limited planning.

He was supposed to be a good fuck. The kind that left her sweaty and heaving. The kind that left her a little scared, heart racing. He was the thrill of being caught. Now he was a boyfriend? She couldn't be sure.

She thinks of Sean before she falls asleep, of the day they met, and wakes thinking of him again.

The first thing she noticed about him was his pale skin, the way the vein in his neck stood out against his dark collar, his dark hair.

Jo would later say it was his voice, the way his long fingers strummed his guitar in the stairwell she followed him to later, but the truth was more sincere, more honest. And she didn't do honest with anyone unless it was on her terms.

Her hair was blue when she first saw him, reflecting her life in that particular season. As she fell for him, she lightened.

One night, he hitched a ride with a friend to her motel and watched her rinse the blue conditioner she used to color it from her hair.

He smiled when she asked him to don the gloves, apply the pink color she wanted to try out. A reflection of the color he turned her skin when he blushed himself.

He was so soft, and she was tired of being cut on the jagged edges of the men she always fell for.

She was being cut now.

She rolls over in Apollo's bed, alone. She can hear him, possibly in the kitchen. He is an early riser, and she likes to sleep late. So she tries to meet him in the middle when she can. He says she sleeps the day away too much, and she'll never accomplish anything in life that way, especially now that the world can turn against her if Sean —or Calliope—lets everyone know what she did.

He always says against *her*. Not *them*. As if he isn't half of this freak show they have created.

She knows he calls Calliope early in the mornings. His estranged wife is an early riser, too, their routines, possibly, still in sync.

Jo never was a jealous girlfriend. Sean didn't plant the seed. His trust in her was offered freely.

Apollo didn't give her a reason at first, after being caught—when they could finally be free to be together.

His house was free of Calliope's belongings since they were separated for some time before Sean caught her and Apollo together, but sometimes she thought it still smelled like the other woman.

There's a blanket in the corner, thrown over a chair. Whenever she walked by it, talked to Apollo near it, just by the bathroom door, as he brushed his teeth, it was like she could hear the older woman, the wife's voice. She could hear her words from five years ago.

She liked to dissect the disdain, the dripping sarcasm. The two women were never friends, rarely friendly. When she arrived on Apollo and Calliope's doorstep clutching Sean's hand she felt the other woman's hesitation, intermingled with her desire to help. It was short-lived, she felt, when it came to her. When she sniffed out their age difference, a gap that wouldn't matter when they were older, but was recognizably inappropriate while Sean was a teenager.

Jo didn't care about appropriateness, about what the world thought, at least back then, before Sean's fame thrust them in the spotlight, put them under the microscope.

What pissed her off more than anything was the deeply rooted instinct that Calliope didn't care what was appropriate either when it came down to it. When carnal instincts took over.

She waits for Apollo's voice to end its booming barrage of questions in the kitchen before swinging her legs over the edge of his bed. Grabbing a shirt from the floor—one of his—she joins him.

When he sees her walk out of the bedroom, his eyes meeting hers from across the living room, he smiles, but it doesn't meet his eyes. His smiles have been lessening, losing their luster.

His arms are on the countertop, even across the distance she can see the faint indention on his finger, the loss still unable to be given up by his skin.

"You're up early," he says, reaching for a white coffee mug, steam rising.

"You woke me," Jo replies, walking across the carpet, only letting her weight rest on the balls of her feet as she goes.

He notices, his eyes roaming her legs, falling downward. "Why do you walk like that? It's annoying."

She stops just past the coffee table, digging her toes into the carpet. These little critiques have been coming out, more and more.

She blamed the stress at first, the hiding.

They both locked down their social media after Sean caught them, too fearful of what he may do and say.

Jo tried to convince Apollo they were safe, at least he was. Sean was not vindictive, one for revenge. He wouldn't out them to the media. He wouldn't offer the details of their split.

He would never look at her, even after everything he saw, the way Apollo was looking at her right now.

FORTY-SIX

CALLIOPE

APOLLO

Every time I turn around, there she is. And the only reason I let her stay around is because you aren't here. The only reason I EVER fucked her, was because you wouldn't anymore.

APOLLO

Why are you doing this to me?

FORTY-SEVEN

SEAN

**PRESENT
TORONTO**

THE LETTER, really just a sentence on a page, arrives on a Saturday. It's in a large envelope, too large for the paper, but large enough to hold the photos inside.

I stare at my face next to Jo's. My eyes are half-closed, the flash is too bright, but the joy I see there, in both of our eyes, wounds me.

He can never be you.

It was a love I thought would never fade away, would never be rooted in falsity.

I don't show the letter, and the attached photos, to Calliope. I shove it all in one of the drawers of a console table in my entryway.

Looking at them makes my stomach want to walk out of my body, and I can't feed the need to feel the anguish it brings me.

Writing sad songs is what songwriters fuel themselves with. I don't need evidence of her regret to fuel my pen.

Calliope and I have been holed up at my place for five days. I have posted evidence of my return home to my Instagram, but I have kept it one way, still removed is the ability for my fans to comment, to speculate. They speculate elsewhere, in places and forums I refuse to look.

I know Calliope does though, I can see it in her furrowed brow, in the way she sets her phone down after looking at it for just a few minutes.

In this haven we make love, eat breakfast, create art in a bubble that is suffocating us.

She takes photos out of my living room window. I hear the click of her camera, her sigh.

I have caged her; this situation has caged her.

I have to set us free.

Calliope is toweling off in the master bath when I find her. She pulls the white towel up, over her breasts, in modesty, and it brings a smile to my face that is so wide, I know she can see the wrinkles around my eyes.

She smiles and drops the towel, walking to me, damp. "What are you smiling about?" Her hands are in my hair, her toes on the tops of my feet.

She's so little, and I wonder if I can break her just by being who I am, by being tied to the life we pretended didn't exist away from the lake.

"I want to go away," I say, wrapping my hands around her frame, burying my face into the space just behind her ear.

I feel her trying to climb my tall frame, so I grab her, spin her around, and set her on the countertop. She falls back a little into the sink and laughs, it's something musical, something I haven't heard all day.

When she speaks again, she has pulled away. Her head is against the glass and I can see every bit of her. "Where do you want to go outside of this room, Sean?"

I want to taste her, get lost in everything, but I can't let her distract me. I know she is going dark and can put on a show here now, but the truth always has a way of crawling out.

I spent too many years ignoring the subtle signs the woman I loved was giving me.

My hands grip her hips, soft flesh, and a soft sigh escapes her.

"We can't stay here forever. We have to get out of here. We'll go mad, and I can't be scared forever of what the world will think," I say.

"You already know what the world is going to think." She leans forward, forfeits her seduction, her distraction. "But I'm not going to say I haven't been going a little mad."

"Are we ever going to talk about the fire?" I can still feel the morning, the panic.

We packed, boarded the plane in a hurry, fled. My heart was beating fast and the thought of seeing my uncle face-to-face, no matter who was to blame for the turn our lives had taken, terrified me.

He was my father's brother, his father's son. Even if his hands, in the past, never caused violence, I still wondered if he was capable of all they were.

"You don't know what he's capable of," she says. "You don't know what I want to do to him, how I want to hurt him. I want to say it's not like me to be mean, cruel even, but it is. It has been."

"You're not mean," I say, pressing my thumb to her bottom lip. I love the feel of it. The way it pushes out when she's animated.

"I have mean thoughts. I've let the venom of others seep into me. You don't know what your uncle is like. I mean, you know now he is the kind of man who would fuck his nephew's girlfriend, but that's not it."

"What else is there? Did he do something to you?" I know he's the kind of man to send dozens and dozens of texts to his wife, even when she hasn't sent a single reply back.

"He did a lot of things to me."

"Did he hit you?" When the words leave, I know the truth of how I feel. That it isn't a preposterous thought, an idle wondering. It's something I would believe in a second.

"You can hurt someone without hitting them."

My phone rings in my pocket, pulling my eyes from her, from the melancholy there. It's my manager, Jesse, and I don't want to take it, but Calliope is already hopping off the counter, moving around me for the towel she abandoned. Leaving me with too many questions, answers inside of her I'm afraid to find.

FORTY-EIGHT

CALLIOPE

**PAST
THE LAKE**

"ARE you ever going to fuck me again?" Apollo asked.

He was shaving, leaning over the sink, as I stepped out of the shower, reaching for my towel, avoiding his eyes.

Any pleasure my body felt no longer came from him. I came for myself and was trying to make myself happy, for a moment, when he walked into our bedroom.

When I heard the heavy door shut, I put my hand to the water—washed away the evidence. I cleaned up as he plugged in his razor, whistled a familiar tune.

Apollo hummed, and it tuned me into his moods. Warned me, before he spoke, of what was to come.

I tried to walk past him but was too slow. He reached out and pinched the back of my arm.

I jerked away, showing him a scowl. All he did was shrug, and that eased me. He seemed bored, his question and my answer not really what was on his mind.

It was a ripple. When he brought up fucking, I thought of why I wasn't fucking him. I thought of Nick, of the way Apollo made me believe it was something I brought on myself. Made me think I must have liked it.

And I did like it. The gray of it made my stomach turn.

Now, when Apollo was inside of me, I felt like I was losing my mind. Like I was dreaming, and I would blink my eyes, any moment, to find another man there.

So I needed to be drunk to fuck my own husband. I needed to be so far gone; it didn't matter who it was.

It wasn't the first time I'd been there. Inviting the feel of flesh, the cool quiver down my throat of glass after glass of wine, to dull myself, to make me feel. Back then, I just wanted to feel something. Now, I just wanted to turn it all off. The way it hit me depended on my mood.

I liked how the liquor could mold and meld into whatever I needed it to be sometimes.

Apollo finished up, walking into the bedroom with a hand towel at his face, wiping away any stray shaving cream. "The only way to live a full life is to offer forgiveness. When we offer forgiveness to others, we offer it to ourselves."

I listened to him as I pulled on my panties, my bra, applied lotion to my skin—but I didn't look at him. I knew it pissed him off when it seemed like I wasn't listening.

"When you are unforgiving, you punish yourself and others. You're punishing me, limiting me. Do you want to make my life harder? When I make your life better?" he asked.

I slipped my feet into a pair of flip-flops by the bed, finally, done dressing, done pretending.

I took a breath, then looked up into his eyes. "Who do I need to forgive?"

"Nick was like a brother to me."

He hadn't said his friend's name in months. It hit me like a slap to the face, though I suspected it was coming. I could feel it every time I looked at a calendar. I could feel my teeth, every one of them, as I clenched my jaw.

He threw the towel in the hamper, annoyed at my muted response. "My birthday is next week, as you know, and I want him there for the party."

I didn't speak, still. Instead, I listened to my breathing, the acceleration, the way my shoulders moved with each exhale, the way my chest inflated, expanded with each breath.

The panic attacks stopped, and it'd been so long since I felt one coming on.

Not since we took the kids in. It was if my body told me I couldn't alarm them, couldn't let them see me crack.

They changed the dynamic of the house. My arguments with Apollo were reserved for the bathroom, the bedroom, the walk-in closet. They were only performed out in the open when Sean and Jo left the property. And that was a new thing, now that Jo had a car. It almost felt like Apollo wanted the girl gone. He wasn't done with her, but he was bored with her.

I liked knowing the main house, lawn, and pool were all safe places as long as they were home.

They were gone now. Out to get ice cream. There was nowhere for me to escape.

My husband looked at the walk-in closet, then at me. "I think you need some time to think about us."

I thought about us all the time. But I knew that wasn't what he meant. He meant I needed a lesson. I needed to start acting more in love with him.

"What do I need to think about?" I asked, venom creeping in. I didn't always lay low. I didn't always back down. I looked at the closet again, wondering how long I could stomach it.

"You need to think about your life here. Before I met you. In that trailer," he pointed to the right, likely south, where my old trailer was. He always knew exactly where he stood, while I always felt off-balance around him. "You need to think about this beautiful house that I gave you. You need to think about my needs, too. You need to think about *my birthday* and what *I* want for it. You need to clean up the mess you made." His voice was cracking. I knew he was about to cry, and I felt nothing.

"And how do I clean up the mess?" my voice was flat.

"Plan the party."

"I'll plan the party."

"You don't have to invite Nick if you're too embarrassed to talk to him. I'll invite him."

I shook my head. The tears were coming now. My life, the one I actively created here, would fall apart if his friend stepped on our property.

"Stop that fucking shit, Cal," he warned, but I didn't stop shaking my head.

I didn't stop when he walked across the room to me. I didn't stop when he grabbed me by the arm and pulled me to the closet, pushing me inside. I knelt down in the dark as he closed the door, my head still shaking as he pulled the chair next to the bathroom door to it, shoving it under the doorknob.

My head was still shaking as I screamed at him through the dark.

FORTY-NINE

CALLIOPE

APOLLO

You never did want to face shit. Face your mistakes. You think you can just run away from them? Again?

APOLLO

I'm always going to be waiting for you. Because I love you. Can't you see that?

FIFTY

SEAN

**PRESENT
ON THE ROAD**

I SPENT JUST shy of a month at the lake house in the Ozark woods with Calliope, mapping her body, pretending she would one day be open with me, terrified of being caught in our scandal. And I was only scared of being caught by the one person, even more so than Jo, that couldn't say a damn thing to me about what I was doing. He had done worse.

One part of my body was in ecstasy, one was in torment, waiting for the owner of the life I was tasting, to come back and claim it. Though Calliope was no longer his to take. I hoped.

We spent less than two weeks at my place before we left. Every day Calliope was becoming more withdrawn, drifting away from me.

At first, I sat on the bench near the largest window in my place, staring out, writing, asking for her input. She was my muse and I wanted her thoughts on the way I was painting her, but she didn't critique, offer alterations or little endearments the way Jo did. It took me a few days, but I finally let what I was doing hit me. I wanted her to fill a role she didn't want to fill, to take over, to do the way the former couldn't.

I received two more letters from Jo before we left. Though I wanted them to stop, I couldn't reach out to her. I was afraid of what I might say to her. I was afraid she would cry and I would forgive her.

I knew I would never take her back, but I didn't want to give her the chance to claim my forgiveness. It was something that fell out of me, unbidden, at times. Even when I was so sure I felt no intention of offering it.

The first time I saw Jo her hair was blue. It changed with her mood, though she favored pink. She said it was the aura she wanted others to see. She was so good at manipulating me, right from the start.

I look over at Calliope. Trying to read her aura.

I am not at ease behind the wheel of a car. Finding fame so early in life allowed me to avoid losing myself in that rite of passage.

Jo taught me to drive after she got her car when we lived at the lake house.

The car she ended up getting was out of her price range, far beyond what she had saved, and I see now, it was a gift from Apollo.

I wonder now at what I didn't see back then, how naive I was. I wonder at when they started, and how Calliope reacted to the news of their affair, the way she seemed resigned, not shocked.

I have so many questions to ask her, but I bottle them up, decide to lose myself in this idea of our future instead.

We leave my house in my Jeep, Calliope behind the wheel. In charge.

"Where are we going?" I ask, my fingers playing with a hole in my jeans.

"I don't know for sure." She glances at me, smiles. "I have an idea, though. I think it's a good one. How long can we be gone again?"

I look at her, her small body on the black leather, her white legs in her shorts. She is dainty, like a small bird. My index finger runs down her arm, and I see her shiver. "I don't have anywhere I need to be for a long while. So, that's up to you."

When it comes to control, and my life, I offer it up freely in anything other than my music, my words, and the stories I want to tell.

In the beginning, I let Jo take the reins when it came to promotion, plans, ways to get my name out there. When people started to take notice, she let go of that responsibility, reaping the rewards of my sudden and scary ascent into stardom.

Whatever Calliope's plan is right now, I don't even care what it is. Just to be near her, to pretend there is nothing that can't be overcome here, is all I want to do.

When Canada is behind us, and the open road of the States stretches out ahead of us, I reach into the backseat, grab my notebook.

Scraps of paper flitter out in my lap when I turn around. Little pieces of my sadness stare back at me, and I have a strong desire to throw them out the window. I don't want to release songs about Jo. There are only three of them, surprisingly, but I know they are strong. Pulling them from the dam was difficult, but I did it, late at night, when Calliope slept beside me.

Being split in two, straddling the line of heartbreak and desire for someone new, is a flood. I don't know how to stop flowing.

I shove the papers into the back of the notebook, flip to the middle, and stare at the blank page. The radio is low, the sound of the large tires on the Jeep is lulling me.

When we stop at a stop sign my eyes jump to a flash of white fur. From the corner of my eye, I see Calliope look, too. She doesn't drive forward, and luckily there are no other vehicles at the four-way stop in the small town we are passing through. The owner of the white husky eyes us, unable to see our faces through the dark tint of my passenger window.

"What happened back then?" I ask, still watching the dog, his fluffy tail waving goodbye as his owner guides it away from us.

"He ran away," she says, and it feels like a lie.

"What happened?" I ask, again, turning to her. "How'd you get him back?"

"He ran away," she says, rehearsed, and then, "My friend Ethan found him after we left that summer. He called me and I told him to keep him safe. He's more his dog than mine now, but sometimes I take him back for a bit because I miss him."

We had dropped Kanuk off at a small white house before we left Missouri, boarding a small plane headed to Toronto.

She clutched the dog tightly, burying her face in his fur then. He was a small bundle of white fur when I met her, now a full-grown dog. Always by her side, watching me with cool blue eyes.

"Why didn't you bring him with you? He would have loved a road trip, I'm sure."

"I just want it to be us," she says, turning her eyes to the road, taking her foot off the brake.

I want it to be just us, too, but I know it's not.

FIFTY-ONE

CALLIOPE

**PAST
THE LAKE**

"DON'T BRING HIM HERE! If you do, I'll leave!"

Those were the words I screamed before Apollo left. He packed slowly later that night, in our bedroom, only letting me out of the closet when he needed to get his shirts. I hugged my knees when he walked in, flipping on the light.

He didn't say a word, and I didn't move, making him walk around me for whatever he needed.

Finally, as he was zipping up his suitcase, I untangled myself from the floor.

I was dizzy, trying desperately to gain control of myself.

I didn't want to hurt. To feel the blinding pain. To feel nausea. So I counted in my head, each step taking me closer to my bed. When I was next to it, I pulled the covers back, sliding my body in slowly. Never looking at Apollo, though, I could see him staring at me.

"I hope you thought about us, about how much I love you, while you were in there."

I didn't respond, just nodded at the ceiling. My heart stopped racing when he was gone again, boarding a plane, granting Nick's request to see him.

My husband commanded every room he entered, commanded every situation, every bit of his own fate. But Nick was the true alpha in their friendship.

Apollo had not severed ties with his longtime friend, had not pushed him away completely, but they weren't as close as they used to be.

Nick wasn't the best man when Apollo and I were married, but I knew he was his dearest friend.

I felt that places could carry your pain. So Chicago was the haven I escaped to, no longer able to endure the pain the Ozarks held, every place, every person a reminder of my brother.

Now, Chicago was a prison. When I drove down to my favorite coffee shop, I passed a billboard with Nick's face on it. An advertisement for his real estate developmental company.

A company that aided Apollo's, and in turn, benefited my life.

I stopped going to the shop after that September night. I stopped leaving the house.

I started seeing a therapist against my husband's wishes. I considered going to the police station, but I didn't know what to say.

He didn't hold me down. He didn't force me to do anything.

He tricked me. And I wasn't sure the law could help me.

———

The water was cool on my toes; I moved them back and forth in the Ozark lake that night, the red of my toenails peeking out.

My brain was fuzzy from the wine, vision blurry at the edges.

I liked the numb. The numbness was comforting. Years ago, I wanted to feel something, anything, to erase the numb.

Now I envied that girl who was able to fall into vices, lose herself.

I wanted to fall into the water.

Not fight for air.

I wanted to disappear.

But even dying took a strength I didn't have at that moment.

Sean found me like that, down by the water. I heard his footfalls on the wooden planks of the dock. My eyes were closed, and I didn't open them when he sat down next to me. I could feel his eyes on my profile; knew he would see the salt there. I caught sight of his guitar.

"Are you okay?"

Three words, but the intimacy there was damning.

We had been spending too much time together. Our lovers left us alone too often. Whether they were sneaking off with each other or just abandoning the ones they claimed to love, it didn't matter. They left us alone together. One large house and secrets I wanted to share, but never would.

I could break his heart that way.

"No," I said, unable to lie. I opened my eyes and looked at Sean and his guitar, wiping my face, pushing my wine glass into the lake. "Fuck." my mouth felt like it was filled with cotton balls, muffled and mixed with saliva and sugar.

"Let me get it." He moved to his knees, extended his long arm out to the water. His fingers brushed the edge of the glass, and then it sunk, the trapped air bubbling out.

"I have plenty more in the house. It's fine," I said, knowing I didn't need to drink any more anyway.

The framework was there. Something beautiful was growing next to me. Someone beautiful.

I thought of my brother. How beautiful he was. How my friends loved him, some only friends with me to get closer to him. Who will weasel their way into Sean's life if he makes a name for himself?

"Have you been writing?" I asked, removing my feet from the water, tucking them under my dress. It was warm that night, still, even without the sun shining, and I wanted the rain to come back. Something to match my insides.

"Yes," he said, running a hand along strings absentmindedly.

"Who have you been writing about? Jo? Does she work all night?" The questions fell from my mouth, and my stomach rumbled. It was nearly midnight, and I always ate dinner early when Apollo was gone. I hadn't eaten dinner tonight at all.

"No, and yes. Where's Apollo?"

"Spending his birthday in the city," I replied, thinking of the relief I felt in his absence, and the way one word lingered, poison in my belly.

He said the word I grew to hate, over and over. *Cherish*. I no longer *cherished him* the way my vows promised, so he no longer cherished me.

He said I stopped after that night, but he was wrong.

I stopped cherishing him before Nick tricked me.

It was gradual, a slow-moving threat.

Slow-moving like this dangerous pull toward the boy next to me.

"I'll go get you another glass," Sean said.

FIFTY-TWO

CALLIOPE

APOLLO

I wanted you to be the mother of my children. Didn't you want that? Do you want me to make her the mother of my children? She's like a bitch in heat, just like you were. It'd be so fucking easy. Keep ignoring me. Keep it up.

APOLLO

I can feel you. I can fucking feel you.

FIFTY-THREE

SEAN

**PRESENT
ON THE ROAD**

WHEN WE ARRIVE in Chicago I hold my breath. I sensed we were going this direction but didn't voice my concerns, my questions.

Once, I looked at Calliope as we passed a sign telling us how many miles we needed to go before we reached the city where we met, and she looked at me briefly, smiling. It didn't reassure me, but when her hand traveled over the center console and grabbed mine, resting on my thigh, I warmed.

I turn the radio down when she pulls onto Adams Street. The air conditioner is making the hairs falling from the ponytail she's wearing at the crown of her head dance.

When the Jeep is in park, after an impressive parallel parking job I am certain I could never pull off myself, she turns to me.

"Do you trust me?" she asks, her face a little pink.

I nod, and she shows me her teeth, smiling in a way I haven't seen in a while. The lake house stifled it. My place stifled it. She looks younger than I know she is, closer to my twenty-one years, closer to the twenty-five years she was when I showed up on that doorstep in this city.

She turns from me, and reaches for her door handle, so I step outside as well. When she walks around the front of the Jeep I see her gaze isn't on me, but staring ahead. I follow the line of sight, walk to her.

Her right hand is fidgeting with the hem of the light flannel she is wearing, one she stole from my closet before we left.

"What are we looking at?" I ask, pressing my mouth to her hair.

We are on a busy street, the sun hasn't set yet, and I know someone could see this.

The cap I put on in the car is pulled back, exposing my face. And I don't care in this moment.

She is raising her other arm, extending her index finger.

I feel the beginnings of the panic I am too familiar with, the shudder that ripples through me when I fear the unknown, the way it can bite me.

I wish my anxiety would leave this flesh, but I don't know if it ever will.

My eyes follow her finger, expecting to see a man with a long-lensed camera, or worse, Jo and Apollo.

Instead I see a sign. **HISTORIC ILLINOIS US ROUTE 66**, it reads. My eyes travel down to the sign below it. **BEGIN.**

I feel Calliope's hand reach for my belt loop, the press of her mouth to my neck, the way her body feels at ease, too, unable to hide in this moment, despite where we are. Despite who else is in this city.

"You remember that night?" she asks, stepping on my foot, unable to get any closer to me.

"Yes." It was the beginning, for me, of the freefall. The descent into our unnatural attraction. I didn't know why she was looking at me the way she did back then, but I see it now. The way my uncle spoke to her didn't sit well with me, and he thought I didn't hear it. But his voice carried, much like my father's did.

My body's reaction to the bass of it always made me aware of his presence.

She was running then, even when she was trapped, standing still.

What she was proposing now didn't feel like running, though we both knew we were outrunning the truth of the way society would react to us if they knew.

When I turn to her, her arms wrap around me, snaking under my jean jacket, one hand dipping into my waistband.

I rest my chin on her head and close my eyes, open my ears when I hear her clear her throat.

"People can see us, you know."

"I don't care," I say, but she is shrinking away, walking backward. Her hand goes to her eye and before I can ask if she is crying—something I have never seen her do, not even when Kanuk went missing years ago—she has turned and is walking around the front of the Jeep.

I join her inside, letting the hum of traffic drown out my fears.

"The main route is gone, as you probably remember, but there is so much we can see. The minute you need to go though, we will cut it short."

"I don't want to cut it short," I say, reaching for her hand, hating that they are both already on the wheel.

"People need you."

"I need this," I reply, though I didn't know what I needed until this moment. I haven't known what I've needed since I saw our exes together. I haven't known but my body has been pulling me toward her. Toward some answer I hoped she could give me.

"I know," she says, still holding the wheel. "I need it, too. I need something I can be in control of. Something I can do that doesn't require me to stand still, or follow."

"I want you to have control," I say. Images of her on top of me, guiding my body, make me flush. "I want you."

FIFTY-FOUR

SEAN

PAST
THE LAKE

SHE SPENT a lot of time in the water. It was distracting to me when Jo was gone.

I liked to write by the pool, or down by the lake. But my safe places were also Calliope's safe places. We began to get up earlier, tried to beat each other to our spots because once one took claim, the other forfeited to another area of the property.

Some people filled rooms with their energy, with their voices. Some people took up space. And those people were people I couldn't be around often, or for long periods without needing a break.

When I met Jo in the library stairwell, I thought *yes, finally I have found someone who is the same as me. Someone who does not drain. Someone who listens, and watches.*

But it was a trick, and maybe she was just a chameleon. It should have been evident from the start, with the way she changed her hair color to suit her mood.

When the four of us were in a room, my uncle and Jo would compete for the floor. They would fight for the air around us. Talking over each other, loudly, trying to drown the other out.

Today there was no race.

Today, there was rain. A lot of it, and I liked it. It was quiet, and I was alone, to write.

But when the sun set, the rain stopped, and the heat came back.

Jo left for work to do a late shift, and my uncle had flown out unexpectedly, earlier.

I'd spent all morning locked inside. The sliding glass door was open; water came through the screen, but not enough to make me close it.

I could see Calliope across the yard, across the pool, in the main house as the hours went by.

She was in the kitchen, listening to music. I could barely hear it over the rain, but I still knew she was playing something loud.

She had a bandana wrapped around her forehead. Red.

I went back to what I was doing before she caught my eye. The notebook in my lap was covered in notes, not lyrics, nothing romantic. Stats about my latest video upload, future plans.

I couldn't concentrate on it; my eyes were drawn back to Calliope.

I could admit to myself that I thought she was hot. I was a fifteen-year-old boy, and she was beautiful. It was apparent why my uncle picked her, changed her life, took her away from this place.

They struck me as an odd pair, though. He was so big, so gruff, so loud. And she did not try to steal all the space in the room, not the way he did. The way Jo did.

She was like me. If she were ten years younger and found me in that stairwell, she wouldn't have needed to change a single thing about herself.

It was an idiotic thought. I hated myself for having it.

My uncle's wife was not someone I should be thinking about. But she was always there, always swimming in the pool, always swimming in the lake. Always pulling herself out of the water, in that tiny black bikini she wore.

She was not flashy, not loud, not like them.

Maybe that's why I couldn't stop staring at the house.

Maybe that's why I saw her go down to the water that night.

Maybe that's why I followed her.

FIFTY-FIVE

CALLIOPE

APOLLO

I'm sorry. I'm sorry, okay? Why do you make me this way? We are meant to be together. Look at our names. Do you remember the night we met?

APOLLO

Just come home. Come back to Chicago. Come back to me.

FIFTY-SIX

SEAN

**PRESENT
ON THE ROAD**

WHEN WE PULL into the motel, Calliope pushes her seat back, letting me know she is tired of driving. I often drive us around the small towns we visit. The quiet lull of their slow Sunday feeling calms my nerves.

Her phone stayed tucked under her leg while she drove, by her window, away from me. I heard it buzz from time to time, and she didn't look at it, but her body reacted.

My own phone has been plugged into the charger between us, navigating us to each stop, each diner, taking us to the motel we are parked in front of right now. It's open, for her to see.

I erased Jo's number, and I don't believe there is any message that will come to me from her worth hiding, worth being ashamed of. Because Jo is careful. That's why she sent a letter, not a text.

My best friend, August, supports this trip, and all it means. My manager, Jesse, is resigned to my decisions. He has given up the prying questions, given up trying to talk me out of anything.

He has accepted the fact that I will not be led by the nose anymore.

In the back of the Jeep sits Calliope's camera bag. She has a DSLR, two lenses, and a second camera. A Polaroid.

Before Calliope can go check us in, I hand her a wad of cash. We use nothing that can be traced. Me, to hide my name. Her, to leave no trail for Apollo to find, I muse.

Jo's letter gives me reason to believe her relationship with my uncle is over, or in jeopardy. Though he and Calliope ended before I caught him with Jo, my naivety washes away more and more each day. I wonder at their beginnings one minute, and don't care the next.

When Calliope returns, she is smiling and skips the passenger door on her side. "Don't move from that spot!" she yells.

Her Polaroid camera is in her hands when she walks around the Jeep, her hair falling in waves as she fiddles with the film. I throw my head back, squint into the midday sun. She is so fast, so sure of the images she wants. She captures me that way. With smile lines around my eyes. When the film pops out, she clutches it to her chest, protecting it from the light that would ruin my still self.

"Let me take one of you," I sing, reaching for her, but she dances away.

"I don't like being the subject." She walks to the back of the Jeep, away, and I try to remember if I ever saw a photo of her in her Chicago home or the lake house.

The walls were decorated in black and white art, crisp photos blown up, that she took of Chicago landmarks. Never any of her. I think of the photo in my pocket of her, what it means, that she let me take it.

I gather my things, a bag of clothes, my notebooks. The one I was scribbling in earlier is heavy in my hand. I pull it to my lips, let it linger there.

Images of her are in there, script and song, ways she may not see herself. I want to show the world how I see her. Even if she doesn't want to accept that.

Later, after a shower, before the movie, I pull out a pen she got me before I knew the meaning of gifts like these. Gifts that did not beg a gift in return, because those weren't gifts at all.

"Did I get you that?" she asks, knowing, her wet hair turning the white pillow a shade or two darker.

"Yes," I say, pressing her leg into the sheets, running the tip of the pen along delicate flesh.

"What are you doing?" she asks, reaching for me.

I pull away, loving the feel of her clean fingers on my wrist, too slow. "I'm writing a song here."

"I just got clean." I can hear her smile, and she doesn't reach for me again, but she doesn't pull away.

The ball of the pen presses into the soft skin of her inner thigh. A lulling hook is inked there, slowly. When I'm done I push back. The cap clicks loudly in our room as I press it on.

It is a few seconds before she pushes up. "Look at you," she says, avoiding the words I've left on her.

I have nothing on but a white pair of boxer briefs. She is close suddenly, running her fingertips down my stomach, pressing her lips to my nipple.

"You're different out here," I say with a sigh, my head falling back.

"I'm different with you," she says, slipping her hand inside, wrapping around me.

I am so hard for her, already.

. . .

Hours later, after I've heard my muffled name from her lips, over and over, Calliope backs the Jeep into a spot on the edge of the drive-in movie theater field.

Back at the motel, we had taken all our belongings out of the back, then inflated a mattress made for the Jeep, quickly running to a general store for blankets after testing out the softness, and finding it lacking.

We open the back to the twilight, then hang white lights—another general store find—in the back, plugging them into an adapter.

The movie won't start for another half hour, so I busy myself with Calliope's lips, distracting her from the prying eyes of the teenager manning the entrance of the field.

"What do you miss right now?" I ask, taking a break from her mouth, moving to her neck. She presses against me, trying to distract me, but I pull away, run a thumb over her jaw.

"I don't miss anything right now," she says, and I know it's a lie.

I reach over her, grab my phone, and watch her pull her hands to her face, simply because the camera is turned in her direction. With my other hand I reach for her wrists, give them a gentle tug.

"I don't want to forget anything," I say, wanting to add more. *I don't want to forget anything if you don't let us be together after we reach California, the end of Route 66.*

She lets her hands fall away, licks her lips, and closes her eyes.

She looks like a fantasy, something I made up.

I take a picture. Her face is split down the middle. You can see the end of one of the strands of lights, the waning daylight in the window behind her.

When I put my phone down, she opens her eyes.

"I would never post something without your permission. That's not why I took it."

"I know," she says.

"I've always shared my stories, my life, lyrics and bits and pieces with them." My fans get to share my life with me. I share it with them, because without them, I wouldn't have the life they've given me. "I'm going to start posting pictures more often," I say. "They won't be of you, but they'll be of what I'm doing. I can't hide forever."

"I didn't expect you to."

"It's not fair," I murmur, my mouth brushing against her shoulder. She wraps her arms around me, pulling me close. "How do they get a life, and we don't?"

"They can't go out in public. They can't be seen. They get to live a half-life, until they think the coast is clear. Then they'll make it public," she says.

"You think they are still together?"

"You don't?" She maintains a casual tone.

I want to break her open. I want her to be vulnerable with me, but I can't break down this wall unless she lets me.

"Maybe not." I think of the letter, lost in the bottom of a drawer.

"You talk to Jo?"

"No," I say, not elaborating. Then chastising myself for not being more forthcoming, the way I wish she would be. "I never want to hear her voice again. And it's not because I'm still mad. I feel nothing when I think of her now." The low hum of hurt has fallen away. I decide to be open. "She sent me a letter. Do you still talk to Apollo? Do you answer him?" I don't call him my uncle anymore.

"He's still sending me messages, yes." She doesn't say more. She doesn't offer an alternate reality for us. She gives me a fact. "When this summer is over, I'll be a divorced woman. I'll take my name back. A name I don't share with you. Maybe things will seem a little less fucked up then, maybe they won't. But that's at the end of this summer. It's a lifetime from now, and I'm not going to wish it away, no matter what's on the other side of this."

FIFTY-SEVEN

CALLIOPE

**PAST
CHICAGO**

I THOUGHT FAKING it was over. That I could figure out who I really was after I got married. Or at the least, create a new version of myself.

I thought freedom was on the other side of this when I boarded a plane for Chicago, leaving everything behind.

The party girl. That's what I appeared to be when he met me. And that was what he expected me to be when he snapped his fingers. But only then.

When I was not expected to perform in that way, I was expected to be his pristine wife. Long brown hair tied close to my neck. Neutral makeup. White blouses and perfect manners.

I thought being a trophy wife would be a leisurely life. I thought I would spend my days doing whatever I wanted.

That hadn't been the case. There were parties to plan, there were trips to plan. There was our huge house to care for.

Even with the aid of a full-time housekeeper, it was hard for me to keep up. And I wanted nothing more than to keep up, to keep him happy, to be everything he needed.

Apollo wore different faces, and he wore them well. Tonight, he was more like the man I met. So free, fewer lines on his face. He was with his college friends. The ones attached to his side when he visited the Ozarks, finding me, rescuing me.

And among those friends was a new friend. One who hadn't been there the night I met my husband.

I felt Nick eyeing me the whole night. The hair on the back of my neck would raise, I would feel warm. It would never get easier, being in the same room as him.

He was attractive. Long blond hair he pulled up into a messy bun most days, his eyelashes were dark, and when they fluttered over his blue eyes, women fell.

I found him attractive, yes, but I didn't flirt back. I kept my attraction locked down.

I would not bite the hand that fed me.

I looked across the room to my husband. He was laughing, his hand on the fireplace, the other holding a glass of red wine. He loved me in the hue, surrounded himself with it. I looked down at my red dress, my hand involuntarily crept to my mouth; I wanted to smudge the perfect lines of my red, red lips.

When Nick found me, I was drumming my fingertips on the marble countertop, staring across the room at the rest of the guests. The kitchen was rarely empty, but at the moment, it was, so I escaped there. Escaped within myself, within eyesight of Apollo.

"You look lovely tonight, Cal," Nick said, using my husband's moniker for me.

"And so do you," I replied, turning my body toward him. I felt my pulse between my legs, that steady beating women felt when they were near someone they found attractive.

He ran his hand through his hair then, it was down, a little wild looking, and it seemed like he knew I felt it, and I wondered if he could hear my heart beating.

"Will you be taking Apollo away this summer?" he asked, taking a long sip of his drink.

We spent the last two summers back in Missouri. Apollo built a home in the woods, near the lake, for me. We would fly out Memorial Day weekend—stay past Labor Day. Apollo would fly in on the weekends, and I would rarely leave the vacation home.

"Yes," I said with a smile. "It's his present to me every year."

"It looks like he got you another present." He laughed, looking into the living room.

A fluffy ball of white fur was on the back of the couch, lounging like a cat. I'd never owned a husky, or my own dog for that matter, but I was already in love with the puppy's quirks.

"Yes." my voice squeaked in my excitement. "His name is Kanuk."

"He's spoiled you. Must feel good, considering where you came from."

I didn't like his word choice, his implications, and my stomach dipped at the words, but I wouldn't let my face flinch. No wincing moved my flesh.

Men loved to be knights in shining armor. Men loved to save women like me. Men loved to reap the rewards of their saving, their white hope rescues.

"It does feel good," I said flatly. I would excuse myself from this when the opportunity presented itself, retreat to the master bedroom's bathroom for a moment. I was allowed moments.

The old me would have used my sharp tongue now, would have put him in his place, no matter how beautiful he was. But that girl, that woman, was gone.

Everyone says they're afraid to be themselves with the person they love, because what if you are, and the person you love leaves you?

But that's not what you're really afraid of. You're afraid you'll be yourself, and the one you love won't leave. Instead, they'll stay and break you down. They'll kill the real you, and you'll be the one who doesn't leave.

I knew the real me had been dead for years. The death happened slowly, and it started the night I met Apollo.

I excused myself from my conversation with Nick. Instead of finding solace in a solitary moment, I found my husband. I orbited him often after moments that I lamented the night we met. I imagined I deserved this life due to my inability to leave.

I thought about Nick's question as I sat next to Apollo, who made his way to the formal dining room. I thought of the children I didn't want to bring into this. My phone buzzed in my hand, under the table. An email, most likely, but my heart raced a little at the vibration. I could always sense when it would be an issue. It was the tone of Apollo's voice next to me. He moved his head slightly when I looked down.

"Who are you talking to?" he asked, low, so no one else at the table could hear him.

I pulled my phone to the side, and he looked down at it.

My heartbeat in my chest, even though I knew I wasn't doing anything wrong. And I knew the procedure.

I showed him my phone when he asked. And in company, I was discreet. His reputation was not a jealous man, and I wouldn't taint his image. It was too closely tied to mine.

And if not him, who would I have in this city? Where would I go?

When he was satisfied with his glance at my phone, he found my eyes. He smiled, and I eased. It was a reward, and I took them where I could.

My hair was pulled back into a tight bun, my fingernails were red, rashly done. I stared at a smudge on my thumb, then tucked it into my fist, resting it on my thigh. I learned to control my breathing when he sent my heart fluttering. Such a different fluttering than the one I felt when we met.

Tell this story in reverse, and it would all be there.

The first night we met, Apollo's hand slipped between my legs. Large hands. Dark skin and black hair. He pinched the soft flesh there.

I looked at his face and saw nothing.

I saw him smiling at his friend, his happiness. The pressure increased, and I flinched, grabbing his wrist.

My eyes teared up.

He turned to me, furrowed brow and pouting lip. "Are you okay?" he asked.

I moved my mouth to his ear. "What the fuck? You just pinched me."

He looked down at his hand like it didn't belong to him. Some phantom appendage. He pulled it back. "Shit. I didn't even know I did. I'm sorry. Are you okay?"

That should have been it. I had ditched men for less. But back then, I was hollow. The weeks leading up to the sight of his smile—a blur.

The funeral.

The black dress.

The red shoes my mother wore. Tacky. And now the color I wore to make my adoring husband happy.

Her yellow pinto pulling out of the driveway. The return I never saw.

I felt something then. When he touched me, when he hurt me. I felt. And I didn't want to let it go.

Those who have never felt grief, the heavyweight on your chest every morning as you try to crawl out from beneath it, will balk at your release. I didn't care that it wasn't healthy. I cared that there was a chance I wouldn't be alone if I took Apollo's hand. I cared that he was a doorway. I just needed to step through.

I looked down. His hand had made it to me under the table. He squeezed, and I felt nothing.

FIFTY-EIGHT

SEAN

**PRESENT
ON THE ROAD**

THE SKY VIEW Drive-In Theater in Litchfield, Illinois is the last operating drive-in theater on Route 66.

We decide we need to see it, to fall as deep into this nostalgia surrounding us as we could.

She is smiling now, her shoes are off, and the night is cool.

Seeing her so at ease quiets the voice in my head, telling me what I did earlier in the night was wrong, crossing a line.

I heard Calliope in the shower; she was singing one of my songs and I was smiling at the ceiling. It was nice to hear her so free, and it was something Jo would rarely do around me. As if I would laugh at her voice because it didn't sound like mine. It was the only time I saw her insecurity.

Our motel wasn't historic, the walls were white, the art was forgettable.

It was a canvas. We were the colors.

I believe you can be in love with the idea of someone, and never know who the person you've fallen for truly is.

I don't think I ever truly knew my uncle.

With my father, I knew the monster I was battling. I knew his weakness. His weakness was me. The man he thought I was—or wasn't—growing up to be. I was his weakness and his punching bag. I was who he wanted me to be, the name he gave me at birth. *Das Dores*. It meant *of sorrows*. My father was full of sorrows, so I, in turn, was full of sorrows. An echo of his rage.

My smile had faded when I heard the buzzing. I reached for my pocket and found my phone. The screen showed me a text from Jesse, but it was twenty minutes old. The buzzing reached my ears again, from the nightstand.

I knew I shouldn't look at Calliope's phone, but I wanted to anyway. My shame and curiosity warred with the heavy weight in my stomach.

I saw my uncle's name when I stood up and stared down.

The messages were rapid fire. I'd seen it before, but hoped it was just a one-time thing. I'd been lying to myself. The preview was off so I couldn't see the content, but the sheer volume and speed of the messages made the hair on the back of my neck stand on end.

I wanted to throw it out the door. I imagined it. The phone shattering on the white motel hallway wall.

Black and glass, broken and unable to reach her.

I still didn't know why she hadn't changed the number. Blocked him, the way I did, but I quickly banished the thoughts. I didn't know their marriage, but what little she said made me fear he was worse than a man who would sleep with his nephew's girlfriend.

I pulled my phone back out, sat down on the bed, and looked for his contact in my phone.

I unblocked his number.

I could hear the voice in my head as my leg started to shake. I bobbed it on the floor, my anxiety spiking.

It happened so quickly.

The voice sounded like my uncle's, but it wasn't. It was my father's.

Don't be a pussy, it said.

The voice came when I least expected it. When I was fearful, full of worry.

I heard Calliope's voice, off-key and beautiful in its imperfection as she sang lyrics I penned for the girl she replaced.

I know she knows who the words were for, and I know she doesn't care.

Her worry and whatever consumes her when she is silent has nothing to do with me. And everything to do with the man texting her when I stared at that phone, hours ago.

I no longer feel guilty about what happened years ago by the water. I no longer carry that, because now, here with her in this Jeep, I can feel all the reasons she kissed me back then.

The threat was easy to type, because in that moment, I knew I would never follow through. I just hoped he feared I would.

If you don't leave her alone, I'll tell everyone what you did.

I look over at Calliope, at her closed eyes as she brushes the hair from her face, and know I was lying to myself. I would follow through.

I would expose him to the world, to protect her.

FIFTY-NINE

CALLIOPE

PAST
THE LAKE

THE REALIZATION that I didn't want to have children with Apollo didn't come swiftly. Instead, it was gradual, beginning long before the Chicago night that refused to leave me, even when I escaped to the summer house.

I woke up in my bedroom in the city past noon, a rarity, with a bruise on the inside of my thigh. It wasn't the first, and I knew then, it wouldn't be the last.

Our dinner the night before came flashing back when I ran my fingers over the purple flesh, and my throat was sore when I looked over to his side of the bed, seeing it empty. I was too young to feel that way. Like life beat me down, wore me out.

I felt the same way now, this morning. Just older, much older than I should. I eventually swung my legs over the side of my bed and leaned forward. Kanuk didn't run in from the hallway the way he always did when I needed comfort, and that's when the tears came.

Eventually, I reached for my phone and saw a text from my husband.

> **APOLLO**
> I caught an early flight. I'm so sorry about last night. I just love you so much that you make me so mad I can't see. I never understood passion until I met you.

I locked my phone, deciding I would talk to him when he got back. I wanted to run, to clear my head. But what if Sean was outside? I couldn't face him, not after the night before.

The covers flew back. I ran as quickly as I could and barely made it to the toilet, throwing up wine, acid, and popcorn. *When did I make popcorn?*

I spent the rest of the day in bed, hiding from my husband's nephew, strangely desiring Apollo's presence.

I felt guilty, dirty, and lonely.

When my husband got back, I hugged him. Consoled him. Because that's how it went. He would hurt me, and I would comfort him, would apologize for making him so crazy, so angry.

I knew I couldn't fit into the box he created for me forever. It got smaller and smaller every day. One day I'll find myself inside of it with no way out. I am going to lose myself in there. I wanted to lose myself more often than I wanted to admit, but not in the box he created.

When I walked into the kitchen that night as Apollo napped, zapped from his flight, I found the windows open, a song coming from the guest house.

Something was happening at our house that none of us adequately prepared for.

Sean was posting videos online, and they were going viral.

Apollo let Jo and the boy do whatever they wanted with the guest house's interior. They painted the lone wall with no windows a stark white. As he sang, Sean sat on an antique trunk with a stack of records next to him. Jo set the camera up on a tripod. This was the only time I saw genuine affection between them that didn't seem lopsided, altered.

I could read people, and I often wondered if others could see what I saw or if they were all in denial, or complicit with the using.

Apollo was still fucking the girl. I knew, but I also knew I was powerless to stop it. I even knew a small part of me didn't want to stop it. If I stopped it, I would be rewarded with his full attention.

And now, a new emotion lived in my gut. Guilt.

I no longer craved Apollo's attention but played the part when he desired it. So when he doted on me over the loss of my dog, a lie I burned with, it brought me a strange comfort. I wasn't sure if it was because he was using the face I loved, the side of the coin he was landing on less and less, or if I was proud of myself for tricking him. For being in control of something for a change.

Ethan waved at me the last time we ate dinner at the bar he worked at, but I didn't indulge him in small talk. I couldn't risk talking to him in front of my husband anymore.

I was afraid Apollo would punish me again.

Later that night, the four of us sat down to dinner.

It was the night I realized Apollo would use Sean. Would use him up the way I suspected Jo would.

"I have friends in the city who would love to throw some money at you, but I told them it wasn't necessary. I told them I would make sure every video you record from here on out would be seen, and that I'd make sure you got the best representation back home."

Sean smiled over his plate of Alfredo, reaching for Jo's hand on the table. She let him hold it for a moment before pulling away.

He wouldn't look at me.

Was Apollo jealous with Jo? Did he treat her like a girlfriend? Jealousy worked me; a strange cocktail of despair and disgust whirled within me that I hadn't felt in a while.

I wanted to take my husband into our bedroom, fuck him wildly, finally, the way he wanted.

I wanted to let the windows leak our secret to the younger girl. This desire, so red and pulling, made me feel sick again, causing me to raise a hand to my mouth.

Apollo looked at me, and I smiled, then downed the last of my wine, excusing myself from the table. I walked to the kitchen, filling a glass with water, embarrassed.

I wouldn't give in to those thoughts, those lows.

Besides, I didn't want sounds like those to reach Sean.

I didn't want to admit he was the reason for my black jealousy, my deep loneliness.

SIXTY

SEAN

**PRESENT
ON THE ROAD**

"TELL ME ABOUT YOUR BROTHER," I say.

She smiles. "You know, I've said he was my older brother. And that's true, technically. Two minutes older."

"You're a twin?" I exclaim, kissing her collarbone.

"I was a twin."

"You're still a twin."

"It doesn't feel that way. It hasn't for a while." She pauses, brings her hand to her chest. "It's true what they say. When he felt pain, I felt it. Sometimes I feel this pain, right here." She presses two fingers to her heart. "It's like I can feel a flutter of his heart or something. It doesn't feel like my own. And I know it isn't real. He's gone. But maybe he wants me to know wherever he is, he's thinking of me."

I don't stop her. I let her speak, barely breathing. Because she is never like this. She speaks with her body. But I haven't heard her phone going off like crazy since I texted my uncle, so I wonder how alive she will become as each day goes by, if he stays away.

I feel her press her feet to the top of mine. My eyes drag there, away from her profile. The string of lights hung in the Jeep paints her in shadows and romance. But this doesn't feel like romance, more like vulnerability. The kind she has kept from me since that night years ago. The night she won't let me bring up.

"We had different birthdays, too. I was born just after midnight. I love that we both had our own days, and our mom let us have those. She had separate parties for us for years. When we were eighteen, we went out. And an hour before last call he would start playing my favorite songs on the jukebox. He had a fake ID for years, and that was his gift for me, but I never wanted to party like him. I just wanted to go out with him, so I could make sure he got home okay. He had the prettiest voice." She looks at me and smiles, running a finger down my throat. "So pure. I used to stick my hand out the passenger window. I'd let the wind fill my palm, and I would close my eyes and just listen to him sing. It's the thing that stays with me. Sometimes I can't see his face as clearly as the year before. But his voice never fades."

I remember the comparison, her words. And I want to latch on, to use this opportunity, but I pause. Her fingers intertwine with mine, and my eyes are on her face again, her full lips. "What's a song he liked to sing?"

"I don't want to say," she replies.

"Why?"

"Because if you sing it, I know I'll cry. I can feel it." She presses her fingers to her heart again, closing her eyes.

"Maybe that's okay." I take the hand from her heart, bring it to mine.

After a moment of silence, nothing between us but the beating of my heart, she props herself up on her elbow, facing me. The hand on my heart moves, over my neck, to my throat. Her thumb is at the edge of my jaw, her index finger just inches from the scar on my cheek.

Her palm rests over my Adam's apple. "A couple of weeks before he died he started singing one song, over and over. In the shower. In his room when he got ready. Around campfires with his friends, with me."

"What is it?"

"Use Somebody."

I shiver when she says the name of the song. The past is so close. The pieces are falling to the floor, making sense. I feel like I could reach out and touch the boy on the dock. He's buried inside of me, not as deep as before.

Neither of us speak. We can hear cars driving into the field, parking close to the screen. We are parked in the back. Neither of us caring about the movie that'll be starting soon.

I hear her suck in a breath when I start singing. My eyes are closed. I can't look at her, but I can feel her. Her fingers tightening just a little. Her hips moving closer to me. The tenor of my voice echoes into the field.

It's careless. It's stupid. But I can't stop.

I can hear people outside the Jeep singing the echoing background vocals of the Kings of Leon song, so recognizable.

They're just singing because they know the song, I think to myself, as my voice cracks.

My eyes are closed when she moves to the back of the Jeep, pulling the open door down, closing us in.

I lean up on my elbows, stare into her eyes. She's crying, her lips parted, face red.

She looks the way she did that night by the water.

When she doesn't speak, letting the silence swell around us, I almost believe she is daring me to ask. Telling me she will give me an answer this time.

I clear my throat, rock forward, closer to her. "Do you remember that night?"

"Yes," she says, closing her eyes.

"Was it ever about me?" I feel like I'm suffocating, but I get closer, so she can't hide a thing.

"I was married."

"I know." I brush her hair away.

"You were fifteen."

"I know." My thumb traces her jaw.

"You had a girlfriend."

"I know." On down her throat, I can't stop touching her.

"I was drunk."

"That's a lie." My hand retreats. "I watched you. You poured the wine, but never drank it when I brought the second glass down." At this, she turns to me.

"Why were you always watching me? That's the question."

I'm up, on my knees, hovering over her. I taste her skin, pull at her hips, feeling her hands on my chest, pushing. "What?" I ask.

"You're avoiding the question."

"You avoided mine," I reply.

"Is that what this trip is?" She leans back on the glass, voice cracking.

"What do you mean?" I pull at the button on her shorts, watch her hands wrap around my wrist.

"We're all avoiding something, Sean. I know what I'm avoiding," she says.

My phone buzzes in my pocket, as if on cue.

"What are you avoiding?" she asks.

I don't look at my phone until later. Because the life I am avoiding can wait.

We open the back of the Jeep. We watch the movie, and I hear her laugh. I hear every remnant of the tears I pulled from her wash away.

I want everything inside of me to wash away, but it doesn't. My phone is the one buzzing now. My phone is the one ruining everything.

When we get back to the motel, I finally pull it out as Calliope enters the bathroom.

When I open my Instagram I see the usual barrage of notifications, shooting up the screen so fast it's hard to read anything, everything blurs.

Until it doesn't. Until I see my white T-shirt. The one I'm wearing now.

I see the Jeep, pale hands at my back, the dip of my head.

I'm kissing Calliope in an open field, my Jeep one of just three cars there already. The others belonging to couples in their fifties or older, faces I took note of as Calliope drove us in, over the worn-down grass, matted from previous viewings.

The edges of my vision blur and my contradicting feelings make me weak. The account that shared the photo belongs to a seventeen-year-old girl. Her profile says her name is Karmen. I'm tagged in the photo, not just the caption.

It's blowing up.

It's the answer to the question they've been asking. The answer to the question everyone has been asking.

Where has he been?

Where has he been?

Where has he been?

Who is he with?

You can't see Calliope's face, but you can see that whoever is holding me isn't Jo.

SIXTY-ONE

CALLIOPE

**PAST
CHICAGO**

FIVE WEEKS AFTER THAT NIGHT, I arrived at the ER.

Earlier that evening, I fought with my husband about the ways I did not cherish him.

"If you leave me, if you end this before I'm ready for us to be done, you will get nothing." He said it so calmly. Over his green beans. His steak was long gone. He liked to eat one thing on his plate at a time.

His tone was not cruel, not angry. It was matter-of-fact. And when he was calm like that, I feared him.

When he was emotional, I could sway him to either anger or sadness. And when the anger came first, it always led to sadness.

From that night forward, sadness would be what he turned to less and less.

And only then would I truly understand it was never sadness, but the show. One that worked so well.

Something about his words, and his threat, pulled me from the coma I'd been stuck in for those five weeks.

I stood, grabbed my plate from the table, and walked to the sink. I stood in the kitchen, eyes locked with my husband, and threw my plate into the sink, knocking the faucet to the side, breaking the plate. Porcelain clattered across the countertop, and a piece hit my bare foot on the floor.

Apollo smiled, and that pissed me off more.

He could always read me, and the thought of divorcing him had been in my head, pulsing, refusing to go away.

I didn't want to be pulled in, so I gathered myself and walked to the bathroom. Then, I heard him turn up the classical music we often listened to during dinner.

Apollo's dressing box caught my eye as I walked through the bedroom. I walked to it, running my fingers over the mahogany. Inside were the items he slipped on before he started the day. A watch. His wedding ring. Cufflinks.

He often kept a cigar in there as well. His cigar box was in his office, and he liked to sneak single cigars into the bedroom. I never understood why, as he never lit them, and I didn't mind.

Because I liked to find them.

I pulled the one staring back at me from the inside the box to my nose, and inhaled.

I never smoked, and would never smoke.

I spent my childhood smelling like cigarette smoke. Like my mother.

I learned to do my own laundry at an early age and sometimes washed my clothes twice, so they wouldn't smell like my mother's cigarettes. *I don't smell. You're being dramatic,* my mother had said.

My brother smelled like smoke, too, because he took up the habit. But the smoke reacted differently to him. Somehow I associated two very different scents with my long-gone family members.

The cigar I held wasn't the same, and it didn't smell the same, but it was close enough to bring my brother back for a moment.

Apollo found me in the bathroom twenty minutes later.

I was in the tub, soaking. Bubbles surrounded me, and soft music played in the background.

I looked relaxed, and maybe I convinced myself I was, but the opposite would prove to be true later that night.

His cigar was in my hand, dangling over the side.

"Cal, what are you doing with my cigar?"

I blew out a puff of air at the nickname he knew I hated. Then, I dropped it to the floor in my frustration, denting the end.

Apollo knelt down, picked the cigar up, and tucked it into his suit pocket.

"I truly believe we make our own fate in life, Cal. We decide every day how we will feel when we wake up. And when we decide how we are going to feel, we decide how the rest of the day will go. I hate seeing you like this."

"I want to talk to someone," I said, leaning forward in the water.

"A lawyer?" He leaned back against the bathroom counter, crossed his arms.

"No." I looked into his eyes then. It was something I rarely did these days. I busied myself with the social life he insisted I kept full. On days when I felt like I could get away with it, I stayed in bed, feigning sickness.

"Who do you want to talk to? You don't have anyone back home. I'm not sure I get what you mean." He often rattled on like that, barely offering a blank space for me to fill. He especially did it when he was nervous.

"I want to see a therapist."

"And have that get around to our friends? No." He made his decision. It was decided—for him.

I saw the set of his jaw, the dark of his eyes.

I stood from the water, sending a wave over the side of the tub. My hands were clenched at my sides, and it occurred to me, this was the first time Apollo had seen me naked, without the cover of our comforter, my clothes, the darkness of our room, in weeks.

I was hiding from him then, but I didn't care if he saw the damage now.

My ribs were showing. There was a hollow gap between my thighs that hadn't been there since I was a preteen, before I grew fuller in my hips and breasts. Though I was never what one would call voluptuous due to my high school swim career, I used to be fuller than I was now.

I was a shell of myself. My reflection stood next to him in the mirror behind him. I could see the dark circles under my eyes without looking at it.

"I want to talk to someone," I said again. Louder.

"No," he replied again.

We stared at each other for a long while. Until finally, he stood. He ran his hands over his suit and walked to the door.

"I'm going to have a drink. You can stay in here. Think a while."

I didn't plan to camp out in my bathroom and think about whatever *he* felt I needed to think about. But after he shut the bathroom door, his footsteps took him away, and then back to the door.

I heard him press something against the door, then walk away again.

My fingers wrapped around the edge of the towel hanging on the rack on the wall, pulling it over my body, wiping away the suds from the tub.

The floor was wet when I stepped out. I swore at my outburst, at my theatrics.

My hand wrapped around the knob when I reached the door, turning, twisting.

It wouldn't budge, even though there was no lock on the outside.

My thumb fiddled with the lock on my side. I locked and unlocked it, though I knew that wasn't the issue.

Again, the door would not open.

I imagined the red chair I kept by the closet wedged under the knob on the other side.

I imagined my husband out, having drinks for hours, while I stayed locked in our bathroom.

My phone was on the nightstand. My clothes were in the closet.

I was trapped. It wasn't the first time, and it wouldn't be the last.

SIXTY-TWO

SEAN

**PRESENT
ON THE ROAD**

I WAS BORN into a generation that shares their every move with the world, with anyone who will listen. And when I share my life, little places I've seen, grand landscapes, people listen. A lot of people listen.

They listen and they feel like they have a piece of me. My fans have given me my world, they consume my stories and bring me life. So why wouldn't I want to share a bit of mine with them? I've had pictures taken of me without my knowledge shared before, so I try to quiet my mind. To go with it. To drown out Jesse's frantic voice chattering on about addressing the situation, and listen to what August told me when I called him after the picture was leaked.

Just stop thinking. Stop being a puppet. Tell Jesse to shut the fuck up, and just do what you want.

I feel free now that I have been posting on Instagram again. It sounds dumb as hell, a truly superficial problem. But I cannot deny that I felt like there were chains on my heart while I was hiding.

I look at the photo I took at the drive-in theater on my phone. Calliope peeks over my shoulder, running her hand down my chest, making me sigh.

I let my head fall back into her.

"I love that shot," she says into my hair.

"I think I'll post it tonight. They already know I was there, so why not make the memory my own?" I run my fingers through her hair, turn, finding her mouth.

"I know it's important to you. I would never try to control you."

"I know that." I clench my jaw, and Calliope's eyes go there. She takes her index finger and runs it across my chin, and I relax a little, but not completely.

I've held on to a love/hate relationship with it my entire life. It's my father's chin. Strong, cleft.

"I've been playing games in love my entire life. I'm done with that. Did Jo do that?" She walks around, stands between my knees.

I reach forward, running my hands up the back of her thighs, higher and higher.

She stops me. A smile offered. A flash of white against her pale skin, dark hair. I see her smiles, more and more, mile after mile. My uncle is fading from her eyes, I think. His poison isn't reaching her phone.

Stepping back, Calliope reaches forward, presses my knees together, and crawls into my lap, straddling me. "Did she?"

I'd forgotten her question.

I want her. I don't want to talk about Jo. My phone hits the floor, and I'm reaching for her again. The hem of her shirt. Her hip bone, her rib cage, the soft swell of her breast.

She deflects, dodges. "Sean?"

"Yeah. I never knew what she wanted. When she was telling the truth or when she was telling me lies. She's the only woman I've ever been with. The only thing I've known. Until now."

"The girl liked to play games."

"I'm not playing anymore."

Her phone buzzes across the room, and for once, she doesn't flinch. She doesn't move. I don't even know if she hears it.

I hear it, but I, too, don't flinch. Because I don't think it's him.

Calliope presses into me and I am so needful. I want to please her, to make her forget the world waiting for us.

She lets me try.

She lets me, but I'm not sure I can erase her past.

SIXTY-THREE

CALLIOPE

**PAST
CHICAGO**

I DID NOT SCREAM in the bathroom. I did not cry out.

I knew better. I knew that he was gone, likely already on the sidewalk, hailing a cab.

Instead, I looked at my reflection in the mirror. I looked into my eyes, daring myself to remain stoic. Unflinching.

The bath mat on the floor below me was damp; it squished between my toes as I moved them, one by one.

I pulled my hands together, cracked my knuckles. Little sounds to remind herself I was still intact.

The pulsing started when I closed my eyes. The bathroom lights dimmed, then brightened, causing me to grab the sink again to steady myself.

Nothing hurt. My moment of rage earlier was already forgotten from my body. Even breath, empty chest.

My stomach grumbled as it always did after I picked at dinner, eating little of the meals I spent hours preparing for my husband.

When I opened my eyes, I saw the lightning. I didn't know how to describe the pulsing disrupting my vision on my left side.

I brought my palm to my face, covering my left eye. The disturbance electrified on the left side of my right eye. I pulled my hand away, covering the other eye.

My first thought was that I was having a stroke. My mind frantically ran through the symptoms I knew of.

Blurred vision in one eye.

Fatigue.

Lightheadedness.

My body manifested the symptoms, and I tried to convince myself I was overreacting. Creating symptoms as my mind flipped through them.

Frantic, I threw my towel off, reaching for my fuzzy red robe.

The images flashing before my left eye became blurry. I reached up, covering my right eye, assessing my vision.

It was going, and that was something I couldn't manifest. *Could I be doing this to myself?* I crossed the room to the doorknob, twisted again, in vain. "Apollo?" I called, knowing he was gone.

The lights in the bathroom were so bright, blinding me in one eye, fighting to be seen in another. I walked to the towel cabinet, grabbed a handful, and threw them toward the door.

The bathroom often was hotter than the rest of the house, and I was thankful for that. A chill ran through me, not from the temperature but from my anxiety, growing stronger and stronger.

I created a pallet of towels on the floor, curling up onto them. A rolled towel acted as a makeshift pillow as I pulled the front of my robe up, covering my eyes.

I was safe and cozy inside my massive robe, but it didn't save me from the numbness. The arm I was lying on felt like it wasn't there, so I shifted to the other side.

The numbness didn't leave the relieved arm. I tried to push myself up again, and my wrist gave out beneath me, causing my face to slam into the bathroom door in front of me. I tried to reach up, a knee-jerk reaction, to cover my face, but my arms wouldn't work.

It was then that the tears came; a sad wail came from my mouth in the place of my husband's name. Words were not working anymore.

And then, ruthlessly, the pain came.

A blinding hot pain between my eyebrows that shot through my body, down into my belly.

I rocked back and forth for a few minutes, my hips moving when other body parts failed.

The ache assaulted my stomach, bringing what little I ate for dinner back up. Finally, I was able to push forward just a bit. The stomach acid and green beans landed on the bathroom mat, already wet with the bathwater and bubble bath.

I straightened out, twisting my body until my belly was facing the ceiling, then used the last of my strength to rotate again, putting my back to the vomit.

My eyes stayed closed, useless when open. With unusable hands, I felt afraid and so tired. So tired of all of this.

Apollo never locked me in a room this long. Tonight was a first, and a part of me, larger than I cared to admit, hoped I would die in the bathroom. Hoped it would haunt him the way he haunted me. *If anything could.*

I burrowed down into the towels, into the side of my robe. My nose hit the floor, and I could smell my bedroom. Cool air and no humidity. No vomit. No perfume and cigar.

I heaved my body, shoulders moving, until I saw my right hand hit the tile, my long fingers extending beneath the door. I could see them, but I couldn't feel them.

Apollo found me like this. Four hours later. When he opened the bathroom door, I rolled out, and he thought I was dead.

But my wish hadn't been granted.

He dressed me, wiped my face, and took me to the hospital.

I did not have a stroke, as I worried. Instead, it was a severe migraine. When the doctor asked me if I was under a lot of stress, I smiled, but the doctor didn't smile back.

It was determined I was twenty pounds underweight. When the doctor asked me what was causing my stress, I lied. Apollo was in every room I entered, standing next to my bed as every question was asked.

What I offered was a lie but also a truth.

"The anniversary of my twin brother's death is coming up. I always get a little off this time of year. I guess it's worse this time."

It sounded like my only truth, even to me.

SIXTY-FOUR

SEAN

JO
Did something happen between you guys back then? Tell me.

SIXTY-FIVE

SEAN

**PRESENT
ON THE ROAD**

THE ROAD STRETCHES OUT in front of us, and despite the sun, I can see Calliope fading.

"I can drive sometimes, you know."

"You don't like driving."

"I don't like you looking like you may drive us off the road right now and sleep right through it," I say, laughing a little at the end, to soften it.

She glances at me. Her full lips barely smile, it's trapped in the corner, but it's enough.

"Let's just call it a day," she concedes.

She wanted to get through the bulk of Missouri in a day, no plan to linger, and I never argued. This is her trip, though she believes it is an offering to me. I just want to stay with her, any way she will allow me.

We stayed up too late the night before. I can still feel her hand around my throat, the way it thrilled me to see her control my body. After I drifted off, she stayed awake. Before dawn I woke and found her in the bathroom, the light drifting in from the half-open door.

She was bare, her feet pressed into the cheap bathroom mat, her right hand gripping the sink. On the counter, her driver's license sat, the small image of her face the subject of her fixation. In the sink, her hair pooled. She cut it to the shoulder.

I didn't ask her anything, just grabbed the scissors, threw them in the trash with the Walgreens bag from our midday stop.

I look at her little ponytail now, blunt ends sticking out, as she pulls off the interstate. My hand reaches across, runs along her neck, causing her to shiver.

"Quit it," she says, pulling away, winking at me to soften her words.

The hotel is a chain, no history attached that we can claim when we remember the trip like some of our previous stops, but neither of us care. I want her rested.

Later, after we shower together, I let my guard down. I think of Jo's text. I think of the past, the kiss, the wine. The way we buried it.

"I want you to tell people about us," I say, my thumb tracing her knuckles.

Her thumb fiddles with the button on her camera. "People?" She looks through the viewfinder, pulling her hand away. "What people? I don't have any more people."

I don't know what I'm asking, but I'm asking her to take back the rules. I know how to guard the details of my life, but I don't like secrets. Not one of this magnitude, anyway.

"What would you like me to say?" she asks. I hear the click of the camera.

"I don't have any more people either, you know." I cross my arms, staring at the bathroom light, streaming across the floor, petulant.

"Would you like me to tell a story about us?"

"What do you mean?" I ask, looking over at her.

Her plaid top, my plaid top that she is wearing, is open. I can see the curve of her breasts, her belly button, and water trickling from her short hair, all the way down to her black panties. It occurs to me then that maybe I am in love with this woman.

"You know what your uncle said to me once?"

I can't keep up with her sometimes, and I'm afraid of what she is about to say. I shake my head.

"He said art is for the weak minded. He said that after I took up photography. He never said it to you, because he banked on you being valuable. Your talent was apparent the first time you played your guitar for us. He knew you were valuable and a tool he could use. He used your name, your relationship to him, to advance his business after you went viral. 'Do you know who my nephew is?' he would say. The people he told didn't know who you were, but their daughters did, and their granddaughters did. I remember you telling me how much it meant to you that he believed in you because your father didn't, and I couldn't take that away from you. He does that to people. He makes them want to be vital to him. Impressive to him. So I set out to be valuable, too." She holds her camera up.

"I don't like that story," I say.

"That's not what I meant."

"I'm sorry he made you jump through hoops," I say.

"I made myself jump through hoops. And this is my tool." She points the camera at the ceiling, staring at me. "You want me to tell people about us? If I ever did that, this is how I would." Then, the camera is pointed at me.

What she captures is a look of wonder. My mouth turned up slightly at the corner. My hand on my heart, reaching for my neck, where my tension lies.

My uncle used my name to get ahead, though his own ambition got him far in life. He didn't need me, but he used me anyway.

Calliope created a name for her photography that did not include her married surname at the forefront. But my fans still found her when they searched for me.

They followed her. They fawned over her photos, her art. Her name was mentioned, as an afterthought, in articles about my career. They were my only family. My pseudo-parents. And that made this a scandal, as she said.

I didn't want to hear her then, but I was listening her now. I was also choosing not to care.

Because we don't have much time left.

SIXTY-SIX

SEAN

**PAST
THE LAKE**

I WALKED TO THE WATER, her wine in my hand, unsure.

What if Jo comes back and we're still down here?

We would hardly be doing anything wrong, but I knew Jo didn't care much for Calliope.

"She's kind of a cunt," Jo said, once, before bed, as she applied moisturizer to her face.

"Since when do you use that word?" I asked. I would never use that word. No man should ever use that word. I heard my dad use that word.

It sounded gross coming from her mouth. *Do women have different rules for that word?*

"Since she started acting like one," Jo had replied, turning the bathroom light off.

I watched Calliope's silhouette as I walked down. The Tiki torches were lit. The moon was out.

You could see everything.

I could hear everything.

She was crying—sobbing, actually.

I walked faster, setting the wine down on the dock when I reached her, saying nothing. I wasn't sure if she wanted me there or gone. So I waited for her to realize I was there.

It took just a moment.

"Sean, you don't have to stay."

She was standing, and then my hand was on her elbow, her hand was on my chest. Then my hand was on her shoulders, her eyes met mine.

It happened so fast.

It was poetry.

I thought she needed me to stand. I thought she may fall into the water if I wasn't there.

I hadn't felt needed in a long time. It hit me then, a ton of bricks, a cold bucket of water, so many clichés popped into my head. I worried they were littering my notes, my poems, my lyrics.

I knew if I wrote about this moment, it would be raw, real, and something no one could ever read.

Then, just as quickly as we were, we weren't touching. Our hands were at our sides, and her breathing was unsteady.

"What's wrong?" I didn't like how needful my voice was. How hard I thought it may be for her to say nothing when I sounded like that.

Don't be a pussy, my father would say.

"Everything." She laughed, her eyes behind me, on the glass of wine I brought her.

She wasn't like this when I left, not this fragile.

"Do you want to go inside?" I asked.

"No." Her voice was loud, and she caught it, mastered it when she spoke again. "I need to be outside," she replied, crossing her arms.

Her movements told me she was cold, but her sweating brow contradicted that assessment.

"Okay."

"Okay."

We stared at each other for a bit. And I had to admit, it was an overwhelming feeling—to stare into someone's eyes and see them staring back, trying to figure you out.

"I'm sorry you're alone all the time," she said, turning away, sitting down on the dock again. She didn't reach for her wine.

I sat with her again, and reached for my own mask, or armor, whatever you wanted to call it. *My guitar.* "I don't mind it." It was a truth and a lie. When I was alone, I could write whatever I wanted and sing whatever I wanted without Jo offering critique.

I invited notes, I wasn't arrogant. I wanted anything offered to make me better. But sometimes I felt more like a mold Jo was happy to manipulate than the man she loved.

And maybe that was because I wasn't a man at all.

I reached for her glass of wine, to the right of me, and put it next to her.

Calliope didn't look at it, just kept her eyes on the water.

We could hear yelling, loud music, across the water. The house there was lit up. Their laughter echoed across the water, straight to us.

"I've been thinking about that road trip. Route 66. I want to drive it one day," she said. "I want to see California. Ride the Ferris wheel at the end."

"Me too," I said, just as my phone buzzed in my pocket.

It was a text from Jo.

She was heading to a party, not home.

Not back to me.

SIXTY-SEVEN

SEAN

JO
Where are you? I know you're not home anymore.

SIXTY-EIGHT

SEAN

**PRESENT
ON THE ROAD**

WE RENT the last available room at the Blue Swallow Motel in New Mexico. I hand Calliope a wad of cash to take to the reception desk when we arrive. A group of women in their sixties have the rest of the rooms. Their cars have paint on windows, letting us know they're traveling Route 66 together, too.

After my shower I find Calliope gone from our room. The sound of the laughter in the parking lot catches my ear. I hear hoots, hollers, Calliope's laugh, as it cuts through the night, through the walls of the motel, into our room and my chest.

I open our door and peer outside, catching sight of her hair as she laughs, doubling over.

We are almost to the Santa Monica Pier, hours and hours away, but it feels like we're just almost there. We are almost to the end of this. I fear I will lose her when we reach the end, the curtain call.

I fear she wants to lose me and this charade.

People come into your lives in seasons. I will be a short one for her. One of those falls you barely feel, before winter grips you.

Even in this summer heat, I can feel the cold ready to take me.

I can't go out there. I'm afraid I'll be noticed. It happens more and more, every year.

My name is a household name unless the household is just Grandma and Grandpa. And outside, Calliope is making friends with a bunch of grandmas. Parents know my name because their daughters let it roll off their tongues, run through their speakers.

Women Calliope's age and older attend my concerts, write cute messages on neon signs. *I brought my daughter, but she didn't have to twist my arm!*

I retreat back into the room and grab my phone.

I want to text her. But I decide not to.

She's laughing, and though I know I can make her laugh, too, if she comes back here, I don't want to pull her away from some new friends.

As if on cue, as if she knows, Jo texts me.

> **JO**
> Where are you? I know you're not home anymore.

> I know we disagree on this, but we both know we shouldn't talk anymore. You made a choice. Stick to it, or don't, when it comes to him. But when it comes to me, the choice is made.

> **JO**
> He's obsessed with her. Are you with her? They'll end up back together. If you're with her, enjoy it while it lasts.

I don't text Jo back. It's just another game, but the seed has been planted.

When Calliope returns I am under the covers. The lights are off.

She wakes me by running her fingers down my spine. Pressing her lips to the small of my back.

You notice when someone kisses you some place no one has kissed you before. Your skin is alive and every bit of you is sensitive, aware. Sometimes, when she kisses me, I feel like a virgin again. So unsure and alive.

I turn at the waist, grip her throat, and taste her. Liquor and freedom, no fear.

Maybe she wants to be free of me when this is all said and done but at least she will be free of something else. I refuse to believe Jo is right.

I believe they will get a divorce. I'm just not arrogant enough to believe that will cement me in her life, in her future. We are a ticking time bomb.

I hear my phone buzzing across the room as I enter Calliope. Fingers splayed, thumb on hip bone, a slow press in, and her moan.

I sigh and her eyes are on mine as I close them. She can't see it, my vulnerability, the way I do. I really believe she can't see it, and all she can see is me.

SIXTY-NINE

JO

**PAST
THE LAKE**

JO WAS BUZZED when she walked up to the guest house that night, horny and pissed and alive.

Apollo wasn't answering her texts, and he left earlier to spend his birthday in Chicago. Never telling her he was going. She was forced to hear it from his wife. Calliope looked like she was crying, but Jo didn't care. If his wife gave a shit about him, she wouldn't be holding out on him in bed. Allowing Jo to slip into the role she clearly abhorred.

So, Jo picked up a late shift, left the house. Left the suffocating quiet.

She couldn't look at Sean. She couldn't look at Calliope.

She just wanted to make some money, take some shots, flirt with the locals, and forget the house she was forced to live in.

Everything about everyone there pissed her off.

She missed Toronto. It hit her hard when she visited for Honor's funeral, how badly she wanted just to stay and never go back to the Ozarks. But she didn't have anywhere to live there, no ties that were firmly laid out for her. She couldn't squat with friends or live in a motel again.

She was stretching herself thin here with the games and sneaking around. She knew that, but she couldn't stop.

The light from the moon hit Sean's face when she walked in, his eyes open when she looked at him. She questioned how loud she was when she arrived.

"You waited up?" she asked, feeling guilty for a moment, but only for a moment. Her boyfriend's face looked weird.

"Yeah," he replied, and it was the first time she ever wondered if he was lying to her.

He was so easy to read and so easy to believe. Because he wasn't like his uncle. It was what made her unable to take from him. Unable to lose herself in him. Everything that drew her to him also repelled her.

She needed something darker than that to get off. And for that, she blamed the boys from her past.

"Why?" Her hand landed on her hip, her chin up high. She knew he was suspicious, worried all the time. And for good reason. But redirection was something she was skilled at.

"What do you mean why?" he asked, leaning up on his elbows.

It was then she saw it. Sean was fucking hard as a rock under the thin sheet covering his body.

"Were you waiting for me with that?" she asked, pointing at his dick.

"Yes," he replied, guilt in his tone.

She started taking her clothes off then. They smelled like smoke and tequila.

She'd made-out with a regular in the parking lot before she came home. He carried a flask with him and his laugh was husky, sexy. She'd been wondering what his lips would taste like for weeks. She was so pissed at Apollo she decided that night was the night to find out.

Sean leaned back as she walked to him. He always seemed so uncomfortable in his own skin, and she hated it because he was beautiful. So fucking sexy, but if he didn't act like it, she couldn't do it. Couldn't cross the line he was begging her to.

"Get up," she demanded when she made it to the bedside.

He pulled the covers away slowly, swung his legs over, carefully placing one foot on each side of her. His hands were calloused a bit from his guitar. She felt his fingers on her thighs, felt him tremble.

"Were you thinking about me?" she asked, smiling.

When he looked up at her, he said yes.

And it wasn't until after she took his virginity that she realized why she did it.

When he said yes, she didn't believe him.

SEVENTY

SEAN

JO
I was your first. You can never erase that.

SEVENTY-ONE

SEAN

**PRESENT
ON THE ROAD**

I TAKE some of my anxiety medication in Arizona. It's the first time I've needed it since we hit the road.

"I knew it was over before I found them," I say, my hand on the hood of my Jeep.

"How?" Calliope asks, tying her shorter hair up, away from her face.

"We fought so much, this past year. Jo would tell me she hated me. She always made me feel like I was holding her back. She said I was jealous, insecure. But she would be gone for hours, out with her friends. And her stories never added up. I would tell August where she said she was, and he always told me what he heard. All he-said-she-said stuff, nothing concrete. But you can't help your gut feelings, the way they gnaw at you. They hated us together." It's the first time I've told someone outside my bubble.

"Who did?"

"My whole team. On the one hand, they thought it was good for my career, for my image. But she was a loose cannon. Something they couldn't control. And I didn't want them to control her. Maybe that's where it all stemmed from."

"I think it started a long time ago. It was there on the lake, when you were fifteen. I saw it. You felt it, I know you did, and," Calliope hesitated, weighing her words, "maybe Apollo saw it, too. Maybe that's why he chose her."

The desert around us is brutal, blinding, and I want to keep Calliope for myself. Keep her as my muse, never let anyone touch her again. Because she gives me the feeling that no one has ever touched her without bringing her pain as well.

I never want to be one of those men.

"Sometimes I think I want to know more, when it started, why. And sometimes I just don't give a shit. It won't change anything. But I know Jo wants me to hear her side," I say.

"Has she been trying to get ahold of you?" She doesn't sound mad, unsure of anything, and I hate that I hate that.

"Yes." My eyes are squinting in the sun. She couldn't read them if even she wanted to. I want her to want to.

"Talk to her."

"That wouldn't upset you?" I think of Jo's text, how right she is. I can't erase it, and I also can't erase the guilt I feel over that night.

"No, it wouldn't," Calliope says, "and one day you'll realize jealousy and obsession and love are not synonymous."

"What about passion?"

"That's a separate beast. You can have passion without all that disease." She laughs. There is no cheer there. "At least that's what I see in movies and books and songs. I don't know that from personal experience."

I can hear voices by the trail, not far from the Jeep. I turn and see a family of four all dressed in red, white, and blue. The Fourth of July is almost upon us. It's a timer. A countdown I didn't start, but I fear she will make me acknowledge it soon.

I grab Calliope's wrist, pull her toward me. She smiles, and it is genuine. It looks like she could love me if something hadn't been stolen from her.

I lift her up, onto the hood of my Jeep, and her legs are around my waist. My hands are on her hips, and my hair is in her hands.

"Don't leave me," I say. I am unafraid to beg, unafraid to show her what she is doing to me.

My hands travel up her sides, my mouth invites the scandal of us. What she wants to say will break me, so I don't let her.

When she breaks the kiss I see her teeth, then feel them.

"You're more beautiful than they deserve, more pure." Her mouth is traveling, she is tasting my pulse and the salt of my skin. "You made a promise to me, Sean. And I need to know you didn't break it." She presses into me, urging the need to take her here, now.

I want to get her in the Jeep, race back to the motel. "I can't promise that," I say, fingers tangled in her hair. "I never wanted to promise secrets and just this summer. I never wanted to promise that."

"But you did," she says, wrapping her legs around me even tighter.

"We can give them more than hints, we can give them the truth. It won't ruin me. Losing you will ruin me. They'll forget. Eventually, everyone will forget."

"You deserve the fairytale." She pulls away from my skin, from her possession and the ease in which she takes me. "You deserve everything, and that's not anything I can give you."

I straighten the strap on her tank top that has fallen, lean forward and press my lips to the freckle she has there on her shoulder. "Do you know what I learned from my father?"

"What?" She hardens.

"You can't love someone and control them at the same time."

Calliope runs her finger along my jaw. "They didn't deserve you, either."

"He didn't deserve you. I don't think I ever knew you. Who you are now, is not who I grew up knowing. And that scares the shit out of me."

"Scares you?" she asks, fiddling with the button on my shirt.

"Yeah. I never want anyone I love to become so lost inside themselves that they don't even resemble who they were. These last weeks on the road. Is that who you were before?"

"Before?" she asks.

"Before him." I run a thumb across her thigh, and she pulls it away.

"You'll have to be more specific."

I furrow my brow, lost, staring at her fingers wrapped around my thumb.

"Before Apollo? Or before I lost my brother." She untangles herself from me, hops down from the Jeep. "They run together, you know. The loss of one and the gaining of another. I know when I lost myself, and it has nothing to do with those moments in my life. And, Sean..."

I look at her face, every muscle she moves as she speaks, backing away, to the driver's side door.

"There are things about my past I am never going to tell you. And you need to just be okay with that," she says.

"Jesse's been calling me nonstop the past two days," I say later that night, leaning back in the water of the pool outside our motel.

"Call him back."

"I just don't want to deal with him right now."

"It's your life. Your real life. You're going to have to deal with it at some point."

"I like this better," I say.

"Everyone loves a fantasy more. Doesn't make it real."

I open my eyes, stare at her in the moonlight, thankful no other guests are up this late. "You're not a fantasy."

She smiles, moves toward me in the water. When her hips are in my hands, when she is settled over me, teasing, she speaks again, and I can barely hear it. "Did you fantasize about me before?"

"Yes," I admit, red-faced, jaw clenched.

"You shouldn't have."

"What fifteen-year-old doesn't fantasize about an older woman?" I reach between us, move the fabric to the side, slide two fingers in.

Her mouth is on my neck. I dig my finger of my other hand into the soft flesh of her hip, pull her down, feed the need in my stomach.

"What does Jesse want?" she asks, panting, tasting me.

"A concert in California when we arrive. Something small. A surprise," I mumble, not giving a shit about what Jesse wants, just what I want right now.

"Give it to him," she says, pulling my hair, giving herself more access, pulling a small whimper from me.

"Can I sing a song about you?" I sink further into the water, lift her out a little.

She's wearing that tiny black bikini. It could be a different one, but I'm brought back to those years. I see her small body beneath the surface days leading up to the moment we buried.

I can almost feel her lips on my lips, taste the salt of the night.

SEVENTY-TWO

SEAN

PAST
THE LAKE

I FELT ANGER, just like any person. But I always wanted to be in control of it, unlike my father.

I wanted to throw my phone in the lake. I wanted to text Jo and tell her I didn't care if she came back.

Why couldn't she just come pick me up before she went to the party? Why couldn't she blend those two parts of her life?

I shoved my phone in my pocket, watched Calliope from the corner of my eye.

We sat like that, in silence, for a while.

Eventually, I pulled my guitar into my lap, started strumming.

Calliope removed her feet from the water, tucked them beneath her. I didn't sing, I just played songs, one blending into the next. Ten minutes went by, then twenty, then thirty.

I was waiting for Jo. I wouldn't go to sleep until she came home.

It wouldn't be the first night, but unlike other nights, when I just stayed awake until I heard her car, then pretended I was asleep, tonight I planned to confront her. To talk it out. Or scream it out. I didn't care.

I imagined it, what she would say, what I would say. How she would try to calm me down, using tried and true methods.

She used her body to still me. Her mouth around me to make me shut up.

It worked. It always worked.

I almost forgot Calliope was there next to me as I rehearsed our fight until she was standing, staring down at me.

"What are you playing?" she asked, her breathing unsteady.

I couldn't name the song because I didn't even know. I had been on autopilot.

I glanced to the left, my eyes drawn to the second wine glass to be tripped into the water. The red liquid sputtered out, then the glass sank.

"Never mind," she said, walking back up the dock, toward the house.

I sprang up, after her, all thoughts of Jo gone.

My hands made ghost movements at my sides, playing chords, trying to place the song I was strumming.

I thought of Jo, the way I felt used sometimes. It hit me. "Use Somebody!" I yelled into the night air, and Calliope stopped walking.

She turned and smiled and pulled her hands to her face, went down to her knees. I didn't catch her, but before I could stop myself, I was on my knees as well, grabbing her elbows again, pulling her forehead to my chest.

We stayed like that for a moment, as she controlled her tears, pulled herself together.

I hadn't hugged anyone in a while. My uncle didn't hug me, and my father never hugged me, and Jo, Jo hated to be held in the night, in our bed.

Calliope felt small in my arms, every shift made me feel warmer in the hot night. My T-shirt was damp from her tears and sweat.

Her forehead traveled up, it rested on my collarbone, and the arms that were once clutched to her chest hung down, palms resting on my knees.

I ran my hands over her back, over and over, trying to comfort her, until she pulled away. When my arms fell down, hers went up, a palm on each shoulder.

She wasn't looking at me, but I was looking at her. The moon was so bright on her mouth that I couldn't look away. The hair on her face was a mess, stuck to her cheeks, her forehead. My eyes roamed the lines and designs it made, and when she caught me, she pulled her hands from me, putting herself back together.

"I'm sorry," she said.

"It's okay," I replied, leaning back, away from her and the scent of the wine on her breath, away from the heat of her.

When she was done with her hair, with her cheeks and the mascara cleaned up, she leaned forward, then rested her palms on my knees again.

Her hands shouldn't have been there. We both knew it.

I could feel it, so I reached up, grabbing her wrists, and she tugged, embarrassed. But I didn't let go.

"I'm sorry," I said. I was sorry for the song and I was sorry she cried, though I had no idea what it meant to her.

She leaned forward then. Pressed her lips to mine, and it was then that I let her go. When I did, her hands came to my hair, and we both pushed up to our knees.

I could feel her tongue against my teeth, I was hard in an instant, so I opened up to her. When a soft moan escaped my mouth, she pulled away. I tasted salt. I tasted regret. Or maybe it was just the way she was looking at me.

She stood and ran away.

And when Jo found me later that night, I was still lost in that kiss.

SEVENTY-THREE

SEAN

JO
A show in Cali?

JO
If I come, will you talk to me?

SEVENTY-FOUR

SEAN

**PRESENT
SANTA MONICA**

THEY CLOSE down Pacific Park for us in exchange for a show I will play for free, letting the city reap the rewards. I don't need the money, I just need the world to know I am alive, no longer hiding.

I am a kid again when I look at the lights around me, lost in the youth I was unable to enjoy fully.

My eyes rove over the music note tattoo on Calliope's hand, fresh and pink. My hand has hers, and we do not have to worry about being seen, about paparazzi and the hush and whisper of my entourage. Jesse and August are uneasy with us, nervous maybe, wary of her. I don't blame them, I guess. But they don't know her.

This is unnatural, *we* are unnatural, and it's making me dizzy and high.

I pull my phone up as we reach the Ferris wheel. A bored looking man stands by it, waiting for us to give him some work.

I snap a photo and begin fiddling with a filter, looking for the perfect lighting so I can post this moment, immortalize it.

I haven't turned commenting back on yet on Instagram, but my fans know where I am. They know I'm in California. They know I'm happy, because I let them know with my last post. A picture of the ocean. A caption telling them I've missed them.

When we reach the little fence where the line for the ride would have started if the park wasn't deserted, I open my jean jacket.

Calliope slips her hand in, presses her mouth to my chest. "You're always so warm," she says, digging her fingernails into my back, pulling a sigh from my lips.

"And you're always so cold." I trail my lips near her temple. My hands are in her hair, just at the nape of her neck. She shivers, but it's not from the wind.

"Do you think we can exist for long in the world you make?" She has been pressing the issues the last few days—the time, the terms of us.

I am always avoiding it because I just want to stay in this moment for as long as I can. A moment where I know she cares and could want more. She's asking questions because she wants more. That's what I tell myself.

"Yes." I pull away, grab her hand again, and lead her to the ride.

The park attendant lets us in, secures us in our seat, and starts us on our journey upward.

Neither one of us says anything for a while. My phone feels hot in my pocket, it's a window to the world outside, to the reality we will be crushed under. It's proof of the text I sent back to Jo.

"How many times have you been in love?" I ask, turning to the side, one arm in front of me, one behind her.

She can't escape my wingspan, my eyes, and the questions I throw at her when her own scare me.

"Twice, maybe. Your uncle, and the guy I lost my virginity to in high school. You?"

She knows the answer. If I say her name maybe we can break from this insane game. "Once."

"You're going to feel it again," she offers, crossing her leg toward me.

"No. You don't get it. I thought love and need went hand in hand, that you couldn't have one without the other. I needed Jo. I really needed her. And she needed me. Maybe we found each other when we needed each other, to get through a period of our lives that we may not have survived." I can speak about her now with less anger. With the level head everyone always saw on me when my career took off. They applauded me, said I was beyond my years and far beyond the ones Jo had on me. I never saw it, but I tucked those compliments away.

"So you think you didn't love her?"

"I think I thought I did. I was fifteen when I met her."

"So? I was fifteen when I met the first guy I loved. It was a different kind of love than the kind you have as an adult, sure, but not unreal."

"It's not just that. She made me, less." I run my hand through my hair, stare at the glittering lights of the park.

"I know that. I saw that. And maybe you were so hell-bent on proving something to her back then that it's the reason you have this life."

"I don't owe this to her," I say.

"No. You don't. I'm not saying that."

"But do you hear what I'm saying?" I ask, wondering if she even caught the words, the implication.

She looks unsure, beautiful in the flow of the park lights. "Yes," she says, throwing her leg over me.

I grip her hips, listen to what she has to tell me with her skin.

SEVENTY-FIVE

CALLIOPE

**PRESENT
SANTA MONICA**

IT ISN'T his power on the stage that draws me in; it's Sean's vulnerability mixed with his pure joy.

His guitar extends from him, a part of him. Something I knew he missed since we didn't bring one with us on the road trip.

As we made our way across the States, I felt freer out there than I felt in years. It started before Apollo's texts stopped. It began in the lake house when I took his kiss, though the moments of freedom he offered me were fleeting, sometimes only felt when I saw the life he was living as he posted photos online.

And that kiss, that rock bottom moment I regretted for years, I wonder now if I would take it back, given the impossible chance.

I look down at my phone, flipping through photos from the road. Sean's silhouette against the desert. Sean's smile as he sang in the car at a stop sign, his teeth, and his pale skin. The photos damned me. Gave me away. Gave away the fact that I was in love with him.

But the device also brought me a strange form of freedom, or at least, the possibility of it. My gut still warred with my mind, but I felt a peculiar joy when I posted new photos from our trip day by day at Sean's encouragement for the past week.

Were they breadcrumbs? Apollo probably thinks so. That I'm leading him there, to the coast.

And perhaps I was.

I wanted to bury Jo and Apollo when I found them years ago. That was the truth, and I was unashamed of it. It was still the truth now.

He could find me. He could scare me. He could bribe me. He could intimidate me. He could make me throw my phone in the ocean, but he could never erase the evidence.

He always took me for a fool. And the tears I shed for him were real, rehearsed, and exaggerated—a strange combination. The lines blurred, and when I recalled notable scenes, sometimes, I didn't know when the fear was real or when I pretended. Because pretending meant he was satisfied, and he wouldn't push further. It meant he would shed his own tears.

What once caused me to ache, I see so clearly now.

The show of it all.

The way his eyes glazed over when I spoke of my pain.

The way he made me believe I was responsible for his anger, his rage, his sorrow.

I'm the *Muse of Sorrows*. My name weighs heavily. And I just want to shed the sorrow, inspire something pure and alive.

In front of me, Sean is a live wire, bursting. And they devour it.

I want to taste him when he gets off the stage, let him take me in his dressing room, the way he begged to before the crowd started chanting his name.

But that's not part of the plan.

Kissing him again, feeling him inside of me again, none of that is part of the plan.

And nothing is more important than the plan, and the deep sleep I know I'll finally feel again when this is all over.

SEVENTY-SIX

CALLIOPE

**PAST
CHICAGO**

APOLLO ALWAYS JOKED that I slept like the dead, and fell so quickly into it, while he struggled when his mind was full.

I said I was tired, let my head hit the pillow, and was gone. Gone to another world at the snap of a finger. And that night was no different.

The party had been winding down for an hour, and as usual, I grew bored with the business talk, the reminiscing over college years, and stories of people I never knew. The *before* people.

Often Apollo would slip into bed just before dawn, buzzing with energy. He would wrap one of his large arms around my waist—pull me to his needful body.

It was early for him to be slipping in. That was the first clue. One I would cling to later when the numbness set in.

I felt the dip in the bed, his familiar weight, and the rustle of our down comforter.

I opened my eyes just a little, looking at the clock on the nightstand. It was one twenty-three in the morning. One two three. *One, two, three...*

He ran his fingers along my back. It was bare. I was bare for him. Waiting, always waiting and wanting for him when he was ready.

He often took me without words. His breath on my neck and our fingers intertwined.

He didn't smell like whiskey tonight; something sweeter warmed me, woke me a little.

When his hand cupped my sex, it was wet, willing.

Two fingers slipped inside, and I moaned, gripping the pillow. "Don't tease. Just do it," I said. I needed to be up early. The house would be a mess, and he would be sleeping off his hangover. I was having lunch with one of Apollo's co-workers' wives. An attempt to find a new friend in the city.

I'd taken two Ibuprofen before bed. The half-full glass of water on the nightstand was painted red. One twenty-nine AM blurred from the other side as he pushed into me.

I saw stars, the wine still making my mind fuzzy. I'd drank more than I wanted to. One, two, three...glasses?

I couldn't remember.

His breath was on my neck, fingers wrapped around my arm. My face pushed into the pillow as he extended his arms.

He usually pulled me close.

It didn't last long, and most of the time, it didn't when he fucked me like this. He would be drunk; I would be drunk. One, the other, or both. He would finish, I wouldn't, and we would go to sleep.

Tonight was no different.

This was our married life, and I relished it. Because it was a routine.

When he pulled out, I felt his sticky release. I reached for the glass of water, my hands wrapping around it, cool. The room was hot suddenly, my head a rush of stars from the movement. "Fuck. My head still hurts like shit," I said.

Apollo moved, the covers flew back, and I heard him walk across the room to the bathroom. The faucet turned on, but no light came on. Likely to spare my splitting skull.

But light did come on.

It came from my phone on the nightstand.

I fumbled with it, turning it over, staring at the name on the screen.

Apollo.

SEVENTY-SEVEN

CALLIOPE

PRESENT
SANTA MONICA

"ONE, TWO, THREE!" Sean yells at the crowd just before he starts another song.

I feel my heart skip, my vision blur.

We are too often un-alive.

And looking at him on the stage, I know he is so very alive. In a way I haven't been in years.

And it makes me ache. I pull my hand to my chest, clutch the fabric there, wishing it was my heart, that I could squeeze it—end the rapid beating. The fire burning there.

I think of the moments he touched me earlier in his dressing room.

The way he picked me up, set me on the bar, pulling my top down and tasting every hardened peak of me, every soft bit of flesh I offered.

He didn't know how sensual he was. The way he made me wet just by existing. He could walk up to me, press his fingertip to the back of my arm, and I would be pulsing. Unafraid and new, such a foreign feeling to me for so long. It replaced the fear I felt when Apollo walked up behind me.

My phone buzzed in my pocket, but it didn't make my stomach knot like it usually did. I knew who it was. When Apollo stopped texting, I felt free but also frustrated. Wondering if he was over me, over it all.

Soon this phone will no longer ring. There would be no buzz to wake me in the night. No vibration to make my brow bead with sweat.

The fear will end. His name will no longer alter my steps, no longer skip my heart.

I will be free, and the price will be worth it. I'll lie to myself about that until I believe it's true. Until hearts stitch themselves back together, and Sean smiles at some beautiful young girl who can take his hand and not bring him baggage and scars no one can see.

My eyes close. My fingers drum against my heart, a steady beat. *One, two, three...*

His voice is all I hear. He sings about being ready. Waiting forever. Changing plans, and I know he has already.

He's changed his whole world in the aftermath of their betrayals.

He rebounded so quickly, and here I am, years later, holding their sins in my heart, unable to let go.

Not until I get my revenge.

SEVENTY-EIGHT

CALLIOPE

**PAST
CHICAGO**

APOLLO AND NICK had been friends since childhood. Nick was the light to his dark. Had he traveled to the Missouri bar that night, years ago, with Apollo, I may have ended up with him instead.

He drew people in. White teeth, blond hair, tan skin. Wrinkles around his eyes and a dimple on the right side.

His hands were large. When I handed him a drink the first night I met him, I noticed that.

There was a storm in Chicago that night. The rain pelted the window, painted his face in blue and amber, a war with the street lights. I was at war with myself. Finding him so beautiful.

A beautiful man was a beautiful man, and I was not one to stray, but I thought of him that night, just before bed. Apollo locked me in the bathroom earlier that day. Threw away my birth control while I banged my fists on the door, curlers falling out.

My lipstick left a red smear on the door as I tried to speak through the wood, low tones, trying to convince Apollo to let me out. It was the first time he used that punishment, and my frantic words confirmed the power of that move over me. He kept me in there for just a few minutes, and each time after would last longer and longer.

I would later fixate on the meaning of my dream of Nick's hands. If I conjured him there.

Apollo found me in the bathroom at three in the morning.

I heard him enter the home. Heard his fumbling keys and kitchen faucet.

I heard his coat being hung on the four-post bed. My name being called.

I was in my robe. Soft, red. Plush around me. The fuzzy bath mat beneath my sore body.

No words came at first. Apollo held me, gathered me up, carried me to the bed.

The tears soaked his shirt, smelling of whiskey and cigar smoke.

I asked him where he was all night.

"Out," he said.

He did that sometimes. Offered no answer, no matter how much I begged.

He never smelled like a woman, just liquor and smoke.

With the boys, perhaps. One night I didn't ask, just took him in my mouth, desperate for proof. Finding nothing. Just the knowledge that he wanted to get away from me from time to time, and he didn't feel compelled to answer me if he didn't want to.

His wants, above all else, were the most important in the house. Mine—entertained when he saw fit.

Forgiveness was only sought when I shut down, no longer gave him his desires.

My body, and what my body could hold.

SEVENTY-NINE

CALLIOPE

APOLLO
Where are you?

APOLLO
I'm here.

EIGHTY

CALLIOPE

PRESENT
SANTA MONICA

THE CROWD IS SWELLING, getting louder and louder. I can smell the sweat and heat of the women around me. Pheromones and sweet desperation I'm all too familiar with. Sean is lost to them, and I understand why he found the thrill of the crowd better than sex once. They aren't even cheering for me, and I can feel their energy, their thriving desire for him.

This is the moment I've been waiting for. The moment I felt tugging in my chest.

I pull my phone from my pocket. The voices are hushed at his words; it's a new song they have never heard, one he has never played. Words of muses and breaking and the kind of desire you know is foreign and wrong and relatable. He thinks he is alone, but those searching for something find it in his vulnerability.

The message is drafted. The words have been chosen carefully. They will be outraged, sickened, heartbroken…for him. They will dig into my life. Try to track me down. Possibly succeed. But I will keep every truth not offered in the message drafted to myself. My story, with Sean, is a story not for sale, belonging only to us.

I walk off the side of the stage, my face down, the glow illuminating my regret and the tears there.

No one stops me. No one knows I'm not coming back.

He will want to beg me to come back, but it won't take long for him to know why he can't ask me, why I'm undeserving. And maybe then, when it's all broken, perhaps he won't want to ask me.

EIGHTY-ONE

CALLIOPE

**PAST
CHICAGO**

I DIDN'T GO to the police. I didn't report the incident. The devastating truth was I wasn't sure what I would say.

He didn't hold me down. He didn't force his way inside of me. I let him in.

Could you charge someone with a trick? Could you charge someone for being sneaky?

Apollo wept. I thought his tears were for me, for what was stolen. And they were, in a way. He said *I* was stolen from him. Not that something was stolen from *me*. He was a hurricane, a storm of emotions. And before I could figure out why, I was consoling *him*.

"I've lost my best friend," he said, one night, over dinner. The light in his eyes was gone; I saw it. But he wouldn't look me in the eyes, so he didn't see the dimming there.

He was right about many things, a fact he often reminded me of.

I stopped cherishing him. His hands no longer brought blushing. He no longer made me wet and ready.

When we would again have sex, four months later, he would pull out lubrication. I would clench my eyes. I no longer allowed him to take me from behind.

Eight months later, he would express his annoyance over that fact.

"Nothing feels better than fucking you from behind," he said.

Two months later, I would let him again, eyes closed, teeth biting the throw pillow on the couch where I let him convince me he could make me come again.

Biting the pillow, not to stop myself from crying out, but to stop myself from sobbing.

Apollo reconciled his differences with Nick, arguing to me that he was too drunk that night. That he didn't know what he was doing.

Neither of us ever said the word, never said what it was. Me, because I was afraid he would say I was wrong. Apollo, likely because he didn't believe I was raped.

"How many did you have that night? How many glasses? How did you not know it wasn't me?"

Over and over, those questions.

He never yelled. He cried.

And that was worse.

EIGHTY-TWO

SEAN

CALLIOPE
You want us to fit in this world, but we don't. We didn't. There is no way we can.

EIGHTY-THREE

SEAN

**PRESENT
SANTA MONICA**

IT IS A SEA. It is sparkling, tiny lights swaying. A sea shining for me.

My hands are in front of me, steady, finally.

I close my eyes and listen.

Wondering if Calliope is watching from the side of the stage, or the screen in my dressing room.

I want her to see me where I feel at home.

Really see me.

My uncle and Calliope didn't come to my shows together very often when they were together. Three times, if my memory serves me correctly.

My uncle came alone, often. I would fly him out. But Calliope only joined him those three times.

The last time, she had stepped onto the stage, her camera in hand, and captured me.

I remember turning around, my guitar in hand, as she walked away, staring at the little screen on her camera.

I remember the way my uncle looked at her as she walked toward him.

It was a cruel look. I wondered, the rest of the set, what he saw then. What made him so mad.

My profile picture is still the one she caught. The sun and my hair and my guitar.

I was happy. I am happy here, now.

My wrists press down. My fingers hit the piano keys.

I let my lips touch the microphone. I let my voice bring them a favorite, one they can sing along to after the one I just sang, one they'd never heard, about Calliope.

This one makes the little lights on their phones sway back and forth.

I keep my eyes closed until the last verse when my ears catch something.

I don't know what it is I hear, a cry? It's collective, slightly heard above the chorus, to the right of me.

There is a group of girls by the stage, not staring at me anymore, staring at their phones.

They look up at me, at one another, and then it spreads. The girls look behind them.

In the crowd, there are whispers in ears, faces looking at me with sad large eyes.

I continue to sing, heart racing.

The song pours out of me and every time I blink, every time I look into the sea of people, I see more faces lit by their phones, no longer lighting the crowd, no longer singing along.

When the music stops I go on autopilot. I thank the band, I thank the crowd. I do a lap around the stage, touching my fingertips to the hands reaching for me.

When I reach the edge of the stage I see my manager, staring at me, one arm crossed over his chest, one hand over his jaw, his mouth.

When has he ever greeted me with no words? Without updates and opinions and stats, spilling all over me? I can't recall.

I walk ahead of him, hear him trailing. The distant chorus of "Encore, encore, encore" haunts me.

This is when I would be downing a bottle of water, preparing for that encore. But none will come tonight.

"What is it?" I call, over my shoulder, my long legs bringing me closer and closer to my dressing room. Closer to Calliope.

"I told you, I told you, I told you. Messing around with her was a bad idea. Someone was going to get hurt. And who is worth more than any of you? You. You're the one everyone cares about," Jesse says.

"Can you please stop with that bullshit?" I snap, turning back to him just outside the door. "Just tell me what it is." I nod toward the room, and Jesse looks defeated.

"She's not in there. I wouldn't be surprised if you never see Calliope's face again."

I open the door, search for her face even though I know he wouldn't lie to me. My phone is buzzing in one corner.

And in the other corner, I see Jo.

EIGHTY-FOUR

CALLIOPE

**PRESENT
SANTA MONICA**

A HEAD ON A STAKE. That's what I see, what pulls a smile from my tired mouth. The sound of a steady gait on the boardwalk barely reaches my ears. Barely, but it does.

Immobile, I stare at the image, his dark eyes, unblinking, caught in the act, forever immortalized this way.

The crowd cheers, I imagine, from their homes. Dumbstruck and unable to look away from the scandal, the tragedy.

What would a person with everything to lose do with fame if they knew it could be used as a weapon? Anyone can turn the mob on their intended target. They just have to press a button.

The sound of the waves lulls me, I want to jump in, but I know it would be too easy to run now. The men in my life always loved to watch me in the water. Pale skin, limbs that seemed to go on forever, though I was just a slight thing. Five-foot-four, or so.

I'm standing by the edge when my husband finds me. One hand is gripping my neck, one hand gripping my phone.

"Cal, you've lost weight," Apollo calls it from twenty feet away, his pace leisurely until then, halting when I hold my hands up.

He stole words from me often. And though I put miles and time between us, him putting betrayal, I still feel the hold.

It's in his voice.

That leisurely walk.

He's smiling now. Nothing can bother him. As if his frantic texts for weeks have been a joke, an extended April Fools.

We stay like that for a moment. The pier has cleared considerably. The hum of voices behind him is background music.

I can hear my heart—once steady—beating loudly. My phone is gripped tightly. The only weapon I have.

"What are you wearing, love?" he asks.

It's like him to do that—the endearments. To throw them out, trying to pull me back in.

"Where's your girlfriend?" I ask. He will mistake it for jealousy. And it is, but not the kind he wants.

I can't help but wonder if the girl has made her way to Sean. Everyone in the world knows where he is.

I wish I could have stayed to hear him sing. Just a bit longer. It was only a handful of songs, and then I was gone.

Past security, past prying eyes.

One set of eyes caught me, and I held up my phone, pointed to my ear. Why I would have to take a call outside didn't matter. It was enough for the eyes to look elsewhere.

I took a cab to the pier with nothing but a small canvas bag, some cash, my phone.

Nothing in the bag is crucial to me. I look down at it, by my bare feet. My red toenails stand out. I haven't stopped wearing the color.

Haven't shed him. Not yet.

Apollo liked for me to stand out when he sought fit.

Now, I can let the night swallow me whole.

Once, I wanted to let him swallow me whole, pull the last leg in his open mouth.

Letting a man devour you, night after night, year after painful year, is a life some know and can never wake from.

"I know how it is, Cal. They're younger, and they're manipulative. They can pull people like us in. I let myself get pulled in, and I see you let yourself, too. C'mon." He throws his arms open wide, makes a slow circle. "It's you and me, god damn it. It's fucking you and me, forever and ever. All we have to do is just fucking cherish each other again. You know that's all I wanted, right? For us to just cherish each other forever?"

He stops talking. He wants me to fill the space. But I don't.

For years, my silence became a weapon. Apollo became frenzied in it. Wild declarations, threats, tears. He always filled them. I would not stay silent forever, but I wanted him to become unhinged, just enough.

I grip the phone tighter, moving my fingers slowly. Practiced moves.

He takes another step forward, and in response, I shake my head furiously.

"Just say something, Cal. Are you in love with him? How many times did you fuck him? He looks at you like an aunt. You know that's sick, right? Do you really want that reputation? I always tried to save you from that. I took you from that little piss shit town so you wouldn't let yourself become like your mom. Get into shit like your waste of a brother. I saved you, and you know it. You even said it yourself! Did you not?" His hands wave around, his chin juts forward.

I can see the white of his eyes. He seems closer.

Did he move? Did he move on every blink?

I can almost feel him.

My fingers move again. Buttons press.

"Maybe if you had gotten pregnant. Maybe then? Would things have changed then, Cal?"

It's this that pulls me from my stupor, and he sees it. "I didn't want to die young. Not like my brother."

Apollo looks at me with a furrowed brow, cocked head. "What the fuck are you talking about?"

"You're like a drug. Draining, thrilling. A poison. I can't describe it to anyone. The reasons why I never left before."

"You never left me. I pushed you away." He clutches his chest. "I won't do it again."

It's so like him to twist it. He absorbs the blame because it fits the narrative. This is the bait.

"I just want my name back."

"Fuck that!" he yells, wearing his other face at the snap of a finger.

I can see a couple behind him look over at the tone, the volume.

He's quiet for a moment, so they look away, walk hand in hand away from the water.

"We agreed on this months ago. Last year!" My voice rises, and I cross my arms.

"I changed my mind. And I told you before, if you try to leave me, when I don't want you to leave me, you won't get a dime. So if this was what you wanted, we should have filed then. But no, you had to run back to that house. That was the decision you made."

"You're going to give me a divorce. And you're going to give me everything I need to start my life away from you. Apollo, you're not taking anything anymore."

"You can't take shit. You had nothing before me, and you'll have nothing after me."

I smile then, knowing he can see the white of my teeth against the black night behind me. The black water.

I pull my phone to my face. Type, pause, type again. Then pull my hand away.

"You talking to him now?" Apollo calls, the bitter anger back. "Auntie Cal is proud of you. You say that? I should tell everyone about you."

"He wants to tell everyone about us."

He spits then, and shoves his hands in his pockets. Long suspecting, long known, now confirmed. "I didn't think you were actually fucking him. Not until right fucking now. I can't believe it. Okay, I shouldn't have fucked Jo. I'm man enough to admit that. But him? He's like blood to you."

"No," I say firmly. "Sean is blood to you, and you didn't even treat him that way. You didn't expect us to run to each other? You really didn't expect it? I was the first one he wanted to talk to. You built that."

"Were you fucking him then? When he was a kid? They could put you away for that."

"No. I wasn't fucking him when you were fucking Jo five years ago," I say.

"It's just fucking, Cal. Just fucking. It means nothing. We haven't been fucking in ages, it feels like." He motions between us. "And I still love you."

The news finds him then. His phone buzzes in his pocket. He pulls it out, annoyed, an aggressive unlock. Eyes fluttering back and forth. The glow from his phone illuminates his heavy brow.

I smile, then begin undressing as he pulses. I can feel him.

"What the fuck have you done?" he asks, looking up.

I see it. The red, the rare resurgence of his shaky voice. He is controlled, cunning.

I can't outrun the red.

But I can out swim it.

EIGHTY-FIVE

SEAN

CALLIOPE
You'll survive the fallout. We never would have. Because you, with your power, you would never use it to ruin someone's life, even if they deserved it. That's the difference between you and me.

EIGHTY-SIX

SEAN

**PRESENT
SANTA MONICA**

SHE LOOKS like what I once thought love was. Pink and embracing. With thorns I could sense, but never pushed myself to find, because denial is the strongest drug in the world. It's much too hard to find anything unsavory when you really don't want to accept the rot. I only allow myself short glances, and maybe that's worse.

Her eyes are glassy and her full lips look lonely without my gravitational pull toward them. The tug is gone.

I purse my own lips, go to move past her, head down. I hear my phone buzzing, but I can only deal with one disaster at a time, so I don't go to it—yet.

"Can you please talk to me?" Jo asks.

Her voice still makes me tingle. I am not as disconnected from her as I convinced myself I was.

It was love. I tried to lie to myself, convinced myself it was my age and the way she preyed on everything I desired, the way she made me believe the only way I could achieve my dreams was if she was by my side. And maybe she was right.

On the darkest nights, it was her body next to mine that fueled me, kept me warm and ready for the next day.

It was love for me, but I don't know what it was for her. Her sadness is palpable here in this room. So is mine.

"Sean, please."

Is this the first time she's asked me for something with fear of denial?

I don't answer. I close the door, press my body against it, allowing her to ease a little. Her pink hair moves, the scent of lavender and citrus touches me.

She walks across the room to the bar, ducking behind the counter. She always made herself comfortable in a room. Always one to tuck her feet under herself on a couch, jump on a kitchen counter. She let rooms envelope her, invited the eyes of everyone around her.

"What are you doing?" I ask.

"Making us some drinks." The fear is gone from her voice, making it seem like she's in the room without fear of being kicked out now. Like she doesn't need to beg anymore. I think she thinks she has me, but she doesn't know for sure.

"You know I don't really drink." My hands are on the bar, my eyes on her pink hair as she rifles through the mini bar.

"I can make you something you would love. I've always wanted to serve you a drink," she says, as if she couldn't make me a drink at home before I turned twenty-one, as if anything could have held her back.

She offers this to me as if it's a gift. I don't want her gifts anymore.

"You had years to do that. Years when I was begging you to quit reminding me I was younger than you. Years to not shove it down my throat." Everyone gives me whatever I want. The world offers me everything, and I don't take things just to fucking take them. I've had plenty of chances to drink and she was there, in the room. She has seen me turn drinks down, but she didn't pay any attention.

She stands, a glass in her hand, eyes wide. "You never told me."

"Told you what?"

"That it bothered you. What did I say?" Her voice sounds strange, unlike her.

She is playing a role I have never seen her play. The mask doesn't fit well, and I don't want to trample down memory lane, dissect her manufactured words and the way she used to condescend. Even now, her doe eyes make me feel like I've said too much, overstepped a line. Like I've given her reason to think she has a chance.

"It doesn't matter. What does it matter if you made me feel small with words? It doesn't compare to actions." I motion to her. "This bullshit right now. Why are you here? Done fucking my uncle?" I hate the venom there, the hurt seeping out at the edges of my words. I care, I do—still.

She latches on. "Yes, I'm done." She folds one hand over the other, drawing my eyes to her long fingers. They are tan, like the rest of her. She looks like she has been on a long vacation.

"And you think that means we can start again?" I ask her.

She waits a minute to respond, always careful with her words, weighing and measuring the way she can make me smile or wounded. When she reaches across the counter and rests her hand on mine, I don't pull away.

"You're the only family I have. You're not just the person I love, you're my family. Do you know that? I never wanted to be with him. I was just with him because you ended it."

"I ended it because you fucked him. My family. You want to talk about family? You slept with mine." I pull my hand away. Her touch is the last thing I want, and I hate the weakness I allowed myself.

"I don't want him! Let them fight and tear each other apart. Let them get back together if they want! Then you and I, we can start over. I just got lost, Sean. He reminded me of the first guy I was with."

"You told me about him. How was my uncle anything like him?"

"They had the same eyes."

"My uncle and I have the same eyes." I look at the dark pools staring back from the mirror. "I'm not a second choice. I'm not a safety net," I say, shoving my phone in my pocket. Defeated by the sound of Calliope's voicemail. Again.

"I know you're not."

It's then that I look at her, actually look at her. She's wearing a pink dress. Her skin is amber. Small tan lines reach around her neck, which is bare, pink hair in a pile on the top of her head.

I see salt in her eyes, red rims and hands that wring themselves.

She is a mess. And I don't think it's from me. My phone buzzes again.

"You better get that," she says.

"You better leave then," I say, walking toward the door.

When I hear her voice I know she hasn't moved and doesn't intend to leave so easily.

"You don't know, do you?"

I shiver, and I know she sees it. The lump that's been in my stomach since I walked off the stage is still there. "Know what?" I ask, hand on the doorknob.

"What's worse? What I did? Or what she's done to all of us?"

EIGHTY-SEVEN

CALLIOPE

**PRESENT
SANTA MONICA**

THE WATER IS black around me. Black like the pools under my eyes. Black like the nights I would escape to the dock to pretend Apollo wasn't breathing so close to my ear in bed, holding me like he loved me and would never hurt me.

I can't hear him screaming under the water, but I imagine he is. My legs kick, aching from the weeks I've been away from the water, and I think of my brother.

He swam, too, and he was better than me, but he didn't stick with it.

He stuck with dark vices, dark like the water around me.

I can see the lights of the life around me piercing the water, and when I break for air, I turn back, looking at the pier. I don't see my husband, and it brings no peace. I know he is better at this game than I am.

He has always been better, but he underestimated me.

The game was brutal and horrifying and long.

With my arms wrapped around myself on my closet floor, years ago, I passed the time by counting. Counting the seconds and the years that passed. Counting the scars inside me.

And in between those moments of sorrow, I counted all the ways I could ruin him if I just stayed steady, unflinching.

The long game. I vowed to play the long game back then.

I break the surface again, the shore coming closer, the pier growing smaller.

Revenge is a release.

My hand touches the sand, my knees sink in, and into the black night, I scream my red cry.

EIGHTY-EIGHT

SEAN

**PRESENT
SANTA MONICA**

THE PLACE IS UNMISTAKABLE. It's the side of the pool house, the first place I ever felt safe. No matter what was going on with Jo and the partying and the abandonment. I felt safe there, despite my angst. Despite my tears and confusion.

I felt safe in the woods, away from anyone who may hurt me.

Away from anyone who may come home drunk and blacken my eye.

I don't know where I was when this evidence was captured, but my guess is on the other side of that building, asleep.

You can see Jo—pink hair, younger, in a bikini.

You can tell my uncle's hand is inside of her. The arrow tattoo on his forearm is unmistakable.

I skim the *Entertainment Weekly* article.

I see my name.

I see Jo's name.

I see my uncle's name, and I see Calliope's.

The headline reads SEAN AND HIS SORROWS. A play on the meaning of my last name.

The video was sent in from an anonymous person.

But I know who sent it.

I flip over to the last two texts Calliope sent.

My knees hit the floor first, then my forehead. The phone stays clutched in my palm, and I can hear Jo speaking, feel her hands on my back. My name is being pleaded over and over from her mouth, a prayer I can't answer.

I didn't take any medication before this show.

I was high on Calliope and the way she let me touch her in this room.

Now she is gone.

I can hear Jo talking as she rubs my back. She tells me she's missed me and I know she knows what I've seen.

When I push off the floor, tears are streaming down my face. Jo reaches for the scar on my cheek, and I grab her hand.

"You don't miss me." My voice betrays me, my heart, the softness there. I loved her so fully. I'll always love her. But I can never let her touch me again. Not my skin, not my insides, so raw and red.

"How can you say that?" She's on her knees still, and she looks so young and innocent.

I see tears that match mine threatening to fall. The chameleon.

"You don't miss me, and those tears aren't for me. How can they be? You're scared. I know. I didn't know she was going to do that." My phone is buzzing again, but I don't look at it. I know it won't be her. It's my team, hysterical, trying to tie frantic ends.

"Don't you see what they are? He's not a good person. And she isn't a good person, either," she says, pointing at my phone. "They took advantage of us."

I hear the sound of people walking in the halls outside my room. They want to rescue me from everything, even when I say I don't need to be saved. But not from Jo? Their calculating minds don't see this as a threat? Does she not dirty the picture now? No, Calliope is the biggest issue on their minds now.

And I don't blame them. The world is refreshing their phones, waiting for me to say something. They're sharing articles—because there are surely dozens copying the *Entertainment Weekly* article already—dissecting our relationships, drawing family trees on napkins, feeling sick about it all.

They're feeling sorry for me.

I text Jesse. It's a panic moment. I can hear the voices in the hall, the mumbling anxiety in my head taking over, and Jo. She won't stop talking.

"Josephine," I say.

She stops talking, perhaps hears forgiveness. I am resigned to the loneliness I can feel taking over.

Calliope doesn't want to talk to me.

I don't want to talk to Jo.

I don't want to see my uncle ever again.

I want them all to leave me alone, to stop begging, to stop threatening, to stop twisting the knife.

"I need you to leave," I tell her. My voice is calm, steady, as I stand. "You can leave on your own, or you can be escorted out. I texted Jesse. He's on his way. It's your choice."

With my head down—and in her eyes, my guard down—she decides to come to me.

I let her. I hug her, and I wish I didn't as soon as she wraps her arms around me.

"I didn't deserve you," she says, into my shirt.

I can feel the wetness of her face. Her words don't move me, because I see them for what they are now.

When Jo appears to let her guard down, it's because she's begging for affirmations, boosts she can only get from the outside. She wants me to say "Yes you did" or something like that. But I won't. I won't fall into that trap anymore.

Thirty seconds later, Jesse walks in, and Jo is still clutching me while my hands are at my sides. My manager places a hand on Jo's shoulder, and I know she feels it, but she doesn't move.

"Jesse, I fucking know. Give me a moment!" she yells into my shirt.

I reach up and grip her shoulders, pull her away from me. Because I know her. She will milk this for all it's worth, clutch me, beg me, until I have her removed.

"You have to go," I say.

I have to go, too. I have to try to find Calliope.

EIGHTY-NINE

CALLIOPE

PRESENT
SANTA MONICA

I WALK INTO THE BAR, soaking wet, in nothing but a tiny bikini. The bartender nods to me and reaches below, producing a bag. I can feel the eyes of the patrons around me, but I don't look around. They are a blur, a background disturbance of buzzing voices I cannot give my attention to.

I take the bag from his hands and walk to the bathroom, leaving wet footprints behind.

When the door closes, I avoid my reflection as I change into the clean clothes in the bag. Jeans, Converse, a ball cap, and two shirts that smell like Sean.

The white shirt I slip-on, the plaid over-shirt I tie around my waist. His ball cap goes on my head, my short wet hair is tied back, and the saltwater drips down my back, seeping through the fabric of my shirt.

I can feel it, almost hear it. The sea was black and consuming, but I reached the shore. Inside my shoes, I can feel sand and dirt.

When I look up, finally staring into my dark eyes, I am crying, shaking from the cold water and adrenaline.

I allow myself a moment—hands clutching the sink, eyes closed again, accepting the images flooding me.

I can see him, so pure, so beautiful. He's wearing a black undershirt, jumping up and down in his dressing room, mouthing lyrics, running his hands through his hair that's slightly longer again.

I smiled at him then, in love and regretful for the fast-approaching decision I could not steer myself away from.

I look up into the mirror, blinking the images away, and leave the restroom in a hurry because I don't have much time. My careful plan never allowed for tears and regret. There would be time for that later.

The cover he sang for me floods my mind as I walk through the restaurant, nod at the bartender in thanks, and step out into the California night.

There is no phone buzzing in my pocket. There is no way I can be found.

The cab the bartender ordered for me, per my instructions, arrives a few minutes later.

On the way to the airport, my mind betrays me again.

I see Sean's hands moving up my thighs. The thunder of the crowd outside pulses, but my pulse beats louder in my head.

Goodbyes are wounding, regretful, and often swelling. But he didn't know it was goodbye.

"I don't regret what I told you on the Ferris wheel," he had said into my hair, hands moving higher, grip getting more desperate.

He often did that. Used words that had just flittered in my mind. He was so closely tied to me, and I never told him.

I tasted him then, his neck and his salt. His innocence and the way his energy—good or bad—seeped into my soul.

I could feel him when he didn't touch me.

I could feel him through his songs, through his voice. I could feel him in my home when he and Jo visited for holidays. I could feel him when he looked at me in the hallways, slow passings, as we said things with our eyes we shouldn't have.

We kept our unspoken promise for years, to never speak of the night I first kissed him.

He protected me. And I didn't do the same.

I grip the bag in my hands, shifting in the cab, thankful the driver is quiet.

The drive to the airport is long, aching.

All I can think is that he protected me, and in the end, I fed him to those who made him, and hoped I was right. That they would lift him from the dark I drowned him in. His fans chanted his name outside as he took me in the dressing room.

Their love needed to be stronger than mine.

NINETY

CALLIOPE

SEAN
Please don't run.

NINETY-ONE

SEAN

PRESENT
SANTA MONICA

"LISTEN TO ME, Sean. We need to do damage control," Jesse says as he walks back into my dressing room as Jo is escorted down the hallway.

I can hear her yelling at whoever has her.

"Why?" I ask, staring at the text I just sent Calliope. "I can survive this. She said that. She knew it. And she never let it leak that we were together. Even when I wanted it." I look at my manager then, fists clenched at my sides, emotions ripping through me, begging to be voiced.

"Gossip columns are already having a field day with it."

I see concern there. Concern for my image, but also for me. He can see the way I want to fall apart. I am so close to spilling over. "And what are they saying? That I got played? That I have no family left? They're right. And it all fits. Doesn't it?" I throw my hands up, walk to the couch on the side of the room.

"Fits what?"

August walks into the dressing room, looking back in the direction Jo was taken.

I throw my head back, close my eyes. "The story *you* want. The story *we* have been telling this whole time. My fans are going to feel bad for me, they're going to pity me, and then they're going to listen to the next album. Like you want. They're going to hang on every word. They're going to want to be in on the scandal, this *tragic thing*. And, like always, I'm going to let them in. I didn't do anything wrong. Just like you wanted." More salt and more ache in my chest. I can smell Jo in the room. I can smell Calliope on the couch, on the bar. I can still feel her legs around me. The goodbye I didn't know she was giving me.

"I think we all want you to be happy," August says, walking to me, pulling me in for a hug.

"Yeah," Jesse says, "we just want you to be happy. I care about the money, yeah. We all do. It's how we make a living. But I care that you're happy."

"She made me happy," I say, letting go of August, reaching up, pulling my hair.

"Jo?" Jesse asks.

"No." I sit up, glare at him for a second, and then soften. "I mean, yes, Jo did, but not like she does, or like she *did*." I want to turn my phone off. It's blowing up, but I can't cut off the only way Calliope can reach me. "I need another phone," I say, suddenly.

"Okay," Jesse replies, asking no questions.

August hugs me as he leaves, telling me he's getting his car, to take me to my hotel room.

They leave me alone in my dressing room, with the ache and my useless phone, unable to reach the one person I want to reach.

But I'm not alone for long.

NINETY-TWO

CALLIOPE

PRESENT
LAX

"WHAT KIND of monster would do that? It was his uncle. That bitch, Jo. I never liked her for him anyway. I always thought Sean should be dating Carlen Piercy. They killed that duet of Home Again. You could just tell that Jo chick was a hanger-on."

"I don't know, she was with him before he was famous. How could you do that?"

"I don't know. So she was sleeping with his uncle before he was famous. I bet she wouldn't have done that after."

"How could you do it ever? He's sweet, like the sweetest thing ever. I don't get it."

"And what about his uncle's wife? Where is she?"

"I don't know, let me go look. I think I follow her. She has a bunch of photography stuff on there. I remember she took a pic of Sean once on the stage. It's my favorite picture of him."

I bury my face in my book, just one row behind the young girls on the plane.

I wish I had my earbuds, my phone, anything to drown them out. But all I have is a paperback from the airport gift shop.

"It's gone. Her IG is gone. Or maybe I forgot the name? I don't know. I searched, and she doesn't come up."

"Well, if I were her, I would be laying low, too. That's sick, what her husband did. Maybe they'll reach out to each other. Maybe she can make him feel better." The girl looks at her friend, raises an eyebrow, and they both laugh. The joke is obvious.

"Poor Sean," the girl on the right says, the laughter gone from her voice.

"Yeah, poor Sean," the other agrees, scrolling on her phone. "But he's going to survive. Look at him." She pulls up a photo of Sean on stage. It's from earlier that night. A photographer from the side of the stage caught it as he sat at the piano.

He is all white teeth, all sweat, and hair in his eyes. There is confetti in the air, and the glow of phones around him is mesmerizing.

He looks happy and beautiful. And the girls are right. He will survive.

I cling to that notion as the plane takes to the sky.

NINETY-THREE

SEAN

**PRESENT
SANTA MONICA**

THE ROOM EXPANDS with my uncle's presence. He fills rooms, overtakes everything. The way my father did.

He walks to the bar—where Jo was just moments ago—and makes himself a drink. When he turns to me, he takes a long gulp, his Adam's apple moving, the sound of his gulps the only sound in the room.

A little voice in my head tells me I should be afraid, even though I've never seen him lay a hand on another person.

Calliope holds fear inside for the man. It can't be denied.

So maybe I should, too. I sit back on the couch, spread my legs, relax, if only in appearance. "You can't get to her through me," I say after taking a drink of my own. The water in my water bottle is warm. My veins feel like they're on fire. I need him out of my sight. I look at a text from Jesse. I reply, asking him to give us a minute.

"I came to talk to you," my uncle says, walking toward me.

I hold up my hand, showing him my phone, the only weapon I have. In return he shows me his palms, smiles. It's crooked, and I can see the gold wedding band on his hand.

I suspect he hasn't been wearing it but slipped it on for this confrontation.

My eyes don't leave him as he walks around the chair in front of him. He takes a seat, spreading his legs wide as well, relaxed, no fear.

I have fear, and I am unafraid to admit it.

"She was like a mother to you," he states, and it's so laughable I shock him with the noise that comes from my mouth.

Half-laugh, half-cry, some embarrassing exclamation at my disgust over his audacity. "No. That's not true, and you're not turning this around on us."

"So you're an 'us' now?"

I know the answer to that, but this has all been happening so fast I haven't allowed myself to give into that sorrow. But he doesn't have to know that. "Are you an 'us' now?" I ask, knowing Jo is done.

"I did you a favor with that girl, Sean."

"Thanks," I reply, crossing my arms. My eyes don't leave him, and I am struck with how dark they are. How much they look like my father's, and in turn, mine.

"Just tell me where she is," my uncle says.

His voice is low, but his leg is shaking. Like he is full of energy, and he needs to let it out. I wonder if I don't give him what he wants—and I never will—if I'll be the outlet for the energy.

I've been the punching bag before. I've thought I was seconds from losing my life. I can hear my heart racing in my ears. I want it to beat so loudly it drowns him out.

"I don't know where she is." I wish I were lying. I pull out my phone, as my uncle prattles on, and search for her Instagram account. It's gone. *Gone.*

My stomach dares to drop right out of my body. I feel a shiver, a swell of heat. My body is having trouble keeping up.

I lean forward, grip my hair, before closing my eyes. The room spins, I see stars.

"Are you okay?" my uncle asks.

I don't answer. I see it as a movie.

The slow middle, the montage, the sad song playing in the background. Except, it's not just any song.

It's not just any singer.

It's my voice. It's every time I've tried to channel my sadness, the loss of family, into a song.

It's almost humorous. Like I'm in the movie, narrating my own funeral.

I can hear my uncle again, asking if I'm okay.

No answer can be pulled from me.

I see the freckle on Calliope's collarbone. The slow close of her eyes when she was under me when I was inside her.

He pinches me then. On the back of the arm.

I'm pulled from my misery, from the montage flipping through my brain.

My hand hits his as it retreats from my body, and he is smiling. Smiling at my face, I can see it so clearly. The incredulous look I use to aim at my father when he would hit me. As if it hadn't happened a million times before. *Don't look so surprised, you little piece of shit,* he would say. Smiling. The same smile my uncle is wearing right now.

"Got you to stop, right? Don't look at me like that," he says.

I get to my feet, walk around the coffee table, toward him, and he puts his hands up. I know he isn't afraid of me. I've never hit another human being in my life, and I intend to die that way.

I see defeat there, though. In his dark brown eyes. Defeat at the hands of his wife. Finally.

"So she's done with both of us then, huh?" he says.

He's probably right. One for her own good, and one for mine, in her eyes.

"Why were you guys separated? Why didn't you just get a divorce?" I ask him.

"She wanted one. I couldn't commit to it."

"You should have given her what she wanted."

"Sean, you've never been married. And I hate when people give advice to married people on their marriages when they know jack fucking shit about it." His tone is becoming impatient. He doesn't need me anymore, because I am not a doorway to her.

And what would he want from her? There is no taking back what she has told the press. All that's left is his own revenge.

"I know you don't treat the person you're married to the way you did," I say.

"She fill your head with little lies?" He cocks his head to the side.

"I was there," I reply. And I wasn't paying attention. Being around Calliope triggered some memories, but seeing this man before me, my blood, I can feel it. The fear she must have held.

"And what were you doing while you were there? You were busy working on songs, playing that guitar. You were locked away in that pool house, doing anything you could to get this life you have." He spreads his arms wide.

I can still hear the thundering sound of my fans. They've stopped chanting for an encore, but their presence is still large. The sound of their presence can't drown out this moment, though—no matter how much I wish it could.

My father said my head was always up my ass, that I never paid attention.

One time he caught me playing my guitar in the living room. He was saying my name, but I had earbuds in. I was playing and listening and lost, just lost in the music.

He hit me upside the back of my head with his dinner plate. Porcelain and spaghetti went everywhere.

The sauce and my blood stained my shirt.

"If I told you I was sorry, would you believe me?" My uncle stands, his arms are crossed, his stance wide. He is looking at the floor, so I follow his eyes. His shoes are expensive, so is his suit.

He always looked like an adult, and though I didn't trust many adults, I believed in him when he took us in. I believed in the promise of family, despite the hesitation I felt from his wife. I see now why she didn't want us brought into their world.

"Yes," I reply. "Sorry that what you did has come back to hurt you, not that it hurt anyone else."

"I tried to get ahold of you after you saw us. You wouldn't speak to me."

"What did you want to speak about? What could you have said? It was black and white. You are my uncle. She was my girlfriend."

"She wasn't getting what she needed from you." He points at me. A sharp jab into the air. His arms are undone from the knot, and his dark brows are heavy.

"And what was that?" I yell. His anger is infectious. Without fear, I can match it.

"Attention."

"You should have been giving that attention to your wife."

"She didn't want it. Don't I get to be happy, too? Do I just have to beg for scraps from that woman? Oh, I'm sure you had a great summer. I'm sure she gave you everything you wanted. But trust me, it wouldn't have lasted. She would have pulled it away from you. She likes to punish men with that pussy of hers."

I see red, the rest of the room is black and white. "Get the fuck out of here," I say to the floor, my fingers pinching the bridge of my nose.

"I know you were pulling shit back then. I saw you two," he says.

"Saw what?" He's grasping. He wasn't there when she kissed me.

"You were always together when I came back. Your girlfriend was off working, and you were by the pool with my wife. By the dock with my wife. Always with my wife."

"We were the only ones there. And I was a kid. She was my friend. My only friend." I move past him, go to the door.

My hand grips the doorknob when I feel it. He has his hand in my hair, and he is pulling me back.

NINETY-FOUR

CALLIOPE

PRESENT

I WRING my hands when the plane levels out, and I look at the empty seat next to me, thankful for the small plane and the fact that it didn't reach full capacity.

My bag sits next to me in the empty seat, small and filled with nothing but cash, ID, my wet swimsuit, and a few other things.

The girls in front of me have stopped talking about Sean, and it has allowed me too much empty, swelling silence to fill. My thoughts flash through the lake house. Route 66. His dressing room and the way his lips felt when I was telling him a goodbye he didn't hear. One I wouldn't let him hear.

I think of my plan, the final steps.

When I land, Ethan will pick me up.

He will take me to his house.

I will sleep on the couch, with Kanuk next to me.

And in the morning, I will ask him about the destruction.

I will ask him to help me pack up my life at the lake house.

I will ask him to tell me what I did was the only way out.

I won't tell anyone about the letter.

NINETY-FIVE

SEAN

**PRESENT
SANTA MONICA**

I'M NOT GOING to hit him. No matter what he does.

I will not become him. I will not become my father.

The first blow hits my jaw. The second, my cheekbone. I feel it break open. Soft flesh and the warm spread of blood.

I fall to the floor, cover my face, and the blows keep coming.

"Why are you making me do this?" my uncle cries.

And I hear a sob in his throat.

This is how he does it. This is how he did it to Calliope.

He believes I am making him do this.

No. That's just how he sheds the blame.

He wants me to *believe* I am making him do this, that I asked for this. And I know it's what he has been doing to Calliope, for years.

I hear a rib crack when I see her face in my mind. His expensive black shoes hit me again.

Again.

Again.

"I had a plan!" he cries. "I always had a plan. We would be apart, and she would miss me, and then we would come back together, better than ever. The time apart would teach her to *cherish* me. And you ruined that plan."

Each sentence punctuated by another kick.

I feel myself going dark; his voice is fading.

"I didn't want to give her a divorce, because I still love her. And if she wanted time apart, I would give it to her. I would give her all the fucking time she needed to realize she stopped cherishing me. And absence makes the heart grow fonder. She would come back and cherish me again."

He is sobbing. And I know it isn't over the loss of Calliope. It's over the loss of his life, his reputation, his professional career—everything he created from the ground up.

Lives are ruined over scandals like this. She has set everything on fire.

I hear the door open. Moving bodies. No more blows come, and I rock to my side, clutching my ribs, my chest.

There is blood on the white floor.

My blood, my spit.

I've been here before. I've cleaned up my own blood. I've bandaged myself up.

But those days are over.

I feel August's hands on me. He helps me up, as Jesse mutters apologies for not rescuing me sooner.

I brush them both away, walking to the bar. My hands grip the edge, my forehead touches the dark mahogany, and I pretend I am here with Calliope, just hours earlier, before she set everything on fire. Before she ruined lives and set others free.

I am so tired of apologies.

PART TWO
AFTER

NINETY-SIX

SEAN

LIFE IS A SERIES OF MISSTEPS, mistakes, and learning moments.

I do not regret a single mistake I have made. I do not regret the waiting and second-guessing. It is part of the fabric of me.

I do not regret the faith—hard-earned—I have placed in people.

I do not regret a single person I have loved. I do not regret a single person I have pledged myself to.

Love is hard and strange magic, and I cling to it, despite everything. And it would be a lie to say I never fall in love again.

I do. Four years after the scandal.

Her name is Esther. She's a model. The daughter of a Hollywood star.

She messages me on Instagram while I'm in Brazil. I see the blue check mark and decide to open it.

She is in Brazil, too, and we decide to meet up.

Where I am, what I'm doing, while on tour, is open for the public. I keep my heart open for my fans. They lifted me up when everything hit rock bottom.

From that day on, Esther and I keep in touch.

Six months later we meet again, in LA. And from that day on, we're inseparable.

She is the first woman I'm with who is younger than me, and my team believes she's perfect for me. Exactly what I need to leave my past behind.

And they're not wrong.

So, I go along with it.

I post pictures of us from the red carpet of the Met Gala.

I post pictures of us in her yellow convertible as we cruise the coast.

She lives in LA, so I start spending a lot of time there. I like the sun, and her smile is vast and beautiful. I do my best to forget the way California wounded me. Things ended there, so I try to find beginnings there.

Esther reminds me of a porcelain teacup. She has fair skin, delicate edges, and I know she is fragile.

The first time we have sex I know I'm ruined for a younger woman.

It's not thrilling, and while that lets me down, I admit to myself that it's comforting. And I'll take comforting.

She wants to please me, and I let her, making promises to myself that I won't hurt her.

Promises I can't keep.

We are together for nine months before I start to ruin everything. I am in denial, but I see the eyes watching me.

I post the first throwback photo on Instagram and hope no one makes a fuss about it. But I get two texts, right away.

AUGUST

You sure that's a good move?

JESSE

Don't go backward.

No one ever found out about Calliope and me. No one in the press, anyway. There was never any evidence left unless you counted the photo of me with a mystery girl in Illinois. But she remained a mystery girl.

The real evidence was between us. Just photos tucked away on my phone and hers. Polaroids I'm sure she threw away. And the letter. The letter I never let anyone read.

Three weeks later I post the next photo. And the next, one month later.

Each photo is accompanied by lyrics from the album I released after Calliope and I spent our summer together.

An entire album dedicated to her.

My heartache was on display for the world, but they didn't know who broke me.

I let them assume it was all for Jo. I was vague in interviews. Red-faced and tight-lipped. "She knows. She knows," I said, once. My blush taking over where I would not let tears show.

I check Instagram for Calliope's photography account every week. Every week I find nothing.

No one knows where she is, though I do know she is divorced. I never asked her what her maiden name was, and I wonder if she took it back.

She said we wouldn't share a name when she was free of him.

How can you claim to love someone and not beg them of every detail of who they are? I question myself.

I write more.

I post more.

My fans become restless. They think I am reaching out to Jo.

I write new lyrics, but I'm weaving a story I don't understand because I don't know the ending. I doubt I'll ever know.

So I post more.

Every week.

Every week she doesn't reach out to me.

NINETY-SEVEN

CALLIOPE

Sean,

I want to tell you I'm sorry, but it wouldn't be a whole truth, and what use is a muse who tells you boring truths? In order for you to understand why I did what I did, you need to know where I've been. You need to know how buried I was, and who held the shovel.

I SEE THEM—SEAN and the model. In the tabloids. On TV. Red carpets and social media. Hers more than his.

But I know how Sean is. The way he blushes and the way he only comes out in his songs, in low lighting.

Does he miss me? I ask myself this question in low moments. When the solitude I drape myself in is a little too strong.

Healing takes time. And it takes breaking.

I live in places where rain overtakes the world. The Northeast breathes life into me where the Ozark's had suffocated me.

When Sean is in California, I think I can feel him. When he's in the same city as me, I draw the drapes—cocoon myself in regret, remorse, and the resourcefulness I learned from a young age.

And then, he pushes through the radio waves. And he speaks to me in a way he hasn't in years. Not since the back of that Jeep, when he sang into the night, and everyone around us at that drive-in theatre could feel his heart.

The song has his heart in it. They all do, but this one has his heart and mine. A slow piano. Haunting in its ability to cause me to shiver.

I've traveled the world since my divorce. I took back my last name. I'm no longer of sorrows. No longer of the nights when Apollo choked me with his presence.

The tabloids like to dissect Sean's songs. His fans do as well. They think he's singing for Jo. But I know better. And know that girl—a woman in age, but a girl in her grey cunning—has moved on.

Sean's ex is in film now—making a name for herself. And every bit of bitterness I once held for her fades with each passing day.

When you see another woman wear the same fear, the same bruises as you, there is a pull you cannot deny.

I pity the girl and then applaud her when she leaves Apollo, too. We wear many faces.

In the depths of our souls lives the forgiveness we rarely want to give. I have none for the men who made me a shell of myself. But I hope, one day, you have some for Jo. Not for her, but for yourself. I hope you have some for me. You don't have to offer it to me, but just feel it. If you feel it, I will, too. It doesn't matter where you are. I can feel you.

NINETY-EIGHT

SEAN

A FEW YEARS LATER, I go on tour again.

Spain, Portugal, Italy, France, Japan, Switzerland, Poland, Austria, the UK, Ireland, and lastly, the US.

Santa Monica is where it all ends. I lie to myself and tell myself I'm just coming home to California because my girlfriend lives here. And everyone wants to believe a lie when the truth hurts too much.

As usual, I document it all—as does the camera. I open my ribs and let every lyric I'm writing on planes and in hotel rooms flitter out. Every bit of advertising has dogwood flowers on it. I should be ashamed, but I'm not. I want to feel everything. Absolutely everything.

The tour ends on my birthday weekend. It feels like I'm daring fate to fuck me over again, and maybe I am. Perhaps I'm daring fate to give me something that doesn't make me want to rip my heart out.

I don't have to live in my lie for long. In France, Esther and I break up.

It's a scene, in the hallway outside our hotel room.

She causes a scene because she wants to be seen. *You make me look like a fool. Have you seen what they say about me? About us?* I tell her to ignore it the way I do, and she calls me out on the lie. And she isn't wrong about that. Esther knows, even after all this time, I'm susceptible to the things my fans and people on the internet, in general, say about me and my life. But I'm not a teenager or a twenty-one-year-old anymore.

I will always feel. And I'll never apologize for it. I no longer live my life to please the commenters and those who need to shove their opinions down others' throats on the internet. It's the quickest way to unhappiness—an easy river to flow down.

My ex-girlfriend is wrong about one thing, though. She thinks I'm still hung up on Jo, and I tell her the truth, that I'm not, but she sees it in my eyes. The way I can't let go. She just doesn't know who it is I can't let go of.

A camera catches everything, the breakup and the aftermath. But I have final approval on what the world sees.

A documentary will come out about my career before the last show of this tour. The last place I saw her. Where Calliope dove into the ocean, where sirens live, where dark things dive, and never surface.

It almost feels choking, being followed and dissected. I talk about songwriting and how certain feelings can never be brought to life. No matter how hard I try.

The world sees how my friends ground me. They see an orphan boy on tour, with a family of millions cheering him on. They see a rise, an ascent to achieve legendary status, something I know I can never do.

The editing is respectful of my relationship with Calliope. There are hints of her and the scandal with my Uncle, Jo, and Calliope—my Aunt by marriage. It cannot be ignored, but they don't know about *us*.

I watch the finished product in a hotel room overseas, and the clips are telling. I see how it flashes across my mind—something tragic and beautiful, a love you cannot find but once. I see a man who can never recover from a love he should never have tasted. A *woman* he should never have tasted.

There are no small stages in life. But, you make them as big as you want with perseverance. It's magic, this life I have been blessed with. Pure magic and every dark part fuels me.

I will step onto the stage I was singing on when she left. I'll put on a show, break into a million pieces for the crowd to feel.

The past seven years have been a love letter. When I was thinking of Calliope, when I was pretending she never existed, all of it. Love is a vast sea I cannot find a shore in. It's dark as the night she left in, twinkling lights, and the crowd swelling.

I can't breathe when I lose myself to it, the heartbreak. But I can breathe when I think of how I rebuilt myself into a man I can be proud of. Nothing like those who share my blood, nothing like the man who took me in.

But the truth is that when everything spikes, when my emotions are so high I feel like I'll never come down; I do miss the lake house. I miss quiet nights where I would be playing my guitar in my room. I miss the unknown, wishing on stars and hoping people would want to hear what I had to say one day.

I miss those days a lot. I see Calliope walking on the lawn, a drink in her hand. And I remember that feeling—*I can't have her*. My teenage hormones and loneliness took flight inside me like a caged bird. Nowhere to go. So I wrote it down. I wrote it down over and over, and I hid it from the person I was supposed to be in love with.

We all want a forbidden thing sometimes. Its wrongness always felt like something private and pure when I never spoke it. I could make it romantic in the songs, and one day, everyone did hear that want.

They hear me and it's beautiful. I was able to take something that people would judge and turn into something they longed for.

Because when you strip it down, love is love. There is nothing spiteful and cruel about it. It was there at the heart of who I was and who she was. A simple longing I don't feel regret over. I don't feel shame over it. It's a want I will never let anyone take from me.

Calliope's name means *muse*. And though she's divorced herself of my last name, *of sorrows*, I can't let go of it.

I cling to my sadness when no one is looking.

I cling to it as I step onto the stage each night, inching closer to the final show. My last chance.

NINETY-NINE

CALLIOPE

Somewhere in the gray of what happened to me, I let him take my life away. I let him make me believe I was the sum of my parts, and what they could be used for. My mother taught me how to be in charge of this truth, he taught me to fear it. In some stories, there are many villains. In some stories, you feel like the villain. In some stories, revenge is the only release.

THE DOCUMENTARY WAS FILMED for years quietly as Sean toured the world. A crew followed him around as he entertained, filmed interviews, walked red carpets, and as he worked on his new album. Some things are delicate, off-brand, private, and intimate to him. But you can see it all. In the background, there's a foreboding, a solemn lead-up to the ways his past shaped him.

I watch, wrapped in a blanket in my apartment. I watch as images of my lake house fill the screen—intimate phone videos of him and Jo, as I filmed him for YouTube and other streaming platforms.

There's heartbreak, and it's acknowledged, though the documentary focuses more on him and his music, the highs he soared to.

But where he came from can't be ignored.

His sixteen-year-old self is immortalized in front of me. For himself, for me, for the world.

I'd been there, to shows, and I'd seen it firsthand. The way he looked alone on the stage, with a sea of phone lights swaying. It could steal your breath from you. The way they screamed, the cheering, the hum of their voices as they sang his lyrics back to him. Just an ethereal human being and a guitar. The voice of an angel, cliche but true.

I shiver when he climbs the stairs in front of me on the screen, out to a crowd. He's wearing black jeans, a white tank top, and his arms are lean, muscular. Tattoos new and old.

Watching him grow into the strong, long-haired man in front of me on the screen, from afar, is breathtaking and excruciating.

The images change to him on tour, him and his beautiful homes, grown-up and far away from the broken home of Toronto, far from the poison home in the Ozarks, to his own life that he's created.

It's his smile that wounds me the most—bright and vast and devastating. He's beautiful with his soft voice and those eyes—dark, and behind them a heart that only wants to create. To be a man on a stage—be legendary.

He doesn't know it yet, but he is and will be.

I tear up, watching him run around the crowd, hugging fans, touching their hands, smiling.

I can feel myself in the songs, an unspoken thing, my essence cemented forever in lyrics he pens.

When I was a young girl, my favorite story was Alice in Wonderland. And when Sean announces his new album, Wonderland, during the documentary, what can I do but break? To let the sobbing overtake me?

My best friend Cynthia finds me like that as she walks into my apartment with a pizza box balanced on her palm.

She rushes to me, and when I speak, it's almost as if she knows. "You heard it, then? I thought you weren't going to watch this…" she whispers into my hair.

I nod. Slow breaths and beating heart. "I thought he would forget me."

My best friend pulls away, wipes the tears from my eyes. "How could he ever forget someone like you?"

"He's twenty-eight years old. He should be…over foolish dreams and pining, and all the things he sings of."

Cynthia smiles. "Are you over those things?"

It hits my heart then like an arrow. The way his voice often pierced.

I need to see him. I need to tell him I'm sorry I took so long.

When I wanted to live, Apollo made me feel again. When I wanted to die, he made me believe I wanted it. He made me believe something was stolen from him the night his friend tricked me. He made me believe my trauma was an inconvenience. He made me believe the home we built was no longer a safe place, it was a truth come full circle, a ghost from my childhood. He was right. I couldn't find happiness there. Until you stepped through our doors.

ONE HUNDRED

SEAN

WHEN I CLOSE MY EYES, I hear music, and see her.

There's a girl in the crowd of the Santa Monica show who looks like her. My eyes linger there more than they should. Igniting a blush in the young girl. She's my age. Older than Calliope was when I met her. *Did she grow up on my music? Find me posting unedited, raw videos when we were both fifteen?*

I break eye contact with the girl, close myself off, let my voice reach out.

I don't want to write for a while. I don't want to sing for a while.

It hits me hard as the lights go out, as the roar grows louder, deafening.

Sweat beads at my brow, a drop lands on my hand, gripping the mic.

When I exit the stage, hands touch me. My manager, telling me I killed it. August, telling me he already has a trip planned for us. I know he wants to cheer me up. He'll say it's because of Esther, but I know he can see past my bullshit. He's stopped calling me out for my throwback posts.

I smile at them, heart beating fast. It's not the smile they want. August leaves and Jesse follows, always asking me questions when I need quiet. "What's wrong?"

"I need a break. I need a break. A long one," I say, tapping the mic to my chest. I shouldn't still have it in my hand, but I left the stage in a daze.

Jesse walks me to my dressing room, crossing his arms when he shuts the door. "Do you think you'll ever move past that summer?"

"What summer?" I keep my eyes closed as I remove my mic, instinctual, repetitive and comforting.

"I worry you'll never get over it, man."

I smile at Jesse's reflection in the mirror before me when I look up. "You worried I would never get over Jo. You were wrong about that."

He smirks, "well, she certainly got over you."

"Did you ever have any doubt she would?" I don't wish my first love ill will, and I know Apollo hurt her. It was in the tabloids. And luckily, she has been able to move past it. To make a name for herself in the world. But, of course, the tabloids and everyone on social media still dog her. They do it on my accounts still, though it's lessened. The masses have a long memory.

"Nah. She's a little opportunist," Jesse says.

"Maybe." I shrug. I don't care. I know she had a thing with Tristan Kane, the Sexiest Man Alive and Oscar hopeful, and all that. If I were a jealous guy, I would care that she moved on up to the biggest movie star in the world. But it doesn't bother me. I've seen interviews with him. He seems like a decent man. And if there is anything Jo needs in his life, after what she has been through, it's an honorable man.

"God, you're too nice. Well, if it isn't her, what was that about." He motions the direction of the stage I left, sweat stained, with my emotions written all over my face.

I turn around, relenting. "I'll never get over it," I say, staring him in the eye.

"I knew it," he smirks.

"Not what Jo did. Or whatever she's done since then. I wish her nothing but the best."

Jesse sighs, running a hand over his face. "Calliope."

"Yes. I'll write about her until I die. Maybe I'll meet someone new. And it'll stick. Maybe it won't. Maybe I'll get married. Have a family. You know I want that. And, maybe it'll go to the dark place of my mind—way in the back. But I'll always pull it out. Worn words on little scraps of paper, maybe, stuck in my lyric journals. Stuck in songs people sing in stadiums, in crowds like out there. I can't explain it, and you're not going to understand it until you feel it yourself. Maybe some people end up with our soulmates. Maybe I won't."

"You think that's what she was?"

"With everything I am. And I think she knows that too."

Jesse closes his eyes, then looks at the door. He knows me. He knows I don't want to linger on this with him. That I need to be alone. Eventually he claps his hands, the silence too much. "Okay. Let's talk tomorrow."

Let's deflect tomorrow, he means. *Let's talk you off this ledge tomorrow*, he means.

It would be romantic to say I've thought of Calliope every single day since the last day I saw her, here, as she stood on the side of this stage. It would be romantic, but a lie.

Missing comes in waves. Sometimes I'd go months without it. The drug of her.

And then a song would come on my shuffle. Something she loved. My own music wasn't safe. It was full to the brim with her scent, her taste.

I have a box of Polaroids in my hall closet. I've pulled it out. Just twice.

I don't want to capture the world the way she does, I just want to watch her do it.

I hope she's taking beautiful photos somewhere. I hope the notes scribbled underneath make someone yearn. Make someone pull her close.

My phone dings. A girl I went on a date with two weeks ago. A rebound from Esther, but Esther is a rebound herself. I want to text the girl back, but I don't know what to say.

Some women are unimpressed with my fame, they carry their own. And some hang on every word; it's too much pressure, and that's the kind I crumble beneath.

ONE HUNDRED ONE

CALLIOPE

Maybe one day we will meet again, some place I left unsaid words on your collarbone. The map is littered with those places. My chest is full of them.

THE SOUND ECHOED. The fans were hushed, and everyone was a heartbeat away from sweet silence as Sean played the guitar. His beautiful hands, the hands that bled to be this gifted strum.

I've never been able to erase the way his hesitant hands felt on me—delicate, unsure, then desperate. To be touched by violence is to question your wants forever. I craved Apollo's violent embrace once, until the reality of my numbness set in, and the cold sweats told me at night more than any self-help book could.

I craved death, the quiet, once.

Now, I crave this. The stillness and sounds echo out of the stadium, all created by Sean's gentleness.

To listen to his music is to wonder what he can do in a dark room with his mouth and hands. He's molded and shaped his body into what they see on the jumbo screen, a delicate and hard canvas for their eyes to feast on. His fans don't know how he looks bare and undone, and will forever wonder at him. The way I don't have to wonder.

I play with the hem of my dress, trying to steady my heart's beating. Sean left the stage, and as the music fades, a single tear rolls down my cheek. It was breathtaking—his show. When his voice would break, I wondered how far he would push himself to make sure he never let his fans down.

They're lucky to know him this way. When he is white teeth, hard lines, worshiping his guitar and drenched in sweat.

It was strange to watch him the way I did for the past three hours. I wanted to be just off stage with my weapon—a camera to capture him and immortalize him in a permanence that cannot do justice to what he is in my mind.

My phone buzzes, and I pull it out reluctantly, my best friend's message making me smile.

> CYNTHIA
> Don't back out. He misses you. I know it.

I shake my head, shoving my phone back into my pocket. There is no backing out now. I traveled down the coast, listening to his music along the way, searching for myself in words.

Love is timeless between some people. I wish I could write lyrics the way he does, or poetry, anything to describe it. Instead, I think of my favorite author. She said it best when she said of the man she loved—He is music, and I am merely madness and melancholy.

But I know I am more now. More than madness and melancholy, and the muse he told me I was.

I'm meant to be here.

Meet me where we met the sky.

ONE HUNDRED TWO

SEAN

IF YOU LISTEN to what your body is telling you, the answers are clear. But we often mistrust the gut instincts, the tingling tell that so badly wants to tell us something. Anything.

Jesse is gone, and I can finally exhale. Though the show is over, I can still hear it. My ears are ringing, my vision is spotty, as it often is after looking at the lights in the crowd.

I'm finally alone in my dressing room when I peel off my sweat-covered clothes and stand in the room with nothing on but my boxer briefs. The air conditioner gives me goosebumps, but it feels good. My head falls back and it feels like the first time in months I've been alone with my thoughts.

I'm counting in my head. One to ten. Over and over again. My heart is beating so fast, and there is no high like this. Nothing will ever compare to this.

I see my phone on the table across the room. An omen I can't escape. I know what I'll do when I've calmed down.

I'll walk across the room.

I'll check it.

I'll let myself succumb to the sorrow. The letdown.

I imagine Calliope on the lake. I imagine her in a white house with floor-to-ceiling windows. I imagine she sees the dogwood flowers in the spring through those windows.

I imagine a white dog walking next to her in the morning when the air is crisp and no one can touch her.

When my heart calms down, I cross the room to my phone, pulling up the throwback photo of the pier sign from our road trip.

It has millions of likes.

I click on the likes and my thumb flicks up, the accounts that liked it whirl past so fast I can barely see them.

My eyes close and I lean my head back into the seat I've taken. It's the same dressing room. It's the last place I touched her.

Outside, the crowd still thunders. My heart still beats, though not as wildly. When I look at my phone, it's black. So I pull the photo up again. A masochist.

I send the accounts flying again. Something about the way they shoot across the large screen of my phone soothes me.

But I see something in the blur. A word stands out, so I stop the scrolling, go back through the names. Millions of names and something caught my eye. *Sorrow. Did I see the word sorrow?*

I find the account. **sea.of.sorrows**.

My thumb runs absently over my jaw, and I clench my eyes. *Sorrows. Sea of sorrows. Why?*

My last name means *of sorrows*.

Calliope shared that name, but I know she doesn't have it anymore.

I click on the account. It's filled with black and white photography. Snapshots of a hand holding Polaroid photos over the water, over sand.

My vision goes blurry and I nearly drop my phone. I see that I follow this account.

The profile picture is a woman by the water. Her silhouette caught by the setting sun.

She has a camera strung over her shoulder. The device sits at her hip.

Sea of Sorrows. Sea. Of Sorrows. C of Sorrows. Calliope das Dores.

I click on the message button so fast I nearly drop my phone.

And, I see she has already messaged me. Two hours ago.

ONE HUNDRED THREE

SEAN

SHE USES MY WORDS. I find them in a caption, from six weeks ago.

A beacon lighting up the sky, and I was wearing blind eyes, convinced she would never resurface.

I think of all the times I saw her moving through the black water. Her pale skin and her red toes when she would step out of the water, climbing out of the dark, out of my fantasies. I loved to watch her then. Cutting through the black, making her way to me.

At fifteen.

At twenty-one.

She looks the same to me in her photos. An arrow to the heart. Piercing.

The pier is full of people as I walk, slowly. I don't care who sees me. My eyes are flittering between my phone and the people around me, looking for her. I know her hair is long again. I assume she will have her camera on her. She may see me right now, hopeless and searching.

I am stopped three times for photos. I smile and laugh and hug my fans, but I am impatient.

When I untangle myself from the last fan, I see the crowd clearing out at the end of the pier. There, it's empty.

I recheck her photos, then check her message. It's cryptic. The way she often was.

When my hands hit the railing at the end of my search, I close my eyes.

Meet me where we met the sky.

I look at the horizon, the way the sky meets the water.

I can't feel her here, and I worry that we have been apart so long, reading her emotions is no longer a skill I own.

Where we met the sky. I think of planes. I think of high-rise balconies.

I think of the Ferris wheel behind me.

I think of my mouth on her. The way I told her I loved her, without telling her.

I run. I run to her because seven years is a lifetime.

Seven months is a lifetime.

Seven minutes is a lifetime.

Any time away from Calliope is too long.

I see her hands in her hair, adjusting a ponytail. Her eyes are on the crowd, searching, but she can't see me from where I stand. I need a moment. I need a moment. I need a moment to look at her.

There is a canvas bag next to her feet. When her hair is fixed, she doesn't reach for it. She crosses her arms and stares at her shoes. I move closer, and I can see that her toenails are no longer painted red as I walk up—they're aqua. I see a couple next to me eye me, figuring out who I am, recognizing my smile maybe. I can feel it. It hurts, it's so full. I haven't smiled like this in months.

She shifts before I clear my throat, one arm around her waist, one still across her chest. Her thumb is on her chin when she looks at me.

She looks straight into my eyes.

And I look back, frozen, smile gone from fear and a seed in my belly so heavy, and laced with abandonment, I can't ignore it.

I drop my hands to my sides and wait.

Finally, she smiles. "I'm sorry it took me so long."

ONE HUNDRED FOUR

SEAN

A HOTEL. My hotel room.

Is there where reunions take birth?

Calliope trails behind me, one finger interlaced with mine. I let her go, shutting the door behind us. There are lights as far as the eye can see out the expanse of windows on the far wall. I watch her walk to the glow, her hands clasped in front of her.

Seven years and I don't know what to do with myself. With my hands. My mouth wants to taste her. I want to hoist her up on that countertop. But does she want that? I always let her take the lead seven years ago.

I'm not a little boy anymore.

Calliope turns from the windows, smiling. "You look…you look like the man I always knew you would grow into. It's nice to know you're right sometimes."

I've filled it out. I'm not a skinny kid anymore, and my voice has deepened slightly. I smile, and she does, too, reaching up to cover a blush.

"What?" I ask, taking another step toward her.

"One thing you never did was make me nervous. But you're making me nervous now."

"In a bad way?"

She shakes her head. "No. Not in a bad way."

I take another step toward her. I like her words, but I know they're wrong. I remember landing in the Ozarks after I found Apollo and Jo together. I remember that night in her kitchen. I was making her nervous then.

I don't want power over other people that I can use for ill will. But this power I feel over her, after the spell she placed me under and never let go of years ago, this power feels good.

She walks backward, away from me, toward the kitchen as I walk to her. And the smiles we wear are laced with a heat I've never felt, not even in our past.

"Calliope, where are you going?"

"Nowhere you won't follow." She hits the island counter behind her, nestles between two barstools; when I reach her, I move them out of the way. And she doesn't stop me. She just stands there with her dainty fingers interlaced.

"Sean das Dores, you're lovely. You always were. But you're something more now."

I step into her space, my feet planted outside hers, my arms caging her in. My mouth descends to her ear, and I push her hair back. She shivers when I speak. "What am I?"

"Everything," she breathes, her hands reaching for the hem of my shirt.

I pull away far enough to bring my mouth to hers, and the kiss I taste has salt, tears she's shed in the seconds I've been close to her. I savor her whimper, the feel of her throat beneath my hand.

Those dainty hands snake under my shirt, travel up.

I moan, remembering the way those hands felt on my chest, the way she would ease the tension away. I pull away, breaking our kiss; my hands find her waist, lifting her onto the counter. Her legs go around me, pulling me close, but her torso leans back.

"I've missed you," she whispers.

"And?" I've only wanted one thing from her. And no amount of writing can make that urgent desire go away. I want to know her soul mirrors mine. I need confirmations—her affirmations.

"And…" She brings her hand to my jaw, one thumb slowly grazing my lip. "And so many things, Sean."

"Make it one thing. Make it one thing you can tell me and no one else."

She tries to pull my mouth to hers, brings herself close, but now I'm the one pulling away.

"Don't make me beg, Calliope. Don't make me…"

"There isn't a part of me that hasn't missed you in the seven years we've been apart. There isn't a part of me that hasn't loved you since the moment I knew you."

I don't say I love her back. I don't break open yet. I press my forehead to hers, squeeze my eyes shut. My mouth will taste of salt too. Will taste of her. I kiss her, my arms around her, her hands in my hair.

When we break for air, I swear, then pull away, stare into her eyes. "I love you. I love you, I love you. You can't leave again. Please never leave again."

She laughs, but it's shaky. Still, she pulls me in, and there is no warmth like the kind you can bring out of a woman you once thought was made of ice.

She is my muse, everything I was born to need.

I pull her close, press her chest to mine, and breathe in slowly, exhaling by her ear. She is trembling and unsteady, but she stills for a moment, realizing what I'm doing.

I hold her a little longer, allowing her breath to match mine, my mouth by my ear.

For five minutes, we stay like this, breathing in slow, exhaling slowly. Together—skin to skin, chest to chest.

Finally, I feel her pull away; her head goes to my chest, her arms around me. "I love you, Sean. I love you."

I cup her face, bring her mouth to mine, but before I can kiss her, she closes her eyes like I'm about to bring us closer than we have ever been, some place we can never return from. "You're reunion, regret, risk—more than a rebound. More than the road trip, you're red. It's staining me, breaking me open in ways no one will ever be able to chase. I can never be apart from you now, Calliope. This is it. Forever. Whatever it means for you."

She shivers at my words, lyrics I've penned and sang to millions, now confirmed to be about her. For her. I sacrificed futures with women who could never compare, shadows of what I wanted.

I reach for her shirt, pulling it up. She's older now, more beautiful in all her defined lines. The color of her skin and the pink of her lips

I'm wondering—millions of places inside of me break open when she's near. "Tell me you'll never disappear again," I beg, tracing her collarbone with my mouth, moving to the next button.

"I'll never leave you again. Wherever you are, I'm there. Where ever you want to go, we'll make a life."

"Don't be afraid of the world and how they'll tear it apart."

"I don't care. Let them talk. The entire world worships you. Let me worship you now." She unbuttons her blouse, pushing my hands away. I reach behind, pull my shirt over my neck.

We can't move fast enough. We are mouths and hands and humming. We are heat as we both tremble.

I fit into her, and she curves into the notes coming from my mouth.

I remember what it was like to make music with my body, to feel it all.

When we are bare, I lift her, press her against the wall, and ease in slowly. She feels like nothing in my arms, light and like the birds we have tattooed on our skin.

"Sean, I need you until the sun comes up."

I move faster, spurred on by her words, pressing her into the wall with an enthusiasm I worry will push her through it.

I bite her jaw, grip her ribcage, "Okay, yes. Fuck."

"Don't fuck me like I'm delicate. Don't, Sean."

So, I don't.

ONE HUNDRED FIVE

CALLIOPE

I LOVED HIM THEN, in the past. But, it was something I wasn't proud of.

Twenty-one years old, and I undressed him. His insecurities and his heartache. His betrayals and the light wounds he let come to the surface.

It wasn't the right time. It's difficult for flowers to bloom everlasting when the caverns inside of us run too deep.

And I needed to heal. To expose the abuse I endured for years to ears that knew when to pause and give advice.

For years, I went to bi-weekly and eventually weekly therapy sessions.

I broke open every fiber of the scarred being I was and my ache. My mother. My brother. My ex-husband. The way the world would view me if I sought out the love—and man I wanted—when all I wanted to be was the woman behind the lens.

I see my therapist once a month now. Maintenance. Bandage checks.

Now, I look in the mirror at my wrinkles and the sheen of my skin. No longer a girl, no longer a broken woman.

The water in the sink swirls down the drain, and after a moment, I reach in, cup the cold liquid, and throw it on my face.

The sun is peeking in when I return to the bedroom, and the view before me is magnificent.

The covers are pulled down, exposing the expanse of Sean's back.

He was a man before, though young. And now, at twenty-eight, he's broader, more expansive. The timbre of his voice will never be booming, and there's no sound quite like it. But he's all grown up. So practiced and measured in how he made love to me last night.

I stare for as long as I can, knowing that once I touch him, he'll no longer be a photograph but something so much more. Flesh and blood and my soul's magnet.

Sean stirs, wiping his eyes, turning over into the bed. His chest begs to be touched, and I sway before walking to him.

"What are you doing awake?" he asks, voice groggy.

"I needed to use the bathroom. Did I wake you?" I ask, kneeling on the carpet. I reach out, running my hand through his hair. Long again, to his shoulders.

He grabs my wrist, brings the delicate flesh to his mouth. "Yeah, but that's okay. Come back here." He doesn't ask; instead reaches for me, pulling me into the bed, bringing our bodies together, flush. The long length of him solid beneath me.

I straddle him, lean back away from his mouth, my palms resting on his chest. "You're so beautiful, Sean das Dores. I want to take your picture."

He smiles, teeth and closed eyes, his long throat. And God, to photograph him like this, what a gift. "Okay. Like this?"

"Yes," I breathe, already getting up, heading to my bag.

I turn the camera on, walk to the window, open the curtains, letting the early morning light in.

When I turn to Sean, he is up on one elbow, watching me move. "You're wearing my shirt." He smiles, eyes roving my pale legs.

"Yeah."

"What will I wear?"

"Nothing," I reply, adjusting the camera's focus and pointing it his way. I take a shot, recheck the focus.

It's an intimate thing to take someone's photograph. To capture their soul in the stillness of black and white.

He doesn't look scared. He looks confident. How many photographers have captured his essence? He's grown familiar in his body; I've watched it, piece by piece, article by article. So careful with his words, cautious in his movement. Only truly letting go on stage, or inside me. I hope, anyway. I reach the bed, step onto it, and Sean falls back, arms moving up above his head.

"You know what to do, huh?" I tease.

"It's not my first photo shoot," he replies. And it hits me then. He isn't scared of himself anymore. He isn't frightened of his vulnerability, his open heart. Because he knows now what I always knew, the world yearns for this part of him. They see his openness and feel like they aren't alone.

When he sings about his anxiety, his mental warfare, they feel it too. They feel less alone.

I capture him, tell him how to move, speak to him in hushed endearments.

And when the photos are developed, I want to show the world.

And when I ask Sean if that's alright he says yes. He will be my art, if he can show me his.

The studio is dark. A light shining down on Sean, and he has his hand on the keys. There is a man on guitar, a man on the drums. A producer in the room with me.

I sit in the corner on a couch. Shivering in anticipation, as if my body will break open when the first note cries out.

But it doesn't. I'm human and humming as he starts the song. He's singing of wonder—his voice cracks, the tenor intimate and swelling. The music rises, and he pulls away from the mic; echo and keys make me dizzy.

This song is for me. I knew it the first time I heard it. But to hear it like this? God. He wonders what it would be like to be loved by me before the night in the hotel. The reunion and the way he let me into his tender vulnerability.

I love you, I love you, I said, into his hair, as he eased into me, as we breathed together, heartbeats united in a slow rise until they seemed to gallop.

The young man in front of me has long shed that skin. Skilled hands on the piano, capable hands once on me, fingers teasing the keys the way they teased every peak and valley of me as the sun crept up. Mouth to the mic that was once to my flesh, seeking, bringing me to cries and crescendoes.

What is it to be loved that way? In a way that breaks and beats? I gasp, the song swelling to another chorus around me. It's intimate and thrilling, and I need him beneath me, rocking into me.

Everything about him is so breathtakingly beautiful, I think I might cry. When I reach up to my cheek, I realize I already am.

To be loved by him is intimate, a gift you never want to wash off.

As the song ends, I hold my breath. I need Sean alone, away from the prying eyes of those in the building, those close to us now. The people I gave shy hello's to when we arrived.

I can't sing like him, can't do what he does with his mouth, that gorgeous throat, but I can sing to him with my body, with my hands, and the words I'm no longer frightened to spill onto him. This love is an undoing, an ache.

I've spent seven years aching, but this is different.

One by one, the musicians say goodbye, shaking Sean's hand as he darts glances at me over their shoulders, taller.

When we're alone, he walks to me slowly, aware of himself—more aware of his power, impressive gait, and the movement he owns—graceful.

"Were you trying to bring me to my knees with that? Because if they hadn't been here, that's where I would have been."

Sean laughs, falling to his knees, moving between my thighs, placing his hands on my hips. "You're the only one I've ever wanted to hear that song. And the only way I could get it to you was to hand it to the world, and hope you'd hear it and know, I just needed to be loved by you. Still."

I place my hands on his shoulder, move one hand higher, brushing the curls from his forehead, from his dark eyes. "Tell me no one is coming back to this room."

He smiles, and it's never been more real. He's no longer that broken boy. "No one is coming back to this room, Calliope."

EPILOGUE

SEAN

THE BOAT TAKES US OUT, my hand easy on the steering wheel. Calliope smiles at me, almost giddy. I laugh at her happiness, thrilled by it. I'm taking her away, to a villa on Catalina Island. "What? Why are you smiling like that?" I ask.

"I thought someone would take us out to sea. Not that you would be the captain." She touches my shoulder, runs her hand down my chest.

"The only way I can guarantee complete privacy is to take matters into my own hands."

"What else are you going to take into your hands?" She smiles, and I can tell she wants me to take my hands off the steering wheel. I want to put them on her, worship her. But I want to get a little further away from the world. I have plans.

"We're almost there." I smile, running a finger up her thigh.

She retreats to the seat ahead of me, and I try to keep my eye on the destination, but the way the wind whips her brown locks around is distracting.

Calliope applies sunblock with precisions, generosity. And her pale skin deserves to be protected. She deserves to be protected. At all times. Every day, for the rest of her life. After a while, I slow our speed approaching the island ahead.

Calliope sits up, shielding her eyes from the sun. "Where are we?"

"Our own corner of Catalina Island. A place no one can bother us," I reply, cutting the engine as we approach the dock where the crew waits for us.

I can feel her eyes on me as I work, talking to the staff, securing the boat. Finally, I retreat below, grabbing our bags. Calliope protests, but I raise my arms, showing her I have everything.

She follows me closely, and I can feel the question inside her, but she won't dare ask when people surround us.

We enter a black Town-car, and as soon as the door shuts, she kisses me. Her petite frame against me, her hands in my long hair. When she's done, she presses her forehead to mine. "What are we doing here?"

"Vacation. For as long as you want. We'll turn our phones off, pretend the world has stopped. There's seven years of memories between us, and I want to know anything you'll let me know." I kiss her jaw, pull her into my lap.

The driver can't see us with the partition up, and Calliope's mouth finds my ear. "Sean, there's nothing I'll keep the from you ever again. I'm *yours*. And you're finally *mine*. The world can have you when we're done here."

I have to remind myself I can't make love to her here in this car. We have time. And when we're done asking each other questions with our mouths and bodies, I'll ask her the most important question I'll ever ask anyone. I don't care what anyone says or thinks or asks me when we leave here. If she says yes, it's her and I. A team. Friends and lovers and survivors.

I kiss her and pull away. "We better save this for the room." She smiles in return, teeth and a hazy look to her eyes. Few smiles go this deep with her.

I am a safe place for her heart. Fierce and fragile all at once.

We pull up to the villa, and the driver pops the trunk; I join him in the back, grabbing our bags. He hands me a room key, and we walk down the path.

I've wondered about this life for too long. Now I get to have it.

When the door closes on the villa, I drop the bags, reaching for Calliope.

Within these walls, I'll worship her.

I pick her up, and she laughs. "Okay, I guess we are doing this, huh?" She kisses my neck.

"Yeah. I don't know. It felt like the right thing to do." If I'm not careful, I'll reveal my motive for this trip.

The bedroom has floor-to-ceiling windows, a canopy with sheer white fabric blowing in the wind.

I'm from the cold, and I've seen her pretend to be the epitome of the word. We will thaw here, warm, be as bright as our hearts.

I lay Calliope on the bed, but she won't let me stand. "Come here." She claws at my shirt, at my pants, hasty and needy.

I rip my tank top over my head and go for my buckle as she begins to undress below me. Dark hair and white sheets, pale skin, and a little bit of red on her lips.

"God," I whisper, leaning down to her. "You're art. Unreadable, vivid."

She halts me, palms to my chest . "I don't want to be unreadable for you anymore. And I never was; you were just too afraid to be wrong.

No one has ever been able to see into who I am like you, Sean." She moves further up on the bed, hand on my neck, guiding me after her —guiding me into her. Warm and breathtaking.

I rock forward, the walls closing in, tender and tight. "Fuck," I mutter. "I love you. I love being inside of you."

She presses her head into the bed, closes her eyes. Temptress, goddess. The love of my life.

CALLIOPE

The sun peeks into the room; slow-moving white curtains play tricks on my eyes. It's hazy and warm—a vacation from the reality and pressure we'll face.

I reach for Sean in the dark, my eyes now closed. I find his chest, torso, and long hair, and I move over him, my thighs on each side of his hips. "You're beautiful and kind and everything I knew you would be."

His hands travel up, palming my breast, then further, to my neck. "Do you want to swim?" he asks, always hiding from the compliments. Though I can tell he's so much more sure in who he is.

"Yes. Clothes?"

He laughs. "Maybe at least on the way down there. But I don't think anyone is going to see us."

Ten years between a man and a woman when *he* is older, no one bats an eye. But the pressure placed on my shoulder flitters in and out of my mind. I push it away. Running and a steady vegan diet were things I focused on. Control. When the tiny pieces of my life shattered, I managed them the best I could until they became large pieces. Boulders I could move and work until I felt invincible.

"Okay," I say, standing, going to my bag. I pull out a tiny black bikini, then retreat behind a screen in the corner.

Sean laughs. "I've seen every inch of you."

"I know. Let me cling to social norms for a minute," I mock. But the laughter dies in my throat when Sean walks around, helping me take my shirt off, shimming down my panties.

"I want to see the sun," I breathe, going up on tiptoe, reaching for Sean's boxer briefs.

"Okay, okay."

I love him like this, hungry and wrapped around me. A delicate God, unfolding.

When we make it to the water, he goes out further than me, long limbs carrying him. But I can out swim him if I try. I can leave him if I try, but that will never happen again.

When I reach him, he turns in the water, the sun glinting off the necklace I noticed he was wearing when he stripped off his shirt and took off into the ocean.

A silver chain, with another silver circle dangling between his pecs.

I wrap my legs around him, hands steady on his shoulder. "What's that?" I ask, kissing him, pulling away to stare into his dark eyes.

"Something," he breathes, hand traveling up my back, the other keeping us afloat. "Something for you. If you'll have it."

I look down between us. The silver is glinting in the light, the water obscuring my view; I reach between, my fingers pulling the ring up.

A silver band, a black stone. Nothing traditional, screaming *will you marry me. Will you take this name you hate?* But asking *something*.

"Sean?" Our eyes meet, and he looks so sure of his question, as if he knows he won't regret it no matter what I say. "Sean. Say it." I press my forehead to his, the only sound the waves and my beating heart.

"Be my partner forever. Never leave me except for death. Marry me, not my name. Marry the man I am, the one you always knew I would be."

SEAN

There is no home without her. And I imagine she will stretch this out, have to take a moment. And I'm prepared to give her every moment, but she smiles, crushes her mouth to mine, the ring falling to my chest, safe on the chain.

I start moving closer to shore as she kisses me, hungry and desperate.

When we make it to shore, I fall, cradling her close to me, letting her back hit the wet sand.

I pull away, kissing her jaw, her cheeks, her eyelids as she smiles, trying to speak. Laughing or crying, I don't know. I pull back, looking at her. "What? What? Are you okay?"

"Yes. Yes. *Yes*. I'm okay. I'm... I'm okay. I'm..." Calliope reaches up, her hands on my neck, her legs wrapped around me. "I'll marry you. I'll marry you, Sean das Dores."

I kiss her. This woman who halts my heart, keeps me guessing. My muse and my other half. My escape, my open road, my echo.

I hear the song I sang to her in the jeep, how my voice echoed around, and how she cried; I see it.

I knew I loved her then. I knew I was done. I knew I would write whatever we had into the grave or resurrect something; I wasn't sure what then.

But I resurrected *her*, pulled her from the long-gone parts of my life, back into the present.

My mouth reaches hers over and over again. "My muse. You've always been my muse," I say, picking her up and heading back to the steps leading to the villa.

Rebounds and reunions and regret. They're all behind us.

As if she can feel me, Calliope whispers into my ear. "You're worth every risk I've ever taken."

CALLIOPE

There is heaven in this, the lull of the waves, the way he feels beneath me as she rocks back and forth.

I dip down, kissing Sean with the kind of devotion he deserves. "I love you," I say slowly, whispered, hushed as our bodies move in time.

He moves up, caging my ribs with his arms, kissing my breast, my collarbone, stealing my breath away as he moves, sweat-slick on our bodies.

It's unbridled, cosmic, lighting in a bottle. I grip his hair, pull his head back, taste his pulse, his neck, his sweat-stained skin.

There are things you cannot write of, connections the camera cannot capture.

This moment feels like freedom, like the kind of moment hidden deep in the book, past the rage and the breaking of two flawed beings.

"Come with me," he pleads, moving beneath me, pulling me closer until we feel like one person, like one desperate plea to fate.

We break open together, a rush of blood and hope and hands.

When we collapse on the white sheets, he pulls me near, kissing my hair, pulling my thigh around his waist.

I was jealous of the women I knew would get to love him, all the nymphs and worshipping women who would fall to his feet, forever pushing aside the notion that if I just let go, it could be me, forever.

I didn't want to steal his youth, rob him of his future.

And he proved with each song, with each year, that my fears were paper-thin, quickly burned to ash.

Soulmates. That's what we are. And as I press my ear to his chest, listening to his breathing steadily in time with mine, I realize we would have been forever searching for something in other people if I hadn't stopped running, stopped hiding.

The heart is wanting, impossible to feel. Cupid's arrows and myths adorn our legacy. But we write it ourselves. *I* get to choose for myself, for my heart.

I pull away, searching his face, watching his sleepy eyes open.

"We get this, forever." I press my palm to his heart, the ring on my hand cementing my wants.

Sean reaches up, takes my hand. "Yes. We get each other forever. We get to be happy forever."

There are tears on his cheeks, matching mine. And when our lips meet, it is the perfect mixture of desire and unfathomable devotion. Time and its wounding hands can't take this.

When our skin grows old, and our memories fade, we will look back to the songs and the pictures. To our art. And see these young lovers, forever alive, forever like this.

Steady, serene, soulmates.

―――

Read the first two chapters of The Regret, book two in the Red Note series here.

ACKNOWLEDGMENTS

First, my beta readers:

Talon Smith. The best cheerleader. You are such a gem in this industry. Never stop being honest and amazing.

Cynthia Rodriguez! Thank you for talking me off the ledge. I'll keep talking you off yours. Forever.

Amy Vox Libris. Your notes on the beginning of this story helped me TREMENDOUSLY! You are so encouraging. Your love for words is a shining beacon.

Naroba Castillo Lozano, Brittney McHale, and Crystal Aguilar. Thank you for taking time out of your lives to help me with this story. I am indebted to you.

Brooke Anderson. Thank you for loving books as much as I do. I've been waiting for you to come around to share things with. I'll always buy books for you because your excitement over the stories I gift is worth it.

Autasha Calton. ARE YOU HAPPY YOU FINALLY HAVE IT?!?!?!

Kat. Thank you for speed reading this hot mess for me! I can't wait to see what you do next.

My Rebels. I couldn't do this without you behind me. Christina Hart. You are one of the greatest finds of mine in this entire world. I can't wait to hug you, finally.

J.R. Rogue is the author of three Goodreads Choice Awards Nominate poetry collections. She first put pen to paper at the age of fifteen after developing an unrequited high school crush & has never stopped writing about heartache, sorrow, and hope. Rogue has published multiple volumes of poetry & novels. In addition, she is a Certified Yoga Teacher with additional certification in Yoga Nidra & Trauma-Informed Yoga.
She lives in a small town in the midwest with her family, where she enjoys a quiet life reading & telling stories.

Join her mailing list to keep up with everything she's working on.

www.jrrogue.com
contact@jrrogue.com

facebook.com/jrrogueauthor
instagram.com/authorjrrogue
amazon.com/J.-R.-Rogue
bookbub.com/authors/j-r-rogue
pinterest.com/rogueauthor
snapchat.com/add/jenr501

ALSO BY J. R. ROGUE

NOVELS

MUSE & MUSIC SERIES
Breaking Mercy

Burning Muses

Background Music

Blind Melody

SOMETHING LIKE LOVE SERIES
I Like You, I Love Her

I Love You, I Need Him

I Like You, I Hate Her

RED NOTE SERIES
The Rebound

The Regret

STANDALONE NOVELS
Kiss Me Like You Mean It

POETRY

GOODREADS CHOICE AWARDS NOMINEES
The Exquisite Pain of the Unrequited

Exits, Desires, & Slow Fires

I'm Not Your Paper Princess

Tell Me Where it Hurts

Dark Mermaid Song

Songs for the Stars

After The Blackout

I'll Be Your Manic Anxiety Queen

Daddy Issues

Made in the USA
Monee, IL
02 February 2025